Also Available

Wrestling With Love
Meant For Each Other
Meant For Him

Derek hadn't considered food, too content to think of anything but the lingering burn in his ass. As if on cue, his stomach growled, reminding him he hadn't eaten since breakfast. "I could eat."

Scott chuckled, then leaned over to his backpack and pulled out a small washcloth, wiping away cum from his belly and then cleaning Derek's cock.

The sensation of the rough fabric forced a shudder out of Derek which only brought on a new round of laughter from Scott. He became serious just as quickly, staring into Derek's eyes. "That was amazing."

"Yeah, it was!" He leaned over and pressed his lips to Scott's, then stood. "But everything with us is amazing."

He grabbed his jeans and sweatshirt and started to exit the tent, but not before Scott responded to him in a quiet and serious whisper: "It is."

Derek glanced over his shoulder to face Scott and their gazes locked, neither of them saying a word. None were needed for them to know how they felt. After a moment, he turned from Scott and stepped out of the tent.

While he hadn't done much outdoor camping he knew how to put together a fire. By the time Scott joined him with the food, Derek had kindled a healthy flame.

Scott had only packed hotdogs and chips plus they had the water from their visit to the stream. They made quick work of cooking the food and wolfed down two hotdogs each before they even began speaking.

Food in his belly, Derek leaned against Scott. "This was an awesome idea. Still can't believe you and Mom managed to keep this trip such a secret."

"It wasn't the trip that was the secret. It was the promise part that I'd been planning." Scott took the stick he'd used to cook his dinner and dangled the end in flame until the twig caught fire. He waved it back and forth, the orange glow making circles that cut into the darkness. "I wanted it to be special."

"Well, good job. I had no idea and I definitely feel special." Derek glanced at the ring on his finger, then at the matching one on Scott's. The light from the fire flickered over the metal, accentuating the patterns on the band. "But why all the secrecy with my mom? What did she have to do with any of this?"

Scott didn't say anything for a minute and, when Derek looked at him, his cheeks seemed to have become a bit flushed. Maybe the flickering light was casting a hue, but Derek suspected he'd caught Scott in a moment of embarrassment.

Finally, Scott faced him. "You're gonna think I'm stupid, but I wanted her permission to ask for your commitment to me. Kind of like when a groom asks the father of the bride for permission to wed his daughter."

"So, you're saying I'm the girl in all of this?"

Scott's gaze dropped to the ground.

Oh shit. Wrong thing to say! "I'm sorry. It's not stupid. It's sweet."

"Your mom thought so too. She was thrilled." Scott sounded like he was trying to convince Derek rather than sharing information.

"Of course she'd be thrilled. She loves you, Scott. Almost as much as I do." Derek placed his hand on Scott's cheek. "You do know how much I love you, right?"

Scott smiled. "I do. It's just…with all of the instability I've had in my life, I can't help but worry that I might somehow lose you."

"Is that why you wanted us to make this promise to each other?" The realization didn't diminish the gesture, but Derek couldn't deny the tug of sadness to think Scott needed symbols of good faith in order to trust the strength of Derek's commitment.

Scott's father had been a distant man and disapproved of just about everything Scott did. Heck, he'd practically wedged himself between the two of them, almost breaking them apart during their senior year in high school. Was *he* the reason Scott lived with constant fear of losing the things that mattered most to him?

Scott said nothing, but maintained eye contact.

Derek slid closer to him on the log, wrapping his arms around Scott's shoulders and pulling him close. "Scott Thayer, I love you with all that I am, and my promise to you comes from my heart. I want to be with you and there's nothing you could do that would change that. You're stuck with me. Okay?"

Scott leaned into Derek's embrace, resting his head on Derek's shoulder. "Okay."

They remained silent for several minutes, then Scott finally spoke. "I know I might seem a little insecure, but honestly, you haven't done anything to make me feel that way. It's just my own baggage that I have to let go." He kissed Derek's cheek, then stood. "I'm tired. I think I'm going to head into the tent. You ready for some shut eye?"

Derek looked up at Scott. He was tired as well, but wasn't quite ready for sleep. "I'll be there in a few minutes. This fire feels good."

Scott leaned down and brushed his lips against Derek's, then stepped into the tent, disappearing from view.

Derek stared at the flames, processing his day with Scott. From the pseudo-proposal to the sex to Scott's obvious hang-ups, which he'd managed to hide over the past two years, the day had been an emotional ride. Mostly good, but Scott's doubts about the two of them troubled him.

Chapter Four

Scott woke up early the next morning to the serenade of chirping birds. Stretching his arms above his head, a glint of something shiny caught his eyes, drawing his attention. The ring! His heart swelled.

Derek said yes!

He shouldn't have been surprised. After all, if there were any two people who seemed destined to be together, it was the two of them. But that odd sense of insecurity had come over him on the mountaintop, and again by the fire. Under normal circumstances, he would keep those thoughts to himself, but Derek had proven time and again that he accepted Scott just as he was, emotional baggage and all.

He turned to his side, appreciating the peaceful form of his lover. While spending the summer sleeping in their respective homes had given them family bonding time, he'd missed being able to hold Derek close each night as he had during their freshman year.

For several seconds he considered slinking down Derek's body and waking him with a blowjob but decided against it. He looked so peaceful. There'd be time for sex later.

Scott slipped out from under the covers, grateful Derek was so picky about having sheets and pillows. After their romp the night before and the heavy sleep, his body would've been a protesting mass of aches and pains.

He stole one last glance at Derek, absentmindedly stroking his own hard-on. Derek shifted, flipping onto his other side and providing Scott with a nice view of his ass. Oh hell. The invitation was too much to resist, but he'd fucked Derek twice the night before. To try again seemed cruel, especially since he wanted to bring Derek to the summit of the mountain later.

His cock strained even more, protesting against his common sense and courtesy. Without bothering to throw on any clothes, he crept from the tent, ambled to the crest of the path they'd climbed the other day and down to the lake.

Memories of the chilled water forced Scott to stop by the edge. Jumping into frigid water after a long hike and setting up camp was one thing. The idea of jumping into an ice bath after waking up from a restful sleep had his balls pulling up into his body.

Scott counted to three then ran into the water and dove in, ignoring his reservations and his protesting groin. The chill was sharper than the night before, but it helped to wake him up and certainly took care of his morning wood.

He climbed out of the water immediately and sat on a large boulder, allowing his body to air dry. The sheltered lake was breeze free, protecting his wet skin from becoming chilled. The cloudless crystalline blue sky and bright sunshine reflected off the water's surface, giving him the impression of floating in mid-air amongst glittering lights. The perfect kind of dreamy scene to reflect on the previous day.

He'd been so nervous preparing for their trip, right up to the moment when Derek said *yes* to their promise. Life had taught him to doubt commitment and love. His father's rejection of him and the constant moving forced him to question whether he could ever count on anything remaining stable for longer than a year or two. For as long as he could remember, Scott assumed his life was normal…how everyone lived. But when he met Derek he learned how wrong he'd been.

His mother had spent the better part of his youth trying to buffer him from his dad's callousness. It wasn't until he'd met Derek and she'd seen how happy Scott was, then how depressed he'd become when his father pulled him from wrestling and from seeing anyone, that she'd finally stood up for him.

Swallowing back the bitter threads of anger, Scott focused on Derek. His bright smile. His unwavering optimism. His sweet ass.

Scott pushed himself to his feet and returned to the campsite. Derek was up and had the fire going. He must have gotten up just after Scott left because he had a pot of water boiling. He would've had to go back to the stream for that since they'd finished what they'd collected in the canteens.

The scent of instant coffee shook Scott from his thoughts. Two tin mugs rested on the log next to the fire. Derek, dressed in jeans and a tank top, was cooking eggs over the flame. "Morning." Derek greeted him without turning from the fire. When he did, his mouth dropped open. "You look...just wow!"

Scott smiled. "Just taking advantage of our privacy."

Derek jumped to his feet, wincing for a brief second, before rushing to Scott's side. "My ass is a little sore."

Scott strode to Derek and kissed him on the cheek. "I bet it is. Let me get dressed and I'll help with breakfast."

He'd packed foods which were easy to prepare. Bacon, instant scrambled eggs, fruit. Things which they could make with little effort, fill their bellies, and clean up just as quickly. Once fed, Scott brought the cookware to the stream and gave it a quick rinse, using dirt to scrub off the stuck on bits.

When he returned to the campsite, Derek had already tamped out the fire and returned everything into the backpack. "So, what's on the agenda for today?"

Scott sauntered up to Derek and drew him into a hug. "Well, I thought we might fuck around a little and then hike along one of the longer trails that lead to the summit. Since you're complaining of a sore ass, we can skip the sex. It's an amazing view, ten times better than the one we saw yesterday, and one hell of a workout."

Derek nodded, although he said nothing.

"Or we could hang out here, go swimming, whatever you like."

"No." Derek was quick to answer. "I was just thinking it's a shame."

Scott cocked his head to the side. "What's a shame?"

The twinkle in Derek's eyes sent a shiver along Scott's spine. "That you got dressed. 'Cause now I'm gonna have to waste a few minutes taking off your clothes."

"But, I thought you said—"

"That my *ass i*s sore. I didn't say anything about my dick." Derek took Scott's hand and brought it to his groin. Scott's palm pressed against a rigid shaft. He curved his fingers around the width, gently massaging Derek through his pants.

Wordlessly, Derek led Scott back into the tent. Once inside, he pushed with enough force that Scott toppled onto the mattress. Derek wasted no time unbuttoning Scott's shorts and removed them, along with his underwear. He tossed them to the side of the tent, then stripped out of his own clothes and crawled back up Scott's body.

He hooked Scott's legs, an arm behind each knee, and hoisted them up so Scott's ass spread wide and open.

Apparently Derek had no intention of preliminaries before fucking.

"Lube my cock and your ass." Derek's voice, husky and urgent, sparked Scott into action. He reached over the side of the mattress, procuring the bottle of lube. Thank God that it was a pump bottle.

He squirted a generous amount into his palm and reached between their bodies, slicking Derek's cock.

Derek hummed, his eyes closing and a smile curving his lips. "Yeah. Get me good and wet."

Scott sucked in a shallow breath. Derek rarely talked dirty so when he did it sparked all kinds of horniness inside Scott. Using the excess lube, he fingered himself, making quick work of stretching his hole.

Derek sat back on his haunches, watching Scott's preparations. "You don't know how hot you look when you do that to yourself."

Scott stared at Derek. "You don't know how much you turn me on when you get aggressive."

In response, Derek nudged his cock head against Scott's hole. "You think you're ready?"

He'd managed to insert two fingers into his ass and was still a little tight, but after fucking his hot-as-hell boyfriend the previous night, he figured Derek deserved to return the favor. "Ready enough."

A smile spread across Derek's face seconds before he pressed forward, breaching Scott's hole. He didn't thrust, for which Scott was grateful, but he didn't take his time either. With a steady motion, Derek slipped further into Scott's ass.

The burn tore a hiss out of Scott, but they'd made love enough times that he trusted Derek's ability to distinguish between discomfort and actual pain. The burn of Derek's penetration was far from pain and the stretch quickly shifted to a vigorous massage.

Once Derek lodged himself all the way in, he paused, gazing down at Scott. "You're so tight and hot."

"Yeah, well, I aim to please."

That earned him a snap of Derek's hips which forced Derek's cock just a bit deeper inside. Lights flashed behind Scott's eyes as sparks of pleasure fanned throughout his ass. "Holy shit."

"I must have hit your sweet spot. Sweet." Derek bucked his hips a few more times, not withdrawing, but pushing himself further into Scott. Each movement charged the nerves inside Scott. He reached for his own cock which bobbed in time with his racing heart.

"No touching yourself." Derek spoke in a gentle tone, although there was no mistaking the seriousness of his command.

Scott dropped his hands to his sides. "You're evil."

In response, Derek withdrew his cock until only the head remained, then slammed back in."

"Fuck." Scott closed his eyes savoring the sense of fullness with Derek inside him. "Do that again and I might come."

"We can't have that. Not yet." Derek initiated a slow rocking motion, gliding in and out of Scott.

Scott rested his hands on Derek's back, running his fingers along the undulating muscles beneath Derek's skin. Slow rocking built up in speed and force, until Derek's thrusts pounded into Scott. Each time Derek pressed forward, his cock brushed against Scott's prostate, forcing electric waves of pleasure to fan throughout Scott's body.

Derek's grunts turned to ragged breathing. He closed his eyes, his brow crinkling, and he caught his lower lip between his teeth. Increasing his pace, Derek managed a few more strokes before releasing a heaving sigh. "Gonna come soon."

Scott bucked his hips in tandem with Derek, desperate to milk the powerful orgasm out of him. His balls tingled as he observed sweat trickle down Derek's neck. Tingling grew into a sizzling tickle, leaching Scott of his ability to form coherent thoughts. For each downward thrust, Scott arched his back, giving Derek better access and allowing him to savor the friction of hard flesh massaging the inner walls of his ass.

Just as Derek let out a strangled shout and his cock began to pulse, fireworks exploded inside Scott and he came without touching himself. Hot strings of cum pulsed out of him, coating his abdomen. Liquid heat filled him from the inside and leaked out of his ass.

Derek continued to pump, the slippery forward and backward motion ripping a few more spasms out of Scott. Slickness. Sweat. Hard flesh. Derek's muscles quivered through the final bursts of his release and then he collapsed on top of Scott, panting heavily against Scott's neck.

They lay in silence, the only sound in the tent their heaving breath. Slowly, ragged intakes of air subsided until Derek slid off of Scott and rolled onto his back. "Jesus Christ!"

"Yeah. That was pretty awesome." Scott pushed himself into a seated position and winced, the dull ache in his ass flaring as his abused muscles revolted in protest. "Damn. Now we're both sore."

Derek wiped his brow, then pushed himself into a seated position as well. "Totally worth it."

Scott couldn't argue. They'd fucked three times in less than twenty-four hours. Damn but he couldn't wait until they went back to school. Lying in their tent for the next hour seemed an incredible option. Perhaps they could attempt round four. But he wanted Derek to witness the view from the summit before they had to leave the mountain.

Pushing himself off the mattress, Scott collected his underwear and shorts, shimmying back into them. "You up for a hike?"

Derek rolled onto his side. "You're kidding, right?"

"Nope." Scott extended his hand to Derek. "C'mon. I want to take you to the highest peak."

Derek accepted Scott's hand and allowed himself to be drawn to his feet. "I'm just sore, you know, from last night. I hope I'll be able to keep up."

Scott laughed and squeezed Derek tight. "I think you'll survive. Besides, you can't possibly be sorer than I am right now."

Derek nodded. "True." He put on his clothes as well and they left the campsite, heading toward the path leading to the summit.

They stopped by the stream on their way, filling their canteens once again. The hike was less strenuous since they'd already made it to one peak. But the ground was rockier and maintaining solid footing became far more difficult.

About an hour later, they approached the highest peak. "There it is. I should warn you, it's one hell of a climb to get up there, but it's totally worth it."

Derek breathed in deeply, then huffed and smiled. "Lead on."

Scott forged ahead, climbing steep rock walls. Each time they reached a level plain, he stopped for a few minutes to rest and drink some water. When they finally crested the mountain, Scott's heart swelled. "We're here."

Derek gasped and stepped past him, venturing farther out onto the peak. A few moments later he faced Scott, his eyes filled with wonder. "How'd you know about this place?"

"I came up here back in high school."

"Oh really? With friends?"

No. Scott swallowed back the lump in his throat recalling the circumstances bringing him to this spot two years earlier. "When my dad was on business and he'd banned me from wrestling and seeing friends…seeing you…I needed to get away."

Derek stepped beside Scott, taking his hand. "You came here alone?"

There were a few other people on the peak and Scott instinctively glanced in their direction, but didn't pull away. At least old instincts of hiding his sexuality had become mere shadows rather than debilitating obstacles. "Yeah. There weren't many mountains in Iowa so I figured I might as well take advantage of my new surroundings. I wasn't sure how long we'd stay in Massachusetts and didn't know if our next move would allow for hiking."

Derek nodded, frowned slightly. "I didn't mean to bring up bad memories."

"You didn't. Bringing you here is creating new memories for me. Ones that undo everything I experienced before." Scott forced a smile onto his face. Thoughts of his dad and moving from place to place dredged up insecurity.

He didn't want his personal shit to stand in the way of his and Derek's time together.

"You're right about this place. It's beautiful." Derek ambled to this highest point on the mountain, Scott allowing him to lead. "It almost feels like we're flying."

Scott chuckled, recalling the same thought when he sat on the rock by the lake. "I suppose it does." He watched Derek, enjoying the way he took in the panoramic view with boyish awe.

Derek was always so full of wonder and purity, helping Scott to forget his past. At least for a few minutes. "You don't know how happy you've made me, Derek. I don't think you could ever know how happy you've made me."

Derek took Scott's hand and squeezed. "What's going on with you?"

Scott shook his head. "I've just been thinking a lot lately. About how things were and how they are now. Sometimes I think it's a dream that I'll wake up from."

"Scott. You listen to me carefully." Derek paused and Scott stared into his amber eyes. "I love you. So much. We've been through some tough things and come through stronger than ever. Whatever's in the past is in the past. You have me and that's not going to change."

"You've always been so sure. I love that about you." Scott's mother tried to shield him from his father. She'd tried to make each move as easy as possible for him. Amazing a few words from Derek provided far more comfort than years of his mother reassuring him things would work out for him in the end. "I just need a little while to catch up to where you are."

Derek hugged Scott, resting his head on Scott's chest. "I'll be here as you work through whatever you need to.

And I'll be here afterwards too." He turned away from Scott in the direction of the horizon. "And you should give yourself some credit. This time last year the idea of hugging or kissing me publicly was unthinkable to you. Look at us now. Fucking in the wilderness, skinny dipping in ball-shriveling water, and hugging on mountaintops." As if to prove his point, he faced Scott and hugged him close.

"You're right." Of that, Scott felt confident. No matter what old scars needed healing, Derek was a salve that brought life and comfort to him.

Scott stepped out of Derek's embrace and approached a young woman about five years older than them. "Would you mind taking a picture of us?"

"Of course." She smiled and took Scott's camera from him.

Scott led Derek to an area on the peak that showcased the mountain range. The blue and cloudless sky along with the sun reaching its apex created the perfect backdrop and lighting.

"Why don't you guys hug and I'll take a picture of you that way. Then you can take one facing me." The suggestion was delivered as naturally as if she'd asked them if they'd bought their hiking boots at L.L. Bean.

Scott smiled and pulled Derek into a hug. Derek's love filled him just as completely as the warmth of his body penetrated through Scott's clothes. For a few moments, he forgot everything else, leaned forward, and kissed Derek. Their lips grazed against each other with just a hint of pressure.

When he drew back, the woman clapped. "Oh, that was beautiful. You're gonna want to frame that one."

Scott laughed, slightly embarrassed he'd forgotten they had an audience, and threw his arm over Derek's shoulder. The woman didn't miss a beat and snapped another photo of them.

"Damn if you two wouldn't make the best models." She handed Scott his camera. "You have a great visit." And with that she trotted off toward a group of people who were making their way down a path on the other side of the crest.

Scott scrolled through the pictures she'd just taken, Derek leaning in so he could see them as well. The one of them kissing took his breath away. The interplay of light and shadows added an element of magic, as if they were love captured in picture form.

They were cast in partial silhouette, adding an ethereal quality to the picture, but there was enough light to make out their features and know it was the two of them kissing.

Derek kissed Scott's cheek. "She's right you know. I can see myself looking back at this in fifty years and recalling every moment of this trip."

Scott sighed, his vision growing slightly blurry. If Derek only knew how much those words meant to him.

The second picture captured both of them laughing. The sheer happiness radiating off the screen couldn't have been created other than from true feelings. Scott rarely saw himself from the outside in while next to Derek. Did they always look so alive and vibrant when they were together?

"We're printing those the second we get home. Actually, we're stopping at a CVS and printing them before we get home. My mom's going to want the one of us laughing. I want the one of us kissing for our dorm room wall." Derek stared at the pictures for a few more seconds, then ambled to the edge of the precipice and stared out at miles of green and blue.

When Scott glanced at his watch, he couldn't believe thirty minutes had passed. Time seemed to speed by too fast. "Maybe we should head back to the camp site."

They stopped by the lake on their way back, stripping down to nothing and laying their clothes on the rock Scott had used earlier. The water didn't seem quite as cold since they'd just worked up a sweat.

Still naked, Scott scooped up their clothes in one hand and took Derek's in his other, leading him back to the camp site. Once they'd dressed, Derek started up a new fire and Scott retrieved the marshmallows, chocolate, and graham crackers he'd brought for their final day of the trip.

That evening, snuggled together in the tent, they made love two more times and fell asleep wrapped in each other's arms.

The next morning, they packed up, hiked back to the car and drove back to Cambridge, stopping to print the photographs as Derek had requested.

When they arrived at Derek's house, Derek's parents, Claire and Henry, as well as Scott's mother, Shannon, were chatting on the back patio. Claire and Shannon each had a glass of white wine and Henry was wearing a ridiculous blue and white checkered apron reminding Scott of Dorothy from *The Wizard of Oz*.

Claire shot out of her seat when she saw them, rushing over to Derek and grabbing his hand. "Oh, my baby."

She pulled him into a tight embrace, her body shaking. When she finally stopped squeezing, she held him at arm's length, her cheeks wet with tears.

Scott stood back, chuckling at her dramatics. Still, he couldn't deny the sour taste of resentment that he didn't have parents who cared so much they'd cry when their baby boy promised himself to the love of his life. "I'm so happy for you. And you!" Derek's mother released him and pulled Scott into a tight hold. "You shouldn't laugh at the woman you'll someday call 'Mom'."

"I'm sorry, Claire. It's just wonderful to see how happy you are." Scott smiled, his own throat growing tight and his eyes burning, tears threatening to spill over as well. Whether from the show of affection toward Derek or the lack of affection from his own mother, he didn't know, but the acceptance surrounding him had healing power.

Shannon stepped up to Scott and kissed his cheek. "Did it all go as planned?"

Scott swallowed back the guilt at having questioned his mother's excitement. She may not have stood up for him enough growing up, but she certainly worked hard to make up for all those years of instability.

Henry laughed and clapped Scott's shoulder, snapping him from his somber thoughts. "You did good, Scott." He then turned to face Derek. "Get the plates and utensils and set up the table outside. We're having a barbeque in celebration of you two, and of the beginning of your sophomore year. In a few short days, your moms and I will be rid of you."

"Henry!" Claire and Shannon both swatted at him at the same time.

"Hey, we were just talking about it before they showed up." He held his hands up defensively, presumably to ward off any further attacks.

Both mothers dropped their gazes to the ground, a rush of red adorning their cheeks. "We meant we knew how happy they'd be to finally return to the dorms."

"Uh-huh. Sure. You go ahead and convince yourselves of that while I grill the steaks." Henry laughed as he strode away.

Derek took Scott's hand in his. "Come on, help me get the plates and stuff."

Scott followed Derek into the house, only to be pulled off balance the second they entered the kitchen. Derek wrapped his arms around Scott's neck and drew him in for a hungry kiss. When he released Scott, a smile lit up his face. "Thank you for the trip, the promise…for everything."

Scott hugged Derek. "There's nothing to thank me for." Derek couldn't possibly know how one simple word, him saying *yes*, could anchor him, finally steadying his world

An image of Tyrell attacking Derek during their freshman year flashed through his mind, crashing his moment of serenity. Luckily he'd been there to protect Derek and he didn't want to change his lover's tendency to help others, but Derek was too trusting. If he hadn't been there… Scott couldn't even finish the thought. Wouldn't. Derek had said yes. Even considering the possibility of losing the promise of a stable future forced him to shudder.

Derek turned to face Scott. "You okay?"

Scott considered telling him the truth. Just a few words to reveal his insecurity and Derek would likely put his mind at ease. But he'd laid himself bare on the mountaintop. Better to just enjoy the dinner their families prepared for them. "No. Just a little tired from the past two days."

Derek nodded, then returned to gathering the dishes.

Scott watched him, so trusting, so comfortable in his own skin. If Derek only knew how easily Scott's world could crumble, he'd probably stress and fret, taking it upon himself to inspire confidence.

No. He wouldn't lay that burden on Derek. Whatever demons still lingered from his past, they were his own to battle.

Chapter Five

The next few days flew by, what with packing, last minute purchases, and all sorts of family dinners and outings. Derek's mother seemed to need to spend as much time as possible with him. God but the next morning couldn't come soon enough. One more day and he'd return to college and to his daily doses of Scott.

The picture of him and Scott on the mountaintop sat on the mantle next to the picture of the two of them graduating from high school. His mother was nothing if not sentimental.

Derek and his mother sat outside on the patio, reading, when she put her book down and faced him. He flipped his book shut, waiting patiently, but she simply stared.

Several seconds of silence passed. Oh for Christ's sake, whatever she had to say couldn't be *that* bad. "What is it?" he asked.

She smiled and patted his leg. "It's nothing. I'm just amazed by you. That's all."

He had no idea what she was referring to, and said the only thing that came to mind. "Thanks?"

His mother swatted him, then began to chuckle. "You get your sarcasm from your father."

Derek leaned back in his seat, crossing one leg over the other. "Okay. You've obviously got something on your mind. Out with it already."

"I'm just so proud of you, Derek." She placed her hand over her heart and took a deep wavering breath. "The way you've grown into such a strong and courageous man. It's more than I ever could've hoped for. Coming out to me and then your father. Following your heart with Scott. Wanting to help that horrid boy, Tyrell. Your heart is so big and generous."

"Mom." Derek's throat tightened.

"And I couldn't be more thrilled for you and Scott. He's a wonderful young man. Someone I'll be proud to call my son."

"Mom." His voice came out a bit strangled. The outpouring of emotion from his mother wasn't unusual, but for the first time she spoke to him as a man and not just her son.

"But you're also naïve." And there it was. What she really wanted to talk about.

Derek silently berated himself for jumping to premature conclusions.

"Your heart reaches out to others too quickly and I fear for you sometimes. I don't want to see you make another mistake like you did last year. I couldn't bear it if anything happened to you."

Derek hadn't spoken much to his parents about his encounters with Tyrell. He still couldn't believe some of the things that happened himself. The graffiti calling him and Scott faggots on their dorm room door. The attack at the party at the end of the year.

Throughout high school, he'd always been careful, protecting his secret. Once he'd let the world know who he really was, his sense of self-preservation lightened its grip on him, perhaps too much so.

"I don't know what to say. It's not like I *wanted* things to turn out the way they did with Tyrell. Who would have guessed he was so unstable?"

"Scott did." She leveled him with a steady gaze. "You've told me enough that I know he expressed concerns along the way. Why didn't you listen to him?"

Derek couldn't deny the truth. Scott had warned him over and over about Tyrell. Didn't his mother give him credit for learning from past mistakes? He didn't want their last night together focused on such negative memories. "He'll still be there to look out for me. That should give you some comfort, right?"

His mother shook her head. Maybe petulance wasn't the best approach. "It does. But sarcasm isn't the only trait you've inherited. I'm afraid I can be rather single-minded at times. Especially when it comes to you. And I worry. A mother can't escape her nature."

Derek couldn't help the smile crawling across his face. "I'm nineteen, almost twenty. I think you've done your job."

"A mother's work is never done. I'll never stop worrying about you. But there is something you can do to help set my mind at ease." His mother couldn't have appeared more serious if she wore a black robe and held a gavel.

After the years of support and unconditional love, he owed her whatever she might ask. So long as her request didn't require he compromise himself. "Anything. You know that."

"Please be careful. Listen to Scott if he warns you like he did last year. The world may be open-minded, but it's not entirely tolerant yet. There are plenty of people who will dislike you simply for *what* you are without taking the time to learn *who* you are." She took Derek's hands. "Just promise me you'll focus more on you and Scott and not worry so much about all those other lost souls out there who seem to latch onto you."

Derek wasn't sure he could make the promise. At least not to all of what his mother requested. She seemed to need confirmation. "I will, Mom. If I learned anything from last year, it's to trust Scott's judgment." He purposefully avoided the part about focusing on himself. He'd never been able to turn away from a person in need.

"Thank you, honey. That makes me feel so much better." She stood, wiping at her slacks. "I'm going inside to start dinner. Scott and Shannon are coming over."

~~~~~

Derek couldn't shake the heaviness of his earlier conversation with his mom. Probably his overactive mind fucking with him since his mother had returned to her normal buoyant self. Still, she'd struck a nerve. Why did all the stray dogs seem to flock to him? Was he like the Pied Piper of fuck ups?

His dad wore the same ridiculous apron from the other day. Derek made a note to purchase him a new one for Christmas. Maybe one that contained a golf logo or some clever quip like *I Love my Gay Son*. He stared out the window and couldn't stifle his laughter. Smoke billowed from the grill while his dad swatted at the clouds with his spatula.

"Henry, for goodness sake. You'll burn the yard down." Derek's mom rushed outside, stopped a few feet away from the fireworks. "Oh, look at those ribs."

Derek turned from the scene, a smile pulling at his cheeks. For all his father's goofiness and his mother's worrying, he wouldn't trade them for anything in the world. Yeah, he'd lucked out when it came to awesome parents.

Scott slid behind Derek, resting his chin on Derek's shoulder. "Looks like your dad's in his element."

Derek leaned his head back and rested it against Scott's. "Mmmm. You smell good."

Warm breath tickled his neck. "It's just my natural scent."

Derek could think of few things better than Scott's aroma. "Just think, tomorrow I'll get to sniff you all over whenever I like."

That earned him a gratifying swat to his ass. "I like the way you think."

Shannon interrupted their moment, clearing her throat from the entrance of the kitchen. "Can I help with anything?"

With effort, Derek managed not to pull away from Scott. After all, they were only hugging. Plus, Scott served as a barrier to prevent Shannon from seeing the hard-on he now sported. "No, thank you. Scott and I got this. We were about to set the table outside."

"Mmm-hmmm." Shannon eyed them, then crossed the kitchen to the patio door. "I'll go out and visit with your parents while you two…" she raised her hands into the quotation signal, "set up for dinner."

Heat flooded Derek's face.

"Mom!" Scott tightened his grip on Derek. Of course, he was probably trying to use Derek to block his own straining cock if the hard shaft pressed against Derek's ass was anything to go by.

"Back to business, boys." Shannon let herself out and strode down the stairs to Derek's parents.

"I can't believe she just did that." Scott released Derek and rubbed his eyes vigorously.

Derek reached into his own pants and readjusted himself. His cock tangled in his underwear was uncomfortable enough. If his dick managed to weasel through the slit in the front of his boxer-briefs, he'd be sure to scrape against his zipper. "I wouldn't feel too bad. My mom just gave me a talking to before you came over about not getting my bleeding heart involved with all the screw-ups at school."

He didn't know exactly what to expect, but the grim expression on Scott's face didn't match any of the reactions Derek had anticipated. Scott placed a hand on Derek's shoulder. "I hope you listen to her advice. I couldn't bear another year like the one we just experienced. If anything ever happened to you—"

"Stop!" Jesus. Did everyone think he was completely incapable of taking care of himself? "Can't we just enjoy dinner?"

Scott opened his mouth, but closed it and started collecting dishes from the cabinet. Once he'd removed five plates, he rummaged through the utensil drawer with far more energy than necessary.

Derek drew in a deep breath and held it to a count of five. This was supposed to be a fun evening, their last night as a combined family, before Derek and Scott started their lives together for their sophomore year. Why did everyone seem so hell-bent on delivering words of wisdom and warning?

Scott's silence filled the room. Derek closed the few feet between them and kissed the back of Scott's neck. "I'm sorry. I didn't mean to snap. It's just everyone seems to think I'm some helpless victim."

"You're not a victim." Scott turned and gazed directly into Derek's eyes, seriousness barreling into Derek like he'd been hit by a truck. "Victim's aren't in control of what happens to them. You *choose* to put yourself in compromising positions."

What could he say? Scott was right, of course. But it didn't change who Derek was. To deny someone help would be the same as not breathing. Not gonna happen. To argue about events that hadn't yet occurred seemed fruitless. Better to keep the peace and have a confrontation when there was something to argue about. "You're right. I'll make sure I'm more aware of the choices I make."

The promise was vague enough to allow him to continue to support others while satisfying Scott's immediate concerns. His boyfriend and his mother worried too much. Derek had learned some hard lessons during his freshman year. Surely he'd be able to see the warning signs if anything remotely bad were brewing.

Heavy topics melted away as their two families dined together. Conversations about majors and friends dominated the evening. When Derek's mom slunk inside and came out with a sheet cake with *Good luck Derek and Scott* scrawled across the top, Scott dug his hand in and scooped up a huge dollop of frosting and shoved it into Derek's mouth. Most of the buttercream confection ended up on his cheeks and a little lodged in his nose.

Derek returned the favor, sticking a huge fingerful of frosting into Scott's ear. Even Derek's dad joined in, grabbing a piece of cake and forcing it into Claire's mouth.

Once he tried to repeat the process with Shannon, the festivities came to a screeching halt. Shannon dashed around the table, and the parents ended up running in circles trying to paint each other in cake and frosting.

Derek stood back, laughing, Scott by his side. This was how he'd hoped the evening would go, free from heaviness and worry. After all, they were together, safe, and happy.

Derek and Scott had promised themselves to each other. Why worry when there wasn't anything to worry about?

~~~~~

The next morning, Derek woke up early, excited to get to Boston University and settle into his dorm. He carefully placed the picture of him and Scott kissing on the mountaintop in his carry bag and took one last look around his room. "Well, I'm off."

The previous year, his dad had driven him to college and his mother had been an emotional wreck. This year, when he bounced down the stairs, he was greeted by an empty kitchen.

He knew he shouldn't have been surprised since it was six in the morning. No one would be up for a couple hours, and he wasn't going to the campus until ten. But he was leaving. Didn't that warrant his parents getting up early?

Deciding to burn off some of his excess energy, he slipped into his sneakers and workout shorts and trekked outside. The sun hadn't quite crested the horizon, but the dull glow of dawn lit the sky. Taking off at an easy jog, he set a steady pace toward the river, hoping Scott might be there. Maybe he'd been as restless last night as well.

When Derek arrived and no one was there, he ran their regular path, increasing speed as he went. His mother's warning filtered through his mind. Scott's words in the kitchen. Everyone he loved seemed desperate for him to suppress a basic part of his nature.

Why? Because of what Tyrell did the previous year? They couldn't imagine something so horrific would happen again. Tyrell was an extreme case. A self-hating, mentally unstable kid. Most people were normal, with regular problems...whatever that meant.

The sun finally crested over the cityscape, beams of light stretching along the blue of the water and the green of the grassy banks. Tendrils of warmth licked along Derek's skin. With each passing minute his body grew warmer, heat building upon heat.

A hint of a breeze helped to cool him. The interplay of warring temperatures served as an effective distraction from his troubling thoughts. As soon as he began to overheat, the air would brush against his wet skin. The moment a chill set in, rays of sunlight blanketed him.

By the time he arrived back at his starting point, he was coated in a sheen of sweat as he panted heavily.

On his walk back to his house, he continued to think about his mother and Scott. At least the physical exertion of running had served its purpose, and he could think with a level head. He was surrounded by people who cared deeply about him. Still, those same people, especially his mother and Scott, worried about him, concerned he didn't know how to handle himself.

If only they had the same confidence in him that he had in himself. After all, he'd always learned from his mistakes and had come out on top. His family and Scott should realize he knew how to take care of himself.

When he entered his house, the scent of a lavish breakfast floated on the air. His mother and father were chatting in the kitchen. His mother turned to face him and shook her head. "You're always so sweaty."

"Love you too, Mom." He stopped by the bathroom and stripped out of his clothes, took a quick shower, then climbed the stairs to his room to get dressed. The last thing he needed to pack was his sound system, so he bundled that under his arms and lugged it down the stairs and stacked it by the front door.

Returning to the kitchen, the table was decked out. Eggs, pancakes, freshly cut fruit, bacon. His mom had gone all out, as she had the other day. Derek took a seat and started heaping food onto his plate.

"Today's the big day." His mother swept behind him and kissed the top of his head. Derek heard a slight sniffle, but his mom seemed to fare much better than she had the previous year.

"Yeah. Can't wait." He spoke with his mouth full, earning him a sidelong glance from his father.

"You sure you don't want me to go with you?"

"Nah. My car's gonna be full with Scott's and my stuff. We're good."

His dad nodded. "Just offering."

His mother took a seat next to him, silently watching as he ate. After he'd finished his eggs, she grabbed the platter and serving spoon. "Want some more, honey?" Her eyes shimmered with unshed tears.

Oh boy. Maybe she wasn't handling his departure so well after all. "Sure, Mom." She heaped another generous portion on his plate. The act seemed to calm her.

Once he'd finished his breakfast, his parents walked him out to his car, each grabbing a piece of his mixing equipment.

His dad patted him on the back. "Have a great time, son."

His mother pulled him into a hug and clung tightly. Unlike the previous year, she managed to release him instead of clinging to him so hard he couldn't breathe. Still, she had tears streaming down her face. "Have a wonderful time. Study hard. And give Scott a hug and kiss for me." She pressed her lips together. Derek would bet money she was fighting from having a complete breakdown.

Derek nodded, hugging her one last time. "I will." As a conciliatory addition, he added, "And I'll be careful. I promise."

She squeezed him just a bit tighter but when she released him a smile adorned her face. "Thank you."

He climbed into his car and drove a few blocks over to Scott's house.

Scott was waiting on the curb, a broad grin painted across his face as Derek approached. "It's officially our sophomore year."

Derek hopped out of the car, popped the trunk, and helped Scott to maneuver his things alongside his own. It took some creative shifting, but they managed, and after a few minutes, were on their way into the city.

"I'm gonna park by the dorms, and we can walk over to the Student Center to get our courses. That all right?" Derek turned onto Memorial Drive heading into the city.

"Sounds like a plan to me." Scott drummed his fingers on his thighs. "I'm so excited I can't contain myself. You think the lines will be long at the Student Center?"

Derek let out a huff. "You think the sky is blue right now?"

In his periphery, Derek could see Scott staring at him so he kept his eyes glued to the road. Scott gave him a gentle shove, not enough to interfere with driving, but sending a message nonetheless. "Ass."

"Ass is right. The second we get our courses and set up the room, you're fucking mine." Just the thought had his blood racing south and his cock shifting and lengthening in his pants.

"Mmm. I can see you like that idea." Scott reached across the console and cupped Derek's groin. "Oh yeah. If you're gonna be an ass then I'll be a tease."

Derek grabbed the water bottle in the cup holder and brought it to his lips, taking a deep swallow. If Scott kept talking like that, he might forego courses and unpacking and have Scott fuck him on the hard wooden floor the second they arrived at the dorms.

A distraction was definitely needed. "You still free tonight? Jared invited us to dinner." Jared was the leader of The Alliance, BU's GLBTQ student group. Derek had become close to him and his boyfriend, Chad, the previous year. They'd been particularly helpful when Tyrell defaced his and Scott's dorm room door. "He sounded like he had something important to talk about, but wouldn't let on what it was. I could use the moral support."

"Of course. I'm looking forward to dinner. Chad's good people." Scott shifted from drumming his fingers on his lap to fiddling with the stereo. Derek chuckled, not missing Scott's careful wording. Chad was super easy going. Jared, not so much.

Traffic wasn't too bad, and they lucked into a spot in front of their dorm. "Hey, let's unpack first. Then we can find a permanent parking spot and head over to the Student Center."

Scott nodded and hopped out of the car, hauling two large suitcases from the trunk and heading for the dorm entrance. Derek stood back and admired the way his muscles bulged under his t-shirt. After a few seconds, he grabbed a few smaller bags and followed Scott inside.

Unpacking didn't take too long. With their clothes stored in dressers and closets, their sports gear lined up on one wall, Derek's mixing equipment set up in the corner, and the furniture positioned so there was open space in the middle of the room, they headed out.

When they arrived Derek groaned. The line extended outside the building and across the quad. They took their spot in line, and almost immediately old friends stopped by. Elizabeth, their RA from freshman year, bounded up to them, waving her course list in her hand. "Hey guys? How was your summer?"

Scott pulled her into a hug then handed her over to Derek. "Summer was great, but I'm glad to be back."

She took a step back and surveyed the two of them, scanning them from head to toe. "Something's different. Scott, you're much bigger than last year. In a good way. And Derek, you look just as sweet as ever." She continued staring, her eyebrows scrunching together. "But there's something else."

Derek couldn't help himself. He held up his hand and grabbed Scott's, waving their rings in her face. "Scott sort of proposed."

Her face lit up. "You guys are engaged? That's awesome."

Scott corrected her. "Not engaged, but promised to each other."

Her smile faded, replaced by confusion. "What's the difference?"

Derek nudged him with his shoulder. "Yeah, Scott. What's the difference?"

Scott shifted his gaze from Elizabeth to Derek. "The difference is the ring. Do you think I'd propose with sterling silver? You're gonna get at least a carat."

That shut Derek right up while earning a giggle from Elizabeth. "Oh boy, I see the two of you are going to be a handful this year."

Scott simply shrugged, his devilish grin suggesting he agreed. Taking in the playful expression, as well as the promise for their future, Derek's libido jumped into overdrive. Needing a distraction, he reached for Elizabeth's course list. "How long did it take you to get to the front of the line?" They were still standing in the quad outside the Student Center, and the line hadn't seemed to move much at all.

Elizabeth frowned and shook her head. "Shit, took me two hours. I'm ready for a drink." Retrieving the paper, she kissed each of them on the cheek, then flitted in the direction of the dorms. After a few steps, she turned. "Hey, I saw the list of residents, and we're in the same building again. We're having a party tomorrow night. You still mixing, Derek?"

"Of course, Beth. Anything for you."

She squealed and rushed off toward the dorms.

Registering for courses took them about two hours. Derek had nearly worn out the soles of his shoes from shifting back and forth from foot to foot. "Jesus. Took long enough. Let's head back to the room."

He should've been tired, but being back at school, in a shared room with Scott once again, had the opposite effect. Once in their room, he started climbing out of his clothes.

Scott watched him, a perplexed expression on his face. "What're you doing?"

Derek smirked. "Christening the room."

Once he'd stripped, he sauntered over to Scott and placed a hand on each shoulder. "Why are you still dressed?"

Scott's eyes lit up as he fumbled with his belt, shoved his pants down his legs and kicked them to the side of the room. He then pulled his shirt up and over his head, tossing it in a different direction, and faced Derek, his cock standing at full attention.

Derek crept forward, taking in the sight, then lowered to his knees and gripped Scott's cock in his hand. Leaning forward, he sucked the head into his mouth and ran his tongue around the glans. Within seconds, the tangy saltiness of Scott's pre-cum hit his tongue.

He took more of Scott into his mouth, the head pushing at the back of his throat. He concentrated on loosening his muscles before pressing forward a few more inches. He still couldn't fit the whole thing in, but he'd taken more than ever before. His jaw screamed from the strain. One day he'd get the whole thing down his throat.

Scott placed his hands on Derek's shoulders, the muscles in his legs quivering. "Damn, Derek. That's just. Damn."

Derek continued sucking, bobbing on Scott's cock, using his hand to increase the friction. Scott's shaft thickened in his mouth. Derek withdrew and kissed his way up Scott's body. Pushing him backwards, he guided Scott to their bed until they fell onto the mattress. Crawling on top of him, Derek straddled his chest and guided his cock to Scott's mouth.

Scott's eyes widened, but he wrapped his fingers around Derek's member and directed the head to his lips.

Derek groaned as wet heat engulfed him. Scott seemed encouraged and twirled his tongue around Derek's shaft, slurping for all he was worth. Release ignited in Derek's core. Too soon. Derek had other ideas in mind for the two of them. He withdrew his cock from Scott's mouth. "I'm gonna come. Not ready for that yet." His words came out through bated breath.

Scott whimpered, leaning forward and trying to get his prize back, but Derek had already scooted down Scott's body, and within seconds, was kneeling between his legs. Placing his hands behind each of Scott's knees, he applied some pressure, pushing them toward Scott's chest and exposing his ass.

Diving in, Derek licked at Scott's opening, evoking a gasp. "Shit. That's so fucking…aaaahhh—"

Derek drove his tongue into Scott's ass a few times. The pungent odor of sweat surrounded him, likely from the exertion of setting up the room. Once again, the tension of pending release fired along his nerve endings. Derek sat back on his feet and replaced his tongue with a finger. The digit slid in easily, the heat of Scott's insides caressing his skin.

Normally he savored their lovemaking, but Derek could barely control his need. Leaning forward, he stared down at Scott. "I want you to sit on my cock."

Scott's eyes widened, and his mouth pulled into a smirk. "What's gotten into you?"

Derek didn't answer. Instead, he scooted next to Scott, his legs stretched along the length of the bed, and rested his weight on his hands behind him. "I think the question you should be asking is what's getting into you?"

Scott straddled Derek's waist, positioning Derek's cockhead at his hole.

Derek expected him to take his time, but Scott sank down in a smooth motion, barely even grimacing as he did so.

"Oh my God." Scott closed his eyes and sighed, but quickly opened them before Derek had to remind him. *Good.* Placing his hands on either side of Derek's face, Scott captured his mouth while bouncing up and down with greater force and speed. His breath came in short bursts as he panted, grinding and rotating his hips, bringing Derek closer and closer to a point of explosive release.

Using one of the hands he'd been leaning on, Derek gripped Scott's shaft and began to pump, his own release building up inside.

Scott growled as he tore himself from the kiss and gazed at Derek. His eyes blazed with an internal fire. Muscle spasms deep inside Scott's ass caressed Derek's shaft, bringing him closer and closer to the brink of release.

A few more rises and falls of Scott's body and Derek shot deep inside his lover. At the same time, a string of pearly white semen erupted from Scott's shaft, splashing against Derek's chest. The pungent smell of sex perfumed the air as Scott bucked on top of him. The rush of Derek's orgasm continued to rock him as he released several more bursts into Scott's hot ass.

Scott collapsed on top of Derek, wrapping his arms around Derek's torso, his body continuing to rock with after-shocks of his orgasm.

When Scott finally pulled himself together and stared into Derek's eyes, pure joy radiated from him. "That was fucking amazing."

Derek leaned forward and kissed him. "Let's get cleaned up and walk around until dinner."

Scott remained where he was, squeezing his ass a few times around Derek's cock, which was still lodged inside of him. After another few seconds, he lifted himself and slipped off the bed.

The dorm was beginning to buzz with arriving students, some with and others without parents, so their chances of being seen like this were pretty high but Derek didn't care. He dug through his bag and grabbed two towels, wrapping one around his waist. Scott wasted no time in following suit and led them into the hallway.

Just a year earlier Scott would have waited until Derek showered or at least checked the hallway before bounding through the dorm basically naked. Instead, he stepped into an empty shower stall and left the curtain open so Derek could join him. What a difference a year made.

A few female students glanced at them appreciatively as they emerged from the bathroom, and Derek smiled at them before following Scott into their room and closing the door.

Once they were dressed, Derek took Scott by the hand. This new Scott, the one who'd become so comfortable with publicly showing his affection, was one Derek couldn't get enough of.

At least one good thing had come out of Tyrell's attack… Scott had loosened up. Still, being back in the same dorm generated painful memories, and he couldn't help but glance around and take in his surroundings. Maybe he *was* too trusting. Maybe he *should* be a bit more careful.

Pushing the thought aside, he chose to focus on Scott and being back at school. He'd had his fair share of shit the previous year, and one thing was for sure. He wasn't going to let how other people acted change the way he lived his life. He wouldn't cower from fear, and he wouldn't compromise his nature…no matter what the fallout might be.

Chapter Six

Derek and Scott met up with Jared and Chad at a local burger joint. Bean Town Beef was busier than usual. Derek had become spoiled by a summer where the place wasn't overrun by college kids. Of course he still had the same question as he always did when he ate there. Did the *beef* portion of the name refer to the food or the wait staff? A requirement of working in the place seemed to be being buff and beautiful.

Jared wasted no time jumping right into business. "Derek, the reason I invited you to dinner is I was hoping you'd take an office with The Alliance this year."

Chad placed a hand on Jared's arm. "What my charming partner means to say is, it's so good to see the both of you, and how were your summers?"

Jared flushed, but nodded. "I'm sorry. I didn't mean to…like Chad said, how were your summers?"

Scott leaned back in his seat placing an arm over the back of Derek's chair. Derek sneaked a quick glance at him and shook his head when he witnessed the sly smile taking residence there. Looked like he was going to sit back and enjoy the show. "Summer was great. We just went camping last week and…" He held up his hand, "Scott sort of proposed to me."

Chad's eyes widened. "Oh my. The two of you are getting married?"

"Eventually, but Scott bought us matching rings as a promise for our future together." He stared at his ring then looked at the one on Scott's finger as well. "He waited until we were on the mountaintop to…" He turned to Scott, "Was it a proposal?"

Scott shrugged. "I guess that would be the best way to describe it."

Derek turned to face Jared and Chad. "He proposed on the mountaintop. It was incredibly romantic."

Jared smiled although he fidgeted in his seat. Derek could almost make out a slight rocking to his body, like he was about to jump out of his skin. "I'm so happy for the two of you." They were the right words, but looked like he had a stick up his ass. Man, he needed to loosen up.

"As far as taking a position in The Alliance, I'd love to." Derek didn't see any point in prolonging Jared's anxiety. "What office would you like me to run for?"

"Secretary. It's a good starting point, won't take up too much of your time, and will set you up for taking on a position of more responsibility in the future." Jared's entire body sank into his chair, all the tension from moments earlier gone.

Some of Derek's best and worst memories from freshman year stemmed from joining The Alliance. He'd explored living more openly as a gay man, met Tyrell and his lackey friends, and also met Jared, Chad, and a slew of other fantastic men and women.

Scott took a sip of water. "Well, now that we've got *that* settled, why don't we enjoy a nice dinner? I haven't had a burger here in over a month."

"I second that." Chad nodded at Scott with an expression that said *thank you*, then raised his glass. "To a new year and old friends."

Everyone clinked their glasses over the center of the table.

Derek half-listened as Jared prattled on about his hopes for the coming year. His goals were lofty, like the dance at the end of the previous year, aimed at raising awareness and building bridges between disaggregated groups. But Jared's social skills were definitely unpolished. There was a clinical method to his approach which was a bit off-putting. Taking office would allow Derek a chance to bring some of the warmth and humanity to the group's work. Besides, every time he shifted positions his ass throbbed with a dull ache, reminding him of all the sex he and Scott had recently. Certainly a much better focus than Jared's monologue about the annual agenda of The Alliance.

While Derek found the plans exciting, he would've preferred to simply enjoy his first night of sophomore year. Thankfully Chad and Scott were supportive of their more agenda-oriented partners.

All this time, Scott and Chad chatted easily with one another. For a second Derek thought of the two of them as the supportive partners, attending a business function with their men. If *he* couldn't avoid thinking about relationships stereotypically, how could he expect others to? It drove him crazy whenever people asked him who the girl was in their relationship. *Neither, god dammit!*

As secretary of The Alliance, Derek could help to dispel the misconception which existed about relationships, especially gay relationships. Two men were just that, two men, each with their own ways of being masculine, coming together because their personalities meshed. Each bringing his own set of interests and passions. No different than his parents and the way they meshed, or any other couple who was happy and in love.

By the end of dinner, Derek was about ready to stick a knife in his ear. "It sounds like you've got a solid plan, Jared. We'll do some outreach in the community, a couple dances since the one from last year was so successful, and the establishment of a counseling center."

The center initiative touched Derek's core. While he'd need to go through training, he'd be able to help others. Maybe by using a structured system, like a peer counseling center, he could satisfy his need to support others without giving Scott a heart attack at the same time.

Scott pulled out his wallet to pay their part of the bill, but Jared stopped him with a hand on his wrist. "I invited you both, and I'll be taking up some of your boyfriend's time, so please allow me the small concession of paying for dinner."

Replacing his wallet, Scott was gracious enough to agree, although the grimace on his face let Derek know he wasn't happy about it.

As they stepped into the warm evening, lingering heat of a waning summer carried in the air. Chad hailed a cab. "Wanna share?"

Scott interjected before Derek could say anything. "Thank you so much for dinner and the offer, but it's so beautiful out, I think we'll walk back."

Jared nodded and gave both Derek and Scott a hug. Chad did the same and they got into the cab. As soon as the taxi was out of sight, Scott turned to Derek. "That dude seriously needs to lighten up."

No sense in arguing the obvious. Derek took Scott's hand, and they strolled down Columbus Street under the glow of the orange-yellow of the street lamps. "I love the idea about the peer counseling."

Scott stopped, forcing Derek to stop as well. "It *is* a great idea, and I can tell you're excited. I'm totally in support of that, but there was something insistent about

Jared tonight. Just make sure you don't let him push you into anything that you don't want to do."

The warning reminded Derek of his mother's request. She'd asked him to listen to Scott when he shared his concerns. He cupped Scott's cheek. "I won't do anything I don't want to do." *Including allowing you to pressure me into decisions I'm not comfortable with.* "After last year, I think I learned my lesson." His mother and Scott needed to get that through their thick skulls.

Scott smiled, although happiness didn't reach his eyes. "Your heart is too big. I love that about you, but I worry, too. Just go slow. Don't jump head first. Wade into the waters and take your time. See how things play out."

He couldn't see how Jared's excitement about his plans could lead to anything but good things, but if Scott was concerned, listening was the least he could give the both of them. "Okay. I'll go slow."

"That's all I'm asking." Scott started walking once again, Derek's hand still clutched in his own. "Let's head to the subway and get back to campus. I'm sure you're going to want to start planning out tomorrow's set for the party."

"Oh yeah, that's right." How could he have forgotten? "I'll probably just use an old mix. I don't want to waste the first day of the year holed up in our room, mixing. Plus, I want to hang out with people during the party."

When they got back to their dorm room, Derek was glad he'd made the decision he had. Beck was hanging out in the hallway, chatting with someone he didn't recognize.

"Beck!" Derek ran to her and yanked her into a hug, completely ignoring the fact she'd been in the middle of a conversation. "How the hell have you been? When'd you get back from Europe?"

Beck, Derek's best friend from high school and the first person he'd ever come out to, squeezed him back. "I just got back this morning and was pissed to hell I wasn't there for the big reveal."

Derek stared at her, not knowing what she was talking about.

She stood back. "Go on now. Hold that hand out to Mama so she can see your purdy ring."

"Oh. *That's* what you're talking about." He held up his hand, revealing the promise ring.

For a split second, Beck's expression softened, something Derek only witnessed on rare occasions. Then Scott sidled up beside them. She glanced at him and her expression completely changed. "Well, shit on a stick, you turned into a He-man."

Scott stepped forward and slid an arm around her shoulder. "It's so good to see you."

"Did the trip go the way we planned?" She stared at him, eyes wide in anticipation.

"Better. Thanks for helping me. I know you probably had better things to do with your time than Skype with me while backpacking across Europe, but everything went exactly right." Scott kissed her temple.

"Wait, you were in on the whole proposal thing as well?" Derek faced Scott. "Was there anyone besides me who *didn't* know about your plans?"

Scott released Beck and took her bag for her. "Nope. I notified the world so they could all suffer right along with me." He pulled out the key to their room and opened the door.

Beck sauntered past Derek, who remained in the hallway, still processing that she was there and had known about Scott's plans. It wasn't until her strong hand wrapped around his arm and yanked that he started moving. "Chill out. You guys are promised to each other. That's all that matters. And now you're back in the shack. Hope the walls are sturdy in this place."

Scott tossed her bag on the floor. The clanking sound as it made contact with the floor was alarmingly loud.

Beck scowled at Scott. "Careful with that. It's party time." She dug through her bag and procured a bottle of champagne and three plastic flutes. "To sophomore year."

"To sophomore year," Derek and Scott said in unison.

"Hope you guys are thirsty. I've got another bottle in there." She glanced around the room. "What, no fridge?"

Scott took a seat on their couch and downed the drink in one go, ignoring her commentary. "You staying the night?"

Beck rolled her eyes. "Do pigs roll around in their own shit?"

Derek shook his head. "Actually they don't. They only look dirty because they roll around in mud to keep the flies away. And a simple yes would've done."

Beck stared at Derek for a few seconds, then strode across the room and knelt in front of Scott and took his hand. "Dearest Scott. I shall be staying the night if you grant me permission." Before Scott could respond, she faced Derek. "Better?"

"Much." He'd known Beck way too long for her sarcasm to carry any bite.

Within twenty minutes the first bottle was done, and by that time, Derek felt all warm and fuzzy inside, if not a little dizzy.

Scott wrapped an arm around his shoulders and pulled him close. "Where should we go first? The Student Center, the dorm lounge, or should we simply stick around here and see who passes by our room?"

"I prefer the sticking around the room idea." Derek settled onto the couch next to Scott, seeing as Beck had claimed their bed, lounging on her side.

"Suits me fine." Beck stretched her arms and pushed herself into a seated position. "You've got some cuties on this floor." As if summoned, the kid she'd been talking to when they'd arrived passed by their open door. A few seconds later, he ambled by again. When he made a third appearance seconds later, Beck hollered from her perch, "Well stop wearing a tread in the carpet. Come in."

The kid's eyes bugged out and Derek thought he might run and hide, but he took a tentative step into their room.

After about thirty seconds of silence, Beck hopped off the bed and dragged him all the way into the room. "Fucking freshmen. They're like skittish kittens."

He stood in the middle of the room. At about five foot ten and no more than a hundred thirty pounds, the kid looked like a gentle breeze might knock him down. Add to that his shaggy brown hair which covered half his face and Derek's heart bled for him. Last thing a newbie freshman needed was a bodacious loudmouth making him the center of attention.

Scott shook his head. "What's your name?"

Derek rested his head on Scott's shoulder. Leave it to his boyfriend to ease Beck's brazen nature.

He shifted from foot to foot, his hands clasped behind his back, glancing at Derek and Scott before answering. "I'm Tim."

"Well, come on, take a seat." Beck patted a spot on the bed next to her.

Tim looked unsure what to do.

"It's all right. You can come in." Beck spoke with a soothing voice like she was speaking with a toddler, something Derek had rarely witnessed from his friend. The frightened looking freshmen scrambled across the room and sat where Beck had indicated.

Derek felt the corner of his lip creep up, wondering if he'd been anywhere near this shy his freshman year. Of course, he'd had Scott so he was probably ten times more confident than most freshmen. "Tim, which room is yours?"

His cheeks flushed. "I live in the room next door."

"Oh." Derek expected more. "And where are you from?"

"I'm from Washington State. Near Tacoma." He folded his hands on his lap, giving off the appearance of an attentive schoolboy.

"Oh, for shit's sake." Beck cut through the awkwardness of the stilted conversation. "He heard the two of you going at it like bunnies earlier today, then saw you come out of the shower together, and wanted to get to know you since he's gay. He's not out at home. His parents don't know about him."

Tim's cheeks shifted from a slight pink to a deep shade of scarlet. His eyes darted toward the open door and Derek wondered whether the kid was about to make a mad dash from the room.

A flash fire ignited Derek's cheeks. Their sex from earlier hadn't been terribly loud, had it? But then again, he hadn't concentrated on much except for his burning desire to have his cock buried balls-deep inside of Scott. He took a steadying breath. *Note to self, control the volume in the future.*

Time to lighten the awkward mood. "It's nice to meet you, Tim. We have a group on campus that you might be interested in joining called The Alliance. I'm not exactly sure when the first meeting is, but you can come with us if you like." Scott wouldn't be going to all the meetings, but after their freshman year when Tyrell had written faggot on their door, Scott had taken steps toward being more open and proactive in the gay community on campus.

Tim visibly relaxed. "Really? You'd take me to a meeting?" His voice sort of bubbled. He quickly shifted his expression, tilting his head back in a show of indifference. "I mean, that's cool." The ruse might have been effective if his face weren't still beet red.

"Sure. It would be my pleasure." Derek snuggled closer to Scott. Yeah, pretty great start to the year. He was already helping a new kid on his first day of school.

Beck hopped to her feet. "All right, Little Tim, time for you to head off now. Me and these two haven't seen each other in a while and need to catch up."

Scott shook his head. "Beck. He can stick around if he likes."

She opened her mouth to protest, but Scott shot her a glare that shut her up. In all their lives, Derek had never been able to achieve that with her. "Fine."

Tim stared at each of them, his gaze finally settling on his palms. "That's all right. Thanks for being so nice."

Derek smiled. "No problem. We'll see you later."

Tim left, glancing back one last time with a smile aimed at Derek, then disappeared from view.

"I think you have a new admirer." Beck leveled Derek with an unwavering gaze. "And based on your track record with admirers, I think you should be careful."

Fuck! Everyone needed to stop issuing warnings. Didn't they know he'd learned from his experiences? "Whatever. He's a new kid and wants to meet other gay students. Is there any harm in me offering to take him to an Alliance meeting?"

Scott cut Beck off before she could say anything. "No. Beck is just mirroring what I said to you earlier." He rose from the couch. "Why don't we go downstairs and see who's back from last year?" He brushed his lips against Derek's forehead, then extended his hand and helped Derek to his feet.

Beck hopped off the bed. "Sounds like a plan to me."

Derek let Scott drive things in a new direction, but the lingering frustration that everyone seemed to think he was incapable of spotting trouble ate at him.

He listed all of the positive things from his first day of school in an effort to drown his rising irritation. Jared had amazing plans for The Alliance. Tim seemed like a student Derek could help. He and Scott had already fucked like the end of the world was upon them. Beck had made a surprise appearance. And on top of all that, he had champagne coursing through his veins. The evening should've been all relaxation and laughter. But Derek couldn't shake the lingering sense that the people closest to him had little faith in his ability to make responsible decisions.

If Scott planned on babying him for the entire year, they were going to have a serious conversation. For the time being, however, he decided let it go and enjoy their evening.

Chapter Seven

Derek's first class the next day was at eleven-thirty, a course called Sociology of Gender and Sexuality, which would serve as an elective toward his major. That gave him plenty of time to sleep in and even more time to enjoy a solid pounding from Scott. Shit he'd missed starting his days with sex.

Scott didn't have his first class until later in the afternoon, but he had an early morning wrestling practice.

Derek slept in until eight then trekked to the sports complex and caught the last hour of Scott's practice. Surveying a room filled with well-proportioned guys ranging from eighteen to twenty-one didn't do anything to bolster his own self-esteem. Derek's own muscles had become less defined and he made a mental note to hit the school gym. Despite his inferiority complex, he wanted to see Scott in action, especially since Scott was moving up, not one, but two weight classes this year.

The shift didn't seem to faze Scott in the slightest. His competition weighed more than he was used to, but so did Scott. Pride swelled in Derek's chest as he watched his partner's skillful take downs and throws, although he couldn't deny the hint of longing as well. Maybe he'd been hasty in declining to join the BU team. After all, their high school practices, or more precisely, his and Scott's private workout sessions when the rest of the team left the wrestling room to shower, were some of Derek's best memories from his pre-college years.

Between The Alliance, his studies, and mixing, he wasn't sure he'd be able to add wrestling and manage to juggle all of it. At least he could engage in wrestling of a more intimate nature when he had Scott alone in their room.

Once the practice was over, Scott and Hank, one of Jared's friend, joined Derek on the bleachers. Both men dripped with sweat. That didn't stop Derek from inhaling deeply when Scott pulled him into a hug and kissed his temple.

Hank leaned over, bracing himself with his hands on his thighs. "Your man is gonna win us a title this year. I've never seen anything like it. He's a machine. I thought for sure he'd have to work a *little* to keep his spot on the team, but the extra weight seems to be all muscle."

Scott shoved Hank. "Whatever dude. You're just jealous you don't got the moves like I do."

Derek chuckled, pleased Scott could live openly on the team. Scott's fears the previous year that the team would ostracize him when they found out he and Derek were a couple had been completely unfounded. Now, Derek had an open invitation to all the wrestling parties and caught shit from the guys on the team if he missed one. So much for the stereotype that jocks had problems with gays.

Derek followed the two out of the wrestling room. "You don't need to tell me. I used to be able to hold my own against him. Now…forget it."

Scott let out a quiet "Ha!" which Derek chose to ignore.

"How was your first class?" Scott placed an arm around Derek's shoulder, the heat from his body penetrating Derek's shirt and his lover's sweat filtering into his nose like a musky, sensual cologne.

"It was interesting. I'll know more as we go along. The professor is a fruit-loop. Probably did too much LSD at

Woodstock or something. I think I'm gonna be learning a lot about the nature of socially accepted free love."

Scott shook his head. "I'm with your dad on your choice of major. What the hell are you gonna do with a concentration in sociology?"

Derek elbowed Scott in the ribs. "Ass."

Hank paused by the entrance to the locker room. "You two crack me up."

Scott rubbed his ribs. "Yeah, he's a fuckin' laugh riot." Scott shoved Derek, then pulled him close, rubbing sweat onto Derek's clothes. If he thought that was a punishment, he needed better tactics.

"Mmm. Think I'll wear this shirt to bed tonight." Derek lifted a wet spot of his shirt to his nose and inhaled deeply.

"Yeah. I'm taking a shower now." Hank winked at Derek then headed into the locker room.

Scott shook his head. "You're too much."

"And you love it." Derek grabbed Scott's hand and drew it to his lips, kissing Scott's knuckles.

Scott swallowed, a flush creeping up his neck and coloring his cheeks. "If you hang around for about five minutes, I'll meet you out here and we can grab something to eat." Scott faced Derek, lowering his hands to cover his groin.

"I'll wait." Derek took a moment to appreciate Scott's ass in his wrestling singlet, then stepped outside the complex, immediately bathed in sunshine. Ten minutes later, Scott joined him and they went to the cafeteria a few doors down from the athletics building.

During dinner, Scott loaded his plate with macaroni and cheese, a mountain of rice, and a few measly sprigs of broccoli. Derek stared at him. "Got a starch craving?"

"Practice is kicking my ass. I need to refuel. Besides, wrestling in this new weight class requires I eat a lot to keep my weight up. You should join the team. All the guys want you to, and your weight class is open."

"Oh?" Scott probably knew how much he wanted to join the team, which made it all the more difficult to refuse. "C'mon. We talked about this. I don't think I can handle it with everything else I've got on my plate."

"Are you sure? We'd be able to spend more time together."

Low blow. Derek was tempted. He enjoyed using his whole body on the mat. He'd never lost his love of the sport, a perfect blend of team effort and individual skill. But he didn't want to overextend himself. Besides, the idea of serving as a peer counselor had stuck with him since the last Alliance meeting. Certainly that job would take up a lot of his time.

"I'll think about it, but I doubt I'll join. Maybe next year." Derek watched for Scott's reaction, relieved when there was no hint of disappointment.

With their trays loaded, they found seats.

"Whenever you want to join, I'm sure you'll make the first lineup. You're one of the best wrestlers I know. And I'm not talking about our private sessions in the bedroom." He waggled his eyebrows, then burst out laughing. "Sorry. I'm just excited to be back at it."

Derek swallowed back the sense of regret crawling up his esophagus. "Thanks for the vote of confidence."

This was how things were supposed to be. Him and Scott together, supporting each other without any doubts or misgivings. After being tag teamed the previous night by Scott and Beck about Tim, he'd worried he'd have to constantly defend his choices. But alone with Scott, everything lined up just right.

They wolfed down their meals, Derek's burger and fries far more appealing than the pile of calories on Scott's plate, then Scott had to go to his first class. Derek had some time before his so he wandered back to the dorms and went through his stored mixes on his computer.

He had several sets he'd done over the summer. Most of them catered to his personal preferences, mellow rock artists like John Mayer, or his recently discovered favorite Peter Bradley Adams, an accidental gem found through the web-radio station, Pandora.

The somber music wouldn't do for a dorm party. Katy Perry was always a favorite, but totally cliché. Instead he chose to make the evening a tribute to Justin, the Timberlake version since he wouldn't be caught dead honoring Bieber.

He collected several songs to span Justin's career, throwing in Beyoncé, Usher, Maroon 5, and others to give some variety. And he added in a bit of Ariana Grande, just because he loved her.

He worked on the mix until he had to go to his Geology 101 lab course, or "Rocks For Jocks," designed for students, like himself, who seemed to have a learning disability when it came to science. At least it would satisfy his lab requirement.

Saving the mix, he grabbed his notebook and left his room. The moment he stepped into the hallway he bumped into Tim, reeking of weed and eyes bloodshot. Not wanting to seem parental, Derek ignored the signs of being stoned. "Hey Tim. You on your way to class?"

Tim lifted his head in slow motion. After a few moments, a wide grin played across his face. Shit but the kid was high. "Derek. Hey. Yeah. I have a science course. Some class about rocks." His words slurred together, and he didn't maintain direct eye contact.

"Geology 101?" Derek half hoped Tim said *yes* so he could keep an eye on the newbie. The other half hoped he'd say *no* since Derek didn't want to get involved with someone who did drugs. Knowing himself, he'd decide to make Tim his project which cut a little too close to home after he'd done the same thing with Tyrell the previous year. Not to mention the shit he'd get from Scott.

"Yeah. That's the one. What class are you off to?"

A mix of emotions rolled through Derek, both concern and wariness battling for dominance. The fact Tim didn't seem at all concerned that he was starting his school career under the influence of drugs helped Derek to land on the concerned side. "Same one. Let's go."

The science building was a few blocks down from the dorm, As they walked, Derek asked pointed questions while trying to seem casual. If he could figure out what had caused Tim to turn to drugs maybe he could help the kid get onto the right track. "So, how's it feel to be away from home and in college?"

Tim let out a huge sigh. "You don't even know. It's like the weight of the world has been lifted off my shoulders. Back home I had to always watch my back. Whether my parents checked my bag when I got home from school or my classmates followed my every move, trying to see if their suspicions about me were correct, I always felt like I was under a magnifying glass."

"That must have been tough. How'd you cope?" Maybe Tim would volunteer the root of his demons on his own. Family? Friends? Drugs? Something else? "You know, the normal ways." Tim strolled idly next to Derek, staring at guys who passed them. When a man dressed in tight black pants and a leather vest strode by, Tim stopped in his tracks and turned in the direction the man had gone.

Derek followed Tim's gaze and locked eyes with Tight-Pants-Leather-Vest. Maybe it was the intensity of the man's stare that made Derek shudder. Or the way he wet his lips with his tongue while staring at the two of them. Either way, Derek suddenly desired a shower.

Tim continued to stare until the man turned around and sauntered down the street, a swag to his gait. "All I have to say about that is 'da-yum!'"

Derek chuckled, although he found no humor in Tim's brazenness. Even during his freshman year when he wanted to live out loud and proud, he'd never openly gawked at anyone. Then again, he had Scott so he was covered in the *guy* department. "Really?"

"Oh, hell yeah! Back home the only way I could keep from wanting to kill myself was to go to the bars where the old daddy-types went. They paid for my drinks, my weed, the coke. I was really popular with them. I felt special there." Tim turned to face Derek. "Know what I mean?"

"Honestly, no. I'm sorry." And just how serious was Tim when he said he wanted to *kill* himself?

"Huh." The surprise was echoed in Tim's face.

"Maybe I was just lucky. My parents are really cool, and I had Beck."

"Yeah. You're *really* lucky. I couldn't tell anyone about who I was." Was that a hint of jealousy Derek sensed? If so, maybe he was beginning to get to the real Tim instead of the image Tim seemed keen on presenting, bragging about bars, guys, and drugs.

"I grew up in Cambridge, Massachusetts which has to be one of the most liberal cities in the world, and I have Scott."

Tim nodded. "Back home, all I had to do was show up at the bar in my slim cut Levis and a formfitting tank, and the drinks would come all night long."

Derek didn't know what to say, so he let the subject hang in the air. Luckily they'd arrived at the science building, giving him an excuse to change the topic. "We're here. Let's find good seats before we get stuck off to one of the sides or up front."

Tim shrugged, hoisting his bag a little higher on his shoulder. "Sounds good."

As they hiked up two flights of stairs to the lab, Derek tried to sort through all Tim had revealed. As far as he could tell, this was a kid on a fast track to real problems. Beyond the drugs and the underage drinking, he wondered what other experiences Tim had and whether he'd been safe.

In high school, the advisors had gone over basics about narcotics, calling pot the gateway to heavier and more dangerous drugs. Tim mentioned coke. Had he done meth? Had he had sex? Did he use protection?

Not wanting to overthink Tim's situation, he took a seat and flipped his notebook open to a clean page. Tim did the same just as the professor entered the room.

Focusing on class had never been a problem for Derek, so he was able to follow along while other thoughts played out in his head. At the top of the list were his worries about Tim and what kind of trouble the kid could get himself into now that he didn't have the safety net of parents watching over him.

The second thought was more immediate. Once he told Scott about everything Tim had said, he knew the exact response he'd get. *Don't take this on, Derek. He's got problems, and you get too involved.*

Scott was right, of course, and Derek didn't want to hear it, but he also didn't want to keep secrets either. If it came down to an argument, well, they'd had plenty of those and come out fine every time. There was no reason to believe this would end any differently.

~~~~~

This can't be happening again. Scott rubbed his temples where a migraine was getting ready to split his head open. "Derek. Please tell me you're going to steer clear of this."

Derek crossed his arms over his chest. "Scott. We have the same class and sat next to each other. What was I supposed to do? Ignore him?"

Scott opened his mouth but didn't say anything.

"Nice." Derek crossed his arms over his chest. "Look. I told the kid I'd bring him to an Alliance meeting. It's not like I agreed to be his life coach or anything."

"You say the words, but do you really mean them?" Scott took Derek's wrists and peeled his arms from their guarded position. "It's not your job to save every stray puppy that comes your way. If Tim's into drugs, he's bad news. End of story."

"Are you saying you forbid me to help?" Derek's voice carried an edge.

Shit! "Of course I'm not telling you what to do. I learned a while back you'll do exactly the opposite of what I say if I try to *tell* you what to do." The truth was he loved Derek's headstrong ways.

Derek visibly relaxed. "Listen, I know he's trouble. I do." Derek took Scott's hands in his own, squeezing gently. "I won't get too involved. I'll just take him to a meeting. Introduce him to a few people. Maybe help him get started on one of the committees. And that's it. Okay?"

It was more than Scott hoped for and far less than he wanted, but it would have to do...for now. There was always the option of reporting the kid. Drugs weren't permitted on campus and, although many students smoked pot, a freshman flaunting his use on the first day of school would certainly be grounds for disciplinary action. The thought of Derek's disappointment in him if he ratted Tim out was enough to keep him in check. "All right," Scott said. "Why don't we put this behind us for now and enjoy tonight." The party was scheduled to start in about an hour and Derek was in charge of the music. The last thing he needed was an overbearing boyfriend stressing him out.

"Thank you." Derek hugged him and pulled him close, just the way he liked it. The warmth of Derek's touch and the safety of his embrace helped to thaw the chill running up his spine.

Scott wrapped his arms around Derek's waist, sliding his hands down to grip firm ass muscles and giving them a teasing squeeze. Derek yelped, pulling his head back and staring into Scott's eyes. For a second, Scott was lost in the amber depths, before his focus zeroed in on Derek's plump lips.

When Derek leaned in to kiss him, Scott parted his lips sweeping his tongue into Derek's mouth and swirling it in a gentle tumble. Derek's clean, minty flavor filled him, playing against his taste buds.

Hugging their bodies closer together, Scott deepened the kiss, shifting the languid sensuality into something more heated and urgent.

Derek groaned into Scott's mouth, arching forward and sealing their bodies together, torso to torso. Scott's cock lengthened, pressing into Derek's lower abdomen.

After several minutes of frottage, Derek pulled out of the kiss, panting. "As much as I want this, I have to go downstairs and set up." A mischievous gleam shone in his eyes. "But when we get back to the room, we're picking up where we left off."

Scott leaned forward, kissing Derek once more, then released him. *Tease.* "Do you need help bringing everything downstairs?"

"Nope. I got it covered." Derek grabbed his equipment and lugged it toward the door. With his hand on the knob and his mixing stuff precariously balanced, he turned and faced Scott. "Seriously. I promise I'll be careful. I know how hard last year was on you, and I'd never do that to you again." He was out the door before Scott could respond.

Alone in their room, Scott plodded over to the couch and slumped into it with a huff. It was only the first day of school and already worry plagued him. Derek was a magnet for trouble. As sure as he knew the sun would set and rise again, he knew Derek would find some way to try to save Tim. He'd see it as his duty.

Derek's fierce commitment was one of the things which made him special. It's what lit the boundless light inside him. Scott hoped that strength was enough, because the more Derek surrounded himself with darkness, the harder that light would have to work to shine through.

If he stood in Derek's way, even out of a desire to protect him, Derek would understand. He'd even forgive, but there'd be a piece of him resenting Scott's interference. As nervous as butting out made him, Scott would have to do as the singer Tammy Wynette said and *stand by his man*.

But he'd keep a watchful eye on just how deep Derek sank into this new project, and he'd step in if things got to be too much. Maybe not by reporting Tim, but there were other ways to influence Derek. Beck was one. Clair was another. Despite the cowardice of involving others, Scott wouldn't have to bear the sole burden of applying pressure on Derek.

However, those options could wait. Tonight was about celebrations and renewing friendships. He rose from the couch and checked himself one last time in the mirror. Pleased with the carefully constructed casual look he'd achieved, he bounded down the stairs, two at a time.

As he approached the dorm's first floor main lounge, the music became louder and he could hear the din of people talking. Once he entered the room, the noise level escalated.

Elizabeth rushed to his side. "Scott, I was wondering what was taking you so long." She looped her arm in his and led him to a group of other residents who'd been in the dorm the previous year.

Scott bit back the urge to tell her about Tim. One simple comment and she'd be required to deal with the situation.

Instead, he plastered a smile on his face and hugged several of his old friends. Derek was already making his rounds, receiving compliments on his music.

As soon as he spotted Scott, his eyes lit up. Racing to his side, he slid an arm around his waist. The loving action pushed Scott's concerns aside. Nothing helped to ground him like Derek's touch. "Isn't this great? It's like a reunion."

"The party *is* a reunion. Half these people lived here last year." Scott kissed the side of Derek's head and scanned the room. Along with Elizabeth, he recognized about ten or twelve other people who'd lived on their floor the previous year. He spotted many others from the other floors as well. There were also new faces dotted around the fringes of the room. Probably the freshmen trying to figure out the social politics of dorm life.

When he caught sight of Tim, his gut churned. Derek must have sensed something because he tightened his grip. "It's okay, Scott. Just let it be for now."

Scott nodded, but didn't take his eyes off Tim. He seemed fine. None of the telltale signs of being high that Derek had described were present. But Derek had said Tim was practiced at hiding who he really was. Someone like that would surely know it would be a bad idea to reek of pot and have bloodshot eyes at the dorm's first party of the year.

Tim was surrounded by a slew of other people, surprisingly, since he'd seemed so timid the other day. He moved his arms about in an animated fashion as he spoke. Scott had to give the kid credit. He had charisma. If Scott hadn't had inside information, he'd probably find himself wrapped around Tim's little finger, laughing along with the others. But he *wasn't* ignorant of Tim's problems, and he'd never been good at hiding his emotions. Best to stay away until he learned more about the guy.

Derek slipped his hand from around Scott's waist and strode over to the mixing board. With a quick press of a button, the room filled with Scott's favorite song, the one he'd gone to see live in New York at the Bowery Ballroom with Derek the previous summer. Howie Day's song *Madrigal,* the one where he used a mixer to provide his own backup singing and percussion, brought a sense of nostalgia and peace to Scott.

Derek arrived at his side a few seconds later. "Remember?"

Scott hugged Derek in a loose embrace and brushed their lips together. "How could I ever forget?"

That trip had been a series of firsts. Their first road trip, the first time they'd had sex, the first moment he knew, beyond any question, that the two of them would be happy. And it was that trip which had carried him through the turbulence of their freshman year. For a second, he wondered if Derek was trying to remind him that they could weather any storm, but Derek never did have a talent for subtlety.

Not wanting to dampen the evening with his doubts and worries, Scott pushed thoughts of Tim to the side and simply enjoyed Derek's company. An easy task since Derek's broad grin shone with the luminescence of the sun.

They swayed to the melodic thrum, people and conversations blurring into the background. Scott gazed into Derek's eyes, grounded by the pure love radiating back at him. Being with Derek, having him by his side, was all that mattered and all he needed.

For several minutes, Howie wove his spell with beat and melody, people seeming to know to keep their distance. Or perhaps they weren't so much keeping their distance as fading from Scott and Derek's world. They didn't kiss. They barely moved, yet their connection was as strong as if forged out of stone.

Then the music shifted, the somber tune returning to a quick tempo, and they were once again part of the group, surrounded by smiles and laughter and friendship.

Scott was about to suggest they head back upstairs, but before he could utter a word, Tim joined them. "Hey, Derek. Hey, Scott."

Derek smiled at the intruder, tightening his grip around Scott's waist. "Tim." He leaned into Scott's body, nestling his head against Scott's shoulder. "Enjoying the party?"

"Are you kidding? This is great." Tim shifted his attention from their faces to the points where their bodies connected, before continuing. "Someone told me you did the mix for the party. That's so cool." The comment was delivered in a nonchalant manner, although Tim seemed to be studying the two of them more than making polite conversation.

"Thanks. Mixing is kind of a hobby of mine. Always has been." Derek turned to face Scott. "Remember when I first showed you how I put songs together up in my attic?"

Scott leaned forward and rubbed his nose against Derek's. "I do. And I remember our make out session afterwards." The flush adorning Derek's cheeks was gratifying.

When he returned his focus to Tim, Scott observed the smile had waned just a hint. He couldn't help the small sense of satisfaction. Since when had he become petty? Scott shifted topics. "What sorts of things are you into?" The question was supposed to be a casual attempt at making conversation, but as soon as he asked, he found himself paying close attention, waiting to dissect whatever Tim said against what he knew about the kid.

Tim didn't seem to pick up on Scott's discomfort. "Dancing. Not the Dance-with-the-Stars crap, but good old fashioned boogie and sweat kind of dancing."

Scott nodded. It was a good enough answer. He certainly liked to dance and sweat as well. Part of him wished Derek hadn't said anything to him. There was no way he'd be able to view Tim through any other lens than a possible threat to Derek's safety. "The Alliance had a great dance at the end of the year. I'm sure you'll have plenty of opportunities to engage in your favorite hobby while at BU."

Tim perked up at the mention of The Alliance. "I can't wait to go to the first meeting." He shifted his focus to Derek. "Do you know when it will be?"

"Jared hasn't set a date yet, but I'm sure it'll be soon." Derek's attention was diverted to a loud cheer on the other side of the room. Bruce, Elizabeth's new boyfriend, was upside down, hands braced on a keg, and was drinking like a fish. "Oh my God. I've got to go watch that."

Derek took off, leaving Scott and Tim alone in the corner. Scott wanted to follow, but couldn't bring himself to be explicitly rude. Tim watched Derek's retreat, then faced Scott, a nervous smile creeping into place. "How long have you and Derek been together?"

"Since high school. We met when I moved from Iowa to Cambridge my senior year. We were on the wrestling team together." Had it really been two years? Time moved so fast and so slow at the same time. With all that had happened, it felt like ten years, but looking back, he could've blinked and missed the whole thing.

"I'm so jealous." Tim's shoulders slumped, and Scott thought he caught a glimpse of the real person beneath the party-hard exterior. "I bet things would have been different if I'd met a guy as sweet as Derek when I was in high school."

Scott couldn't help it. The opening was too large for him to ignore. "What do you mean? What was it like for you in high school?" He already had some information, so this was a good way to find out whether Tim would come clean like he had with Derek, or if he'd keep secrets.

"It was tough. My parents were always keeping tabs on me, and I couldn't be myself. And the people in the LGBTQ

D.H. Starr ~ 104~Wrestling With Passion

club at school were bullied relentlessly. I didn't want that for myself."

It matched what Derek had said but didn't give much information, at least not the information Scott wanted. "How'd you cope?"

After a few seconds he responded. "I went out on my own, going to bars in Tacoma or Seattle. It wasn't too tough to get a fake ID, and I could be around other gay people and just be myself."

Again, his comments lined up with what Tim had told Derek, although the admission was only partial. "That must have been tough, being younger than all the guys at the bar. I experienced that once, and it was pretty obvious the men wanted to take me or Derek home with them. Maybe even both of us." He hoped sharing this little bit of information might loosen Tim's tongue.

"I don't know. I liked the attention. I wasn't invisible like at school, and they treated me like a person rather than some kid who needed to be protected like my parents did." Tim hugged himself, glancing about the room.

Scott could have continued to push, but it was pretty clear Tim wasn't going to give the same kind of information he'd offered Derek. "Well, now that you're here in Massachusetts and at Boston University, you shouldn't have any problem finding lots of guys who'll treat you like an adult."

Tim smiled. "I'm counting on it." He drummed his fingers on his forearms and didn't maintain eye contact with Scott as he spoke. "Derek sure is sweet. You're lucky to have him."

"Yes. I give thanks every day for having Derek in my life. I'd do *anything* for him." Scott's words came out a bit more forceful than he'd intended, but his initial assessment that Tim would present a problem hadn't been squashed, even if the kid hadn't provided any information to condemn himself either.

"I wish I had someone like him." Tim didn't even seem to be talking to Scott anymore. He stared across the room at Derek. "Look at him. Everyone loves the guy. And his smile."

"Yeah. He makes people happy." Scott placed his hand on Tim's shoulder and gave it a brief squeeze. "Especially me."

Tim pulled back slightly, not enough to break contact, but definitely showing he wasn't comfortable with the uninvited touching. Whether directed at Scott specifically or a general characteristic, Scott had no idea, but he didn't really care either. "I think I'm gonna mosey over to him now."

Tim nodded. "Okay. Catch you later."

Scott wondered whether the words were sincere or if Tim was just being polite. "If you need anything, let us know. We're right next door after all."

Tim shifted from one foot to the other, darting his gaze from one part of the room to another. Without saying anything more, he left Scott and took off through the stairwell door.

Scott joined Derek who was cheering on Elizabeth. She'd replaced her boyfriend on the keg. "Hey. How goes the keg stand watching?"

Derek leaned into Scott. "Oh, my God. I so want to go next."

Scott chuckled. "Your call. Although you've always been a lightweight."

Derek twirled so he faced Scott, an offended expression painted on his face. Within seconds, the seriousness melted into a mirthful grin. "Whatever. It'll make me easier for you to seduce later."

Scott laughed. "Like it would be difficult if you were stone cold sober." The comment caused him to think of Tim. "Speaking of which, Tim didn't seem to be under the influence of anything. That's a good sign."

Derek gave him a reproachful glare, but it softened immediately. "Go easy. I promised you I'd be careful. Give him a chance."

A few minutes later, Derek was upside down, his feet held by two of the guys on the wrestling team who lived in their dorm, and Elizabeth holding the spout to his mouth. Everyone surrounding the keg shouted, "Chug. Chug. Chug."

Scott had nearly pushed Tim from his mind when he appeared by his side. "Holy shit. Derek's doing a keg stand."

Scott glanced at him. All of the jitteriness had disappeared. In fact, Tim seemed to have energized over the course of the few minutes he'd been upstairs. Although Scott had no experience with drugs, he was pretty sure he could make an educated guess as to what had caused Tim's change in behavior, if his sniffles and the way he rubbed his nose were any indicator. *So much for Tim seeming like he's under control.*

He turned from Tim without saying anything and focused on Derek. It took all of his willpower not to pull Derek off the keg so he could corner Elizabeth and tell her what he suspected, but Derek had been clear. For now, he'd have to trust that his boyfriend, the man whom he'd promised himself to, was smart enough to maintain a safe distance from Tim's problems.

Chapter Eight

Derek had gone through a full week of his classes, his favorite being the music class he shared with Scott. The description of the course had been enough to convince him to enroll. After all, music was one of his greatest loves, and his final project would require he put together a mix. Scott had said he wanted to take the class to learn more about Derek's passion. Each time Derek recalled their conversation, his heart skipped a beat. Damn but he loved his man.

The first Alliance meeting was scheduled for Friday. Derek had a shared lab class with Tim and let him know about it. Back in the dorm, Derek kept some distance, not wanting to give Scott any more reason to worry about his getting involved with the kid. At least, that's what he told himself. The truth, when he chose to face it, was he didn't want to deal with Scott's overprotective behavior any time Tim's name came up.

Whenever he and Tim passed each other in the hallway, Derek checked to see if Tim seemed lucid. He hadn't seen the same bloodshot eyes or jittery behaviors from that first day of classes and figured maybe Tim was just a recreational user. While not Derek's thing, he reserved judgment, not wanting to categorize anyone without knowing for sure what they were like.

After their lab, Derek made arrangements to have dinner with Tim at the dining hall nearest the Student Center where the meeting would take place.

At six o'clock, he met Tim in the hallway outside their dorm rooms. The first thing Derek registered was the smell of pot when Tim opened the door.

"Hey, Derek."

Derek kept his thoughts to himself, although he ached to confront Tim. "Ready to go?"

Tim nodded and they headed across the campus. Derek's nerves were already frayed in anticipation of Jared's likely nomination of him to take an office, and Tim's pot use only added to his stress.

"Will there be lots of hot guys at the meeting?" Tim's voice slurred, his movement slow and languid.

Derek drew in a deep breath. "I guess. I've never really paid attention to how the other members looked. There will be lots of really cool people."

"Oh." Was that disappointment in Tim's voice?

Once again, Derek bit back the words itching to come out. After all, The Alliance wasn't a dating service. "Tonight Jared will announce the annual goals, and he'll probably initiate nominations for club offices."

Tim nodded, although he seemed to only half pay attention. "Do many guys date here on campus?"

"I don't keep tabs on who dates who. Some guys are in relationships. Others aren't." He hadn't intended for his tone to come off snappish. One glance at Tim revealed the guy hadn't noticed, or if he had, he didn't seem offended.

Derek heaved a sigh of relief when they entered the dining hall next to the Student Center. There was a wide selection of food. Cheeses, fruit, salad, coffee, water, and soda. The main course was a submarine sandwich stuffed full of different meats accompanied by a bag of chips or pretzels.

Despite the meal options, Derek wasn't hungry. He settled for a salad with a simple oil and vinegar dressing.

Anything more and his stomach would likely rebel during the meeting.

Tim, on the other hand, loaded his plate with at least three thousand calories of carbs and protein. How did he manage to keep the weight from clinging to his sides and gut? The answer wasn't one Derek wanted to contemplate. If Scott's assessment of Tim at the party was correct, Derek was pretty sure he knew what revved Tim's engine and boosted his metabolism.

"You eat like you've never been fed."

"It's the weed. Munchies. Ya know?"

Derek hadn't meant the comment to invite confessions, but Tim seemed eager to share intimate details of his personal life. Since Tim had brought up the topic of drugs, it was time for Derek to address his concerns. "Listen, about that, you should probably go easy with the stuff. If you get caught the campus deans could take disciplinary action against you. They could even decide to kick you out of the school."

Tim huffed and shook his head. "Please. For smokin'? Everyone smokes."

Derek had never used drugs of any sort other than those prescribed by doctors, and he hadn't encountered much drug use in his circles. But there were plenty of times when he'd caught the scent of pot when walking around campus or at various dorm parties. "I'm just sayin'."

"It takes the edge off." Tim's expression grew more serious. "I'm kind of nervous about tonight."

"Why?" Maybe if he could get Tim talking about his concerns, Derek could help to alleviate them. Maybe if he understood Tim better he could help him to see why drug use wasn't the answer.

"Where I come from, being gay means you have a target on your back." Tim's expression softened. Just a hint of his lips parting and his eyes widening. For a second Derek thought he caught a glimpse of the real Tim beneath the outer shell he projected. The moment passed quickly. Tim's shoulders stiffened and a determined glint shone in his eyes.

"Is that why you use drugs? To deal with the stress?" Silence hung between them for a few seconds.

"Yeah, I guess. But also because I like using. It's fun. People drink. What's the difference?" Anger hedged its way into Tim's tone, quickly replaced by a somber countenance. "In high school I knew several kids who came out to their folks and ended up on the street. Do you know what it's like for kids who lose their home and support system overnight?"

Derek shook his head. "I've heard about it, but I don't know anyone who's actually been kicked out of their home."

"It sucks." Tim took a huge bite of his sandwich. A dreamy expression passed over his face. "Damn this is good." He took another huge bite before continuing. "Most of them ended up on the streets in Seattle or Tacoma, hustling just to make enough money to feed themselves. Only a lucky few had friends whose parents were cool enough to take them in. Me, I didn't really have friends in school, so I would've been screwed…literally."

Derek shifted in his seat wondering how this conversation had taken such a dark turn. "I just assumed things were getting better all around." Derek made a mental note to do some research on the current state of gay teens and the struggles they faced. His ignorance weighed on him as he listened.

"Maybe they are, but I wasn't willing to take the risk. I kept my secrets, focused on my classwork, got good grades, and stayed to myself." He took a few large gulps of his soda, covering his mouth and burping. At least he wasn't a pig. "Which is why I went to the bars on the weekends. I would've gone crazy if I didn't have someplace where I could just let off some steam."

The admission was offered so freely and with such genuine honesty it took Derek's breath away. No wonder Tim used drugs. His whole life, at least the way he described it, was about isolation. "I'm sorry it was so hard for you."

Tim hunched his shoulders, almost caving in on himself. Once again, a flash of the Tim beneath the surface emerged, but he seemed to harden himself just as fast. "I'm fine. I got a full ride here. Besides, I found people back home who accepted me just as I was. It wasn't all bad."

From what Tim had shared, it didn't seem like that was the case at all. "Then I'm sorry for making assumptions."

"It's all right. I'm wired to expect the worst from people, and it takes a while for me to let my guard down. You've been super sweet to me from the very first day." He started eating with greater speed, whether out of hunger or to avoid further conversation, Derek had no idea, but he couldn't deny his relief and focused on his salad, allowing silence to settle between them.

Once they'd finished eating, Derek led the way to the Student Center. The second floor had a series of conference rooms for the various campus clubs to use. He and Tim found the Alliance meeting room. A table with water, soda, and snacks was already set up. Tim rushed to the table and grabbed several cookies, shoving one into his mouth before turning back to Derek.

How in the hell could he still be hungry? Derek checked out the room. Rows of chairs lined the middle area and a banner with the university logo and *The Alliance* hung across one wall. Displayed on the Smartboard was a slideshow of events from the previous year. Most of them were of the dance, which had been a screaming success.

Jared was circulating the room. When he spotted Derek, he worked his way over to him.

"Derek. You're here." Jared's smile was warm and genuine, although the corners of his eyes revealed small crinkles. Poor guy probably planned this meeting down to the second and was stressing out.

Derek kissed Jared's cheek. "Jared, I'd like to introduce you to Tim. He's a freshman and lives in the room next to mine and Scott's."

"Where's Scott?" Jared glanced around the room.

Derek mentally scolded Jared for not saying hello first. He spotted Chad talking with a few other upperclassmen. If he'd been there he would've said something. "He's just finishing practice so he couldn't make it. But he'll be at events, and he'll come to meetings when he's able."

"That's a shame. It would have been nice to see him here tonight." Jared patted Derek's shoulder, then extended his hand toward Tim. "Nice to meet you."

There you go, Jared. Derek stepped out of the way.

Tim took his hand and shook it energetically. "You too. I'm so glad to be able to join the group."

Jared smiled, staring at him for a moment. "Everyone's welcome." He shifted his attention to Derek. "You ready for your big night?"

Heat crept up Derek's neck. "So you'll be announcing the candidates for offices?"

"Yup. I'm sure you'll win. Don't worry." He gave a short nod, as if to say *don't worry,* then headed to the podium at the front of the room.

It was like Jared thought he actually *wanted* the position. A second later Jared tapped the mike. "Could I ask everyone to sit? We're going to call the meeting to order."

People ambled to take seats, leaving the first few rows empty and sitting in clumps of two or three. It was obvious who had come with whom, and there was a divided feel to the room.

Once everyone was settled, Jared cleared his throat. "First, I'd like to welcome back members who were part of our group last year. I hope you all had a wonderful summer and are ready for a productive year." He scanned the room and nodded at a few people.

"And I'd also like to welcome new members. It's always good to see how we grow each year. The more who join, the stronger our message of equality and integration." He paused, shuffling a few pieces of paper in his hands. Derek wished Jared could just relax. When he was at ease, his message came across so powerfully. At the moment, he appeared stiff and nervous.

"This year we have a few initiatives that should help to continue our work from last year. First, we're going to sponsor two school-wide dances. The one last spring was an astounding success. We'll hold one before winter recess and another in the spring.

Several members started chatting, and a few people clapped. Jared waited patiently until the crowd settled into silence once again. "The second is a series of community outreach programs so we can strengthen our ties to the various resources in and around the greater Boston area. The community outreach will support the third, and for me, most important initiative." He paused and drew his gaze slowly across the room.

Derek glanced around. Jared commanded everyone's attention. A smile pulled at Derek's cheeks. This was the Jared who led people, and Derek couldn't wait to see how they responded.

"I want to start a peer counseling program," Jared continued. "We'll need training from professionals who know how to prepare us for this important work, but the payoff will far outweigh the investment of time and funding. For the first time we'll have a hotline and walk-in center where students can speak to other students about their feelings and their confusion. Many of you are here because you've either gone through personal experiences of learning about and accepting yourselves or are seeking a supportive group so you can explore your identity within a safe and nurturing environment. We are the people who understand how important it is to be open and honest."

Several people applauded. Jared nodded, his smile giving him an air of warmth and confidence. He glanced at Derek and winked before continuing. "As you may know, this is my senior year and I want to ensure that The Alliance is prepared to continue moving forward after I've graduated. We have three offices on the leadership team that need to be filled, and I'm hoping some of our younger members will step up to take those positions. Tonight we'll nominate candidates for vice president, secretary and events coordinator, and at the next meeting we'll vote. Jeff is a junior and has been with the group since his freshman year. I nominate him for the position of vice president. Do I have a second?"

Charlie, the other junior who'd taken leadership responsibilities the previous year, seconded Jared's nomination.

"Thanks." Jared nodded at Charlie. "Charlie has been with us for one year, and his efforts last year helped to make our dance a resounding success. I'd like to nominate him to be the events coordinator."

Someone Derek didn't recognize seconded the nomination. Derek turned to see who'd spoken. He was a thin, blond guy. He was holding Charlie's hand and Charlie leaned in to kiss his cheek. *Maybe Charlie found himself a man.*

Jared nodded. "Thank you, Evan." He then returned his focus to the whole group. "For the position of secretary, I'd like to nominate someone who joined our group in the middle of last year but in a very short period of time made powerful contributions to our group's visibility and success."

Derek's throat constricted. Damn. He hated when attention was directed at him.

Jared smiled at him. "This person had the fortitude to stand up for himself in the face of extremely unpleasant circumstances, yet he maintained optimism and a belief that things work out for the best. He single-handedly mixed and deejayed the music for our dance and has become well liked by all who know him. I'd like to nominate Derek to be our secretary this year."

Both Jeff and Charlie seconded Jared's nomination without waiting for an invitation to do so. Evan and several others did as well. Derek had expected support, but he'd not imagined so many people would desire his leadership in a group which had done far more for him than he'd given back.

Derek registered movement to his side and glanced at Tim. Puppy dog eyes gazed at him in unabashed adoration. The same adoring look Tyrell had given him when they'd first met freshman year. Alarms rang, accompanied by several red flags.

Derek forced his attention back to the front of the room where Jared stood, a beaming smile adorning his face. "Wonderful. My nominations are by no means the official ballot. Anyone who's been in The Alliance may be nominated for a position. We'll open the floor to others who wish to name people to hold office."

Several minutes later, there were three candidates for each spot. Jared announced that the next meeting would take place the following Friday.

Bringing the meeting to a close, he invited people to stay and enjoy the food and get to know one another.

Derek stuck around for a few minutes, chatting with several people who approached him, but he was eager to get back to Scott. Tim hung by his side wherever he went. When Derek finally decided to leave, Tim left with him.

Night had fully settled over Boston. The paths leading from the Student Center were well lit and the moon glowed brightly in the sky. Luckily September still carried a hint of summer warmth. In another month, the chill of mid-fall would blanket the city.

Tim practically bounced as they crossed the campus in the direction of the dorms. "There were so many cute guys there. Everyone obviously loves you. Did you see how many people seconded your nomination? You're gonna be elected for sure."

Derek smiled. "Thanks." Tim prattled on, but with the meeting over and his nerves settled, he couldn't help thinking about what he and Tim had talked about during dinner.

Tim admitted to believing people were unreliable and were more likely to use him than to help him. He'd also formed a quick and strong connection to Derek, something that reminded Derek all too much of Tyrell. That hadn't ended up well at all. The words of caution he'd been so annoyed by from his mom, Beck, and Scott rang in his head.

If Tim noticed Derek's silence, he didn't let on. "It doesn't surprise me that everyone there is so into you, though. You're hot, smart, and nice. There aren't many guys who I can say that about. Hell, I don't think I've met any guys like you before." The way Tim looked at him and the things he said made it seem like he was worshiping a god rather than speaking to a regular person.

He stopped and waited for Tim to face him. "Listen. The group isn't a dating service. It's a socially oriented group which aims to generate awareness and acceptance for the LGBTQ community at BU." Did he read that from a brochure? Derek sounded stiff even to himself.

Tim's expression soured. "I know."

Derek placed a hand on Tim's shoulder and could see him visibly relax at the touch. "Sorry. That came out wrong. I'm just trying to offer some helpful advice. People might find it a bit overwhelming if you hit on them, at least until they get to know you."

"I guess so. It's just I'm used to using my looks and body to attract attention." He stared at his fingernail, raising his hand to his mouth and nibbling at the nail. "Guess that's not such a good thing, huh?"

"Like I said earlier, I was lucky and had accepting parents." He checked Tim's face, watching for any sign of emotion. Maybe he'd catch a glimpse of the Tim inside one more time. He waited a few seconds and when nothing happened he nodded toward the door. "C'mon. Let's go."

Derek could breathe easier once they arrived at the dorm. Tim had felt like more work than fun. As much as he hated to admit it, Scott might be right about the guy.

Luckily, Scott was waiting for him when he got to their room. Turning to Tim, Derek stood in his doorway, blocking the entrance. "Thanks for coming with me tonight. I guess I'll see you tomorrow."

"Thank *you* for taking me. I was wondering if maybe you wanted to go out tomorrow night. I heard about this bar called The Paw. I hear it caters to bears, and they're my favorite. They'd love you too." He was practically bouncing on his toes as he waited for Derek's response.

"Aw, that's sweet of you, but I think I'm gonna stay in and get some classwork done and maybe do some mixing." Derek had his experience of going to a bar the previous summer with Scott in New York City and was fine with waiting until he was twenty-one before trying one out again. "If you do go, be careful."

Tim shrugged. "I'm used to bars. Nothing to be careful about. But I'll let you know how it is when I get back."

"Okay. Well, Scott's back from practice so I'm gonna spend some time with him. See you later." Tim stood in front of Derek, giving no indication of leaving. Not knowing what else to do, Derek stepped into his room. "'Night."

He closed the door and pressed his back against it once inside. Scott, who'd observed the whole interaction, simply waited for Derek to speak.

Instead of rehashing the evening, he sat on the couch next to Scott and leaned into him. "Have I told you I love you today?"

Scott chuckled. "No. But you don't have to tell me for me to know."

Derek kissed his cheek, grabbed a book from the coffee table, then lay across Scott's lap and started reading. Scott ran his fingers through Derek's hair, a comfortable silence settling between them. For the first time in hours, peace settled around Derek.

When they finally climbed into bed later, Derek snuggled close, wanting to be held. Scott wrapped his arms around him and squeezed. "Wanna tell me how tonight went?"

Derek wanted to, but he still hadn't processed everything himself. "Can we just go to sleep?"

Scott kissed the back of his neck, warm breath washing over Derek and lulling him toward slumber. Safe in Scott's embrace, he allowed his thoughts to flow freely. He was only one week into school, and had already been nominated for a leadership position. On top of that, he had a troubled dorm neighbor who'd seemed to latch onto him.

Fan-fucking-tastic.

Everything in Derek warned him Tim was trouble, but another equally strong part knew he couldn't just shut someone out, especially when they needed help. The real question was did Tim really wanted help or was he stepping into another Tyrell situation? He'd need to figure that out faster than the first time, before any trouble could start.

Chapter Nine

Stretching his arms above his head, Scott savored the way his muscles strained in protest before shaking off the remnants of sleep. A little more annoying was the way his cock tented his boxers.

Slipping his hand along Derek's abdomen, he wriggled his fingers under the waistband of snug briefs, deftly wrapping his slender fingers around Derek's equally erect mast.

Derek groaned and arched his groin into Scott's hand, then cleared his throat. "Morning."

"More like morning glory." Scott felt a smile slip across his face as he imagined several possible ways to greet his lover. A searing kiss. Heated blowjob. Nipple play. Each held alluring potential. Leaning into Derek's neck, he brushed air-light kisses on the soft skin, trailing a path down to his collarbone, along his chest and stomach, until his cheek nestled against Derek's navel. He inhaled deeply, savoring the musky scent of sweat and arousal just below.

Apparently a blowjob was the best of his several options.

He worked the barrier of fabric down Derek's legs, removed and tossed the underwear onto the floor, and decided to stick with his original plans.

In one smooth motion, he swallowed Derek's cock all the way to the base, delighting in the salty tang of his skin. He traveled up and down the length, each trip causing the vein running along the underside of Derek's shaft to thicken and pulse. "Jesus, Scott." Derek's leg muscles tensed, giving Scott a firmer handhold so he could concentrate on devouring his lover.

A droplet of pre-cum entered Scott's mouth, adding Derek's distinct flavor to the mix of tastes. Electric currents ran along his skin as he sank all the way to the base of Derek's cock once again. After a few seconds, before his gag reflex had a chance to kick in, he released Derek's cock and climbed up Derek's body, capturing him in a heated kiss.

Derek tried to withdraw. "Scott. Morning breath. Yuck."

Scott lifted his head enough to look into Derek's eyes. "Does my breath stink? Shit." He hadn't anticipated complaints after waking to a blow job.

"No. *My* breath. I feel like a skunk crawled up another skunk's ass and farted." He smiled, but covered his mouth.

More determined than ever, Scott crawled on top of Derek, straddling his waist. "Do you think I give a shit about that?" He leaned down and kissed Derek once again, reaching behind him so he could fondle the hardened length of flesh brushing against his ass.

More pre-cum adorned the crown, and he used the slickness to coat Derek's dick, then rubbed it against his own hole. Without speaking, he shifted his weight and sank onto Derek until the head popped through his tight ring of muscle. The initial burn lasted a second, followed by blissful warmth.

Derek gasped, rotating his hips and thrusting upwards with shallow movements.

Encouraged, Scott lowered his weight, stopping every inch or so to adjust to the stretch, then continued his journey. When he finally seated himself against Derek's pelvic bone, he paused, luxuriating in the sense of fullness and connection.

Derek's eyes were closed, and his lips pulled into a dreamlike smile. Normally, they maintained eye contact during sex, but this morning wasn't about tenderness. He wanted to feel Derek inside him, rough and manly, until Derek ripped his load out of him. Man he wanted to see his cum painted all over that beautifully toned chest. Or maybe he'd straddle Derek's neck and come on his face. He wouldn't know until the moment was upon him.

Derek bucked in tandem with Scott's rocking, rutting against his sweet spot with each stroke. His breath became ragged, and his eyes squinted the way they always did before Derek exploded with a massive orgasm.

"Scott. Not gonna be able to—" He couldn't even finish his sentence as his cock expanded even more inside of Scott, rocking inside him with each pulse of his release. Gargled sounds emitted from somewhere deep inside Derek's chest as he fought to contain the shout itching to fill the room. Sweat formed on his chest, his skin shining with moisture.

Heat filled Scott from the inside out. Like fireworks, every nerve ending in his body seemed to spark to life until his own limits were reached.

Raising himself, savoring the fullness of semen filling his ass, he crawled up Derek and straddled his neck. He gripped his own cock in his right hand, stroking feverishly as his orgasm built up inside.

Derek tilted his head up and opened his mouth, a clear invitation for what he wanted Scott to do.

All too willing to oblige, Scott angled his cock so the head pointed directly toward Derek's waiting lips just as the first wave of his orgasm hit. The first gush of cum coated Derek's lips, the bulk splashing against his cheek. Derek gripped Scott's ass and pulled him closer, wrapping his lips around Scott's cock and swirling his tongue around the over-sensitized skin just under the crown.

The heat brought on a new rush of need, and Scott bucked a few more times, unleashing more of his fluid into Derek's mouth. Once the waves subsided, he collapsed on top of Derek and licked the stray ropes of white liquid from his lover's cheek, then sealed their mouths together in a sloppy kiss.

Derek skimmed one hand behind Scott's neck, holding him in place as he ran his tongue in circles inside Scott's mouth. The pungent flavor of his own essence danced over Scott's tongue. The thump of his heart eased as he lowered himself so his full weight pressed Derek into the mattress.

With the sense of urgency sated, Scott wriggled into a more comfortable position, his head resting on Derek's chest. "Well, *that* was a great way to wake up."

Derek gave a weak laugh. "Don't I know it? Now if I can get my legs to move, we can shower and grab some breakfast before class."

Scott managed to roll out of bed about five minutes later and haul Derek with him. "You know one of the things I like best about this year?"

Derek rubbed his eyes. "Feeding me cum in bed?"

Scott slapped Derek's ass hard enough to make a soft clapping noise. "*That* and the fact everyone knows we're a couple."

He grabbed two towels. "C'mon. Let's shower."

Derek placed his hands on his hips, looking ridiculously sexy as his cock swayed between his legs. "You suck me off, tell me you love we're a couple, then invite me to take a shower. You're an evil man."

"C'mon. We'll be late for class."

Derek opened his mouth then clamped it shut. Hell, Scott rarely witnessed Derek at a loss for words. He'd have to try the teasing thing more often.

They wrapped towels around their waists, then headed to the bathroom and hopped into the same stall. "And this is another thing I like best about this year."

The two of them had been showering together since the first day of school. Oddly enough, other guys, when in the bathroom, didn't seem to care. The previous year, Scott would have bet his life savings the guys would freak out if they knew the two of them were boyfriends, let alone showering together.

Since Scott had already taken care of their baser needs, the shower was just that...cleaning the sweat and sex stink off, although Scott wouldn't mind the cloud of Derek's aroma surrounding him all day.

Tim was exiting his room as they entered the hallway and his mouth gaped open. Scott leaned over and gave Derek a kiss on the cheek. He knew he was being childish, but he just didn't like the kid and knew it would bug him. Scott added compassion to the list of things he loved about his boyfriend. Derek would never lay claim to anyone simply to spite someone else.

There was a dining hall next door, so they stopped by to fill their bellies before going to class. He'd worked up quite an appetite after his morning exercise, if sex could be considered athletic activity.

"What's going on in that head of yours?" Derek's voice bubbled playfully.

Scott slung his arm over Derek's shoulder. "Just thinking about this awesome way I woke up this morning."

"Really! Tell me about it!" Derek fell into natural banter with Scott. Another thing he loved about the gorgeous man.

"Well, I woke up all horny and decided to wake my boyfriend by blowing him. Then," he leaned in and whispered conspiratorially, "he fucked me."

Derek opened his mouth in an expression of mock horror. "No way! Was he any good?"

"Meh." Scott hugged him before Derek had a chance to shove him away. Once inside he loaded his plate with everything he could fit on it. Eggs, pancakes, bacon, fruit. Derek stared at him, surprise painted across his face. "What? I'm hungry."

"You're not gonna be able to maintain your weight class if you keep eating like that." Derek shook his head.

"Are you kidding? It's work for me to keep my weight *up*. I'll have to train like hell this fall to build a little more muscle just so I won't have to gorge myself for weigh-ins." While he'd worked hard to build his mass over the summer, he'd still drop a few too many pounds to keep his spot if he didn't eat lots on a regular basis.

They took a seat, and Scott dug in. It wasn't until he finished half his meal that he remembered the news he had to share with Derek. "I made plans for us tonight."

That caught Derek's attention. "Really! What are they?"

Scott smirked. "Not gonna tell you. But you'll love it."

"I already said I'd marry you. What other secrets could you possibly have in store for me after the camping trip?" Derek plastered an indignant expression on his face, but his eyes revealed nothing but curiosity.

Scott maintained an air of secrecy. "You're just going to have to wait."

"Bastard!" Derek laughed, then continued eating.

Once done, they grabbed their bags and stepped out into the bright morning sunlight. Scott had an economics course a few buildings down the block, and Derek was scheduled for his lab class across campus.

After their morning sex, Scott was in no mood to sit around for an hour and a half listening to a professor drone on about business, but with each stride, a dull ache throbbed in his ass. At least that would be a good distraction as he suffered through the boring introductory class. Besides, he had better things to think about…like the evening he had planned.

~~~~~

Jillian's was packed by the time Scott and Derek arrived. Scott's stomach hurt from laughing at the hundreds of guesses Derek had made about where they were going, each one more ridiculous than the last. Before they pulled up to the two floor establishment with a bowling alley at ground level and a pool hall upstairs, Derek had questioned whether they were heading to a glass blowing course. Did Boston even have those?

He'd only heard about the place, but had never been, so his excitement level was just about as high as Derek's when they arrived. Scott led him up the stairs, praying the final surprise he'd planned would be waiting for them. He didn't have long to worry.

"Well it sure as shit took you two long enough to get here." Beck stood by the entrance, hands on her hips and decked out like she was going to the opera.

Scott froze, taking in the sight. She wore a velvety, shimmering black dress with a white cardigan covering her top. Her cheekbones looked like they could cut glass, amazing what a good make-up job could accomplish, and her lips would have put Snow White to shame. "Beck, what the hell are you wearing, on your body *and* on your face?"

She pouted, only drawing more attention to her ridiculously apple-red lips. "Nine times out of ten I go to gay bars, or meetings, or whatever with the two of you. Here we're in *my* territory, and you better believe I'll ditch the two of you in a hot minute if a hunk of man candy so much as turns his head my way."

"Oh, I don't think you need to worry about that." Scott bit back laughter. "I have a feeling everyone will be staring at…" He paused for a moment, dragging his gaze to run up and down her body, "…that."

"No you didn't, bitch." Beck stepped forward and swatted Scott on his ass. "Oh my. Now I see what Derek's been talking about."

Her comment drew the attention of several people standing nearby. Heat flooded Scott's cheeks and he suspected their color might rival Beck's lips.

Derek saved him from any further humiliation. "I can't believe you're here." He closed the few feet separating them and pulled her into a tight hug, swaying her back and forth in his arms.

It warmed Scott's heart to see Derek so happy. Plus, he could sense something was up when Derek got back from the Alliance meeting the previous night. Derek poured too much of himself into other people and deserved to be spoiled every once in a while.

They were assigned a table in the middle of the room, which seemed to please Beck. For all her talk, though, she focused on Derek and Scott and not on the others, men and women both, who gawked at her. "Since there are three of us, I assume we're playing cutthroat so no one will have to sit out."

Scott racked the balls. "That was my thought. Derek? You good with that?"

Still beaming by Beck's side, he nodded. "I couldn't care less. I've got my two favorite people with me, and we're having a night out."

Scott bit back the smirk fighting to spread across his face. Derek's happiness was like the sun burning away storm clouds. He only wished his gorgeous, brown-headed man could find this level of freedom more often. Scott added Derek's natural ability to exude positive energy to the seemingly endless list of things he loved.

Beck was the first one to have all her balls pocketed during their first game, so she used the time to distract both Derek and Scott. "Okay. See that guy over there by the bar. The one in the white Polo shirt and black slacks, flanked by a girl and a guy?"

Scott peered at the bar until he found who she was referring to. Easily two hundred pounds of hard muscle, he'd managed to squeeze himself into clothes most likely designed for someone fifty pounds lighter. To his right was another beefy guy and to his left a twig-thin girl dressed in a skimpy tank-top and cutoff jeans.

He turned to face Beck. "Yeah. What about them?"

"I say he's gay." She stared directly at Scott, capturing his eyes.

It wasn't until Derek snickered that his attention was drawn away. "What's so funny?"

Derek feigned an expression of innocence. "Nothing. I'll simply watch since I know where this is headed. She and I played this game all through high school."

Confused, Scott ignored Derek's elusive response and returned his attention to Beck. "So?"

"So, do you agree or disagree?" There was no sarcasm or challenge to her tone, other than the fact she was expecting him to respond definitively to a question with an unknown answer.

He assessed the man once again. Muscled body, designer shirt. Thick arms…actually, thick everything. Tanned. Although the color had an orangey tinge to it so it was probably fake. And a sculpted hairdo. "Gay."

Her shoulders slumped. "Okay. Maybe that one was too easy." She scanned the room once again and pointed out another man a few tables over. He was playing with another guy, and his attention was deeply focused on his shot. "Straight or gay?"

Scott turned to Derek, a question on the tip of his tongue about what the hell Beck was up to, but he figured Derek wouldn't answer based on the evil grin plastered across his face. So he turned back to the indicated man and studied him.

This guy was lankier than the first, but by no means too thin. He had more of a swimmer's body, the trim figure hidden beneath baggy jeans and a football jersey with a Patriots logo on the sleeve. Short black hair, most likely shaved with clippers, crowned his head, and he was pale with a few moles dotting otherwise unblemished skin. He'd caught his lower lip between his teeth, an expression of deep concentration on his face. Right before he took his shot, he glanced at his buddy, or rather at his buddy's groin, then back to the table. Scott would have missed it if he hadn't been watching.

Turning back to Beck, he provided his answer. "Gay."

Beck nodded, a smile forming on her face. "Good. We have a target. Now for the wager." She fished her wallet out of her purse and laid a ten on the table. "Care to make a bet?"

Scott looked to Derek again, but he'd schooled his face into a neutral expression. "I like my balls too much. She'd tear 'em off if I give anything away."

"Yeah? And I won't so much as *touch* them if you don't tell me what this is all about." Maybe Derek wouldn't willingly give information away, but Scott had his ways of coaxing information out of him.

"Empty threat, babe. Like I said, my nads stay with me. If I ruin this game, Beck will put them in her purse after ripping them from my body with one hand." He shuddered, lowering his hands to protectively shield the threatened area.

"Fine." Scott turned back to Beck. Damn Derek for knowing Scott so well. "You want to bet ten dollars to see if he's straight or gay?"

She nodded, but said nothing.

Scott pulled a ten out of his wallet and placed it on the table next to Beck's. "You're on."

Now that the bet was on, Derek finally spoke up. "You're gonna lose."

"Why?" Scott was fairly certain he was correct. What gay guy stares at other guys' cocks?

"I've never won a game. Beck has gaydar like nobody's business. If there's even an ounce of queer in a guy, she can sense it." He picked up his pool stick and took aim at Scott's seven ball, which was near a corner pocket.

Scott was no longer interested in pool. He'd been challenged, and his ego pushed him to focus on the new game in play.

Once the guy in question took his shot, or rather missed his shot, he pushed himself away from the table, standing back so his friend could step forward. As his friend took a shot, the guy checked out his friend's ass, then reached for his groin and readjusted himself. "I win. He just checked his buddy's ass out, and he's springing wood."

Beck shook her head. "That's not definitive, although I'll admit it's suspect." She stopped a waitress who passed by and whispered something into her ear. The waitress nodded, then hustled off in the direction of the bar. "All right, it's probably gonna be a few minutes before she returns, so you two should get back to playing pool."

Scott took his shot, but his attention was still on his wager with Beck. He didn't even come close to sinking a ball. Derek sidled up next to him and placed an arm around his shoulder. "I'll give you a do over on that. But let's wait for your little bet to play out before we continue our game."

Scott slid his hand around Derek's waist and pulled him a bit closer. "You really think I'm going to lose this bet?"

Derek leaned his head on Scott's shoulder. "Yup."

"Whatever. Beck can't always win. I'll be her undoing." His confidence wavered, although he made sure none of his doubt sounded in his voice.

A few minutes later, the waitress returned, heading over to Buzzcut's table. She handed him what looked like a root beer float complete with whipped cream and a cherry on top, then pointed in his and Beck's direction. The guy smiled, laughed a little, whispered something back to the waitress then raised his glass in a friendly salute.

The waitress smiled, her cheeks a bit rosy, probably from embarrassment, and crossed over to Beck. Scott released his hold on Derek and approached the two women.

"Well?" Beck's hand hovered over the twenty dollars sitting on the table.

Rosy Cheeks smiled. "So I did as you asked and brought him the root beer. Then I told him you were interested and wanted to know if he was taken. He said he wasn't, so I asked him the second question you instructed me to ask. Could you buy him a drink because you thought he was cute?"

Beck released a loud *Ha*, grabbing the money in her fist. "I knew it."

The waitress placed a hand on her shoulder. "Not so fast." Her cheeks darkened to a deeper shade of red. "He said he'd be happy to let you buy him another drink if you'd introduce him to them." She pointed at Derek and Scott.

Beck's mouth dropped open. "What? Both of them?"

"Yeah. He told me to ask if they ever invited a third into their bedroom." Her face had become an alarming shade of plum by this point.

Scott nearly jumped onto the table as he realized he'd won. Not only that, but he'd achieved a feat Derek himself said he had never accomplished. That's when the waitress's words sunk in. Victory turned sour as he understood what the guy was proposing. "Hell no."

He turned to face Derek, surprised to see a broad smile still in place. "That's so cute. You're getting all possessive." Stepping forward, Derek wrapped his arms around Scott's neck, and kissed him lightly on the lips.

Scott kissed Derek back, a bit more heatedly than was appropriate for a pool hall, although this particular establishment was located in the heart of Boston where there were equal numbers of every walk of life. Still maintaining his hold on Derek, he turned to face the guy and shook his head mouthing the word *Sorry*.

The guy raised his glass in a silent cheer, took a sip, and returned to his game.

Scott, having calmed down, turned to Beck. "Take the money. That was a lousy game." He delivered the statement with a salty tone, but the smirk creeping across his face let Derek know he wasn't really upset.

Beck wheeled on Scott, forgetting the waitress who used the opportunity to scurry off. "Oh, don't be such a brat. You're the one who won. Besides, don't you have a game to lose to Derek?"

Scott spun on his feet, having forgotten the pool game completely. "You think I'll lose? Care to make another wager?"

Beck looked to Derek, but he provided her with the same blank stare he'd given Scott. She seemed to realize he wouldn't let on whether Scott was good at pool so she glared at him as well. "There was a time when you wouldn't have held out on me."

Derek plastered on a sugar-coated smile, although his next words were pure filth. "When you grow a dick and can fuck me through a mattress, I'll be more than happy to give it up."

That melted the ice and Beck's glower shifted into mirth once again. "Aw, you know I can't resist when you talk all sweet-like with me." She turned to Scott. "See, that's what I love about him. He always knows the perfect thing to say."

Scott leaned in and kissed Beck on the cheek, then waved a new ten dollar bill in her face which earned him a brief scowl. "So, about that wager?"

Beck grunted and placed one of the bills in her hand on the table. "Fine. It's your money anyway."

It was Derek's turn and he cleared the table, ending their game. Scott handed the money over to Beck graciously and racked up the balls for a new game.

For the remainder of the evening, there were no more wagers as they enjoyed each other's company and continued making guesses about who was straight and who was gay.

Outside, Derek and Scott waited with Beck until she got into a cab to take her back to Brandeis. Then they hailed one of their own.

The ride back to campus was filled with idle chatter, and they stopped off to get an ice cream before going back to the dorm. As they rounded the corner onto the second floor, Scott was ready to collapse on their bed and sleep.

Sitting outside their door was Tim, his knees drawn up to his chest and his head resting on his knees. Derek rushed to his side and knelt next to him. "Tim, are you all right?"

Scott froze on the spot. They'd had such a wonderful evening, and all he wanted to do was curl up next to Derek and go to sleep. Seemed that was going to be postponed, and he had the little runt to thank for it.

Chapter Ten

Derek extended his hand to Tim and helped him to his feet. "Come into our room."

Tim looked up at Derek, then over his shoulder at Scott, his expression shifting from relief to apprehension.

Derek glanced over his shoulder at Scott, whose lips were pressed tightly together. Ignoring Scott's displeasure, he helped Tim to his feet and led him into the room. "Come on. Sit down. Tell me what's wrong."

Tim did as instructed and sat on their couch. "I went to that bar I told you about. The Paw. Boston is nothing like back home. No one paid any attention to me. I couldn't even get one free drink."

Scott entered the room. "You're sitting in the hallway because you couldn't get a free drink at a bar and because guys too old for you wouldn't pay attention to you?" Barely disguised repulsion laced his voice.

Derek shot him a warning glare then surveyed Tim.

Tim clasped his hands together so the whites of his knuckles showed through the skin. His eyes shimmered with wetness. "You don't understand. Back home, I was *it*! Guys jumped when I showed up. It was my only way of feeling good about myself."

Derek placed a hand on Tim's shoulder. "You don't need others to make you feel good about yourself. That should come from you."

Tim didn't seem to hear him. "If I can't find that here, then…" He shook his head as if the words were stuck in his throat. "Then I don't know what else I have. Like I told you,

I don't have any friends, and my family doesn't know about me."

Scott huffed. "I'm going downstairs to get a soda."

"Maybe that's a good idea." Derek winced at the venom in his tone. After the door slammed shut he returned his attention to Tim. "Listen. It sounds to me like you're just experiencing insecurity at being in a new place. Why don't you go to bed and tomorrow you can start meeting new people here on campus? Get involved in The Alliance. There are tons of opportunities for you to figure out who you are and what you want."

Tim wiped a stray tear from his cheek. "Could you help me?"

Warning signs flashed again in his head. He had promised Scott he'd be careful and wouldn't get too involved. Still, it couldn't hurt to get Tim started. "Sure. Come to tomorrow's meeting. Officers are being elected, and then the group will start various initiatives. We'll get you hooked up on a team that's working on something social."

Tim nodded, then stood and headed toward the door. Before leaving, he turned to face Derek. "Do you and Scott take showers together a lot?"

Trails of heat flickered up Derek's throat, and he had to swallow them back down. "Not sure what that has to do with anything."

"Nothing. It's just, you two seem so happy. So open. It makes me...jealous." Tim leaned against the wall next to the door.

"Why don't you go to bed? We'll get together tomorrow, and I'm sure you'll find a bunch of people who share your interests." Derek approached the door and held it open for Tim.

A simple nod and Tim left. Derek closed the door behind him and leaned his back against it. *Damn.* His head swam with conflicting messages. On the one hand, he wanted to help Tim get settled into college life. Tim seemed prone to engaging in risky behaviors and needed to learn how to live a safer and healthier lifestyle. Drugs were the most obvious concern, but Tim also seemed to rely on his body to attract attention. From the wrong people. Those two things would lead him down a one way path to unhappiness, possible diseases, or worse.

None of which was Derek's problem, or so everyone he cared about kept reminding him. He'd traveled this road once before and had nearly drowned in the process. If it hadn't been for Scott, he could have been seriously hurt by Tyrell. *Just damn!*

Scott returned a few minutes later. Unable to open the door because Derek was leaning against it, he called out with a hint of panic in his voice. "Derek! You in there?"

Derek stepped aside and Scott rushed in, pulling him into a hug.

After a few seconds, he held Derek at arm's length, scrutinizing him from head to toe, then led him to the couch. "You okay?" He took a seat, dragging Derek down with him.

"Yeah." Derek winced at his own dejected tone. "Tim's gonna be a problem though."

"Ya think?" Sarcasm dripped from Scott's lips, but he immediately backtracked. "Sorry. That was uncalled for."

Derek fought the urge to lash out at Scott for the way he'd treated Tim like a bug, but he didn't have it in him to fight. Scott only acted out of concern. Of that, Derek was certain.

He nestled against Scott. Warmth and safety enveloped him in seconds, and he simply breathed, taking in Scott's scent. "Let's go to bed."

Scott hesitated, then rose and started undressing. Once they were in bed, Derek curled up into Scott's embrace. They lay silently, the only sound their breathing filling the room. Heaviness claimed Derek's limbs and head as he sunk closer and closer toward sleep. His eyes drifted shut and his body melded to Scott, whose arms rested gently around him.

Darkness crowded in on him, peaceful and welcome—

"I don't want you hanging out with him anymore."

The words jarred him from his near slumber. He blinked, fighting to process the words. His head cleared, and the room came back into focus, near sleep replaced by tense alertness. Shifting so he could stare at Scott, he was greeted by an expression of deep concern, eyes pleading and brow furrowed. "Scott. Can't we talk about this tomorrow?"

"No. We need to talk about this now." The urgency of his tone was unmistakable.

Derek sighed, then sat up, drawing his thighs up to his chest and hugging them. "Okay."

"He's bad news. I'm worried he's growing attached to you, and I'm worried you're beginning to see him as a project." Scott remained prone, but his eyes were wide awake, challenging Derek to counter his assumption.

Pride warred with love as Derek fought his instinct to argue. But Scott's concerns mirrored what Derek had just been thinking. "You're right."

That caught Scott's attention. He shifted onto his side. "What?"

Derek chuckled without humor. "I said, you're right."

Impossibly green eyes bored into his, searching for something. "Are you just saying that so I'll leave you alone?"

Derek chuckled again, this time lightness relieving the weight of the last few minutes since they'd returned from playing pool. "No. I think he's growing attached and I don't want that. I'll talk to Jared tomorrow and pass Tim off to him. I'm sure things will settle once he starts making some friends."

Scott stared at him, speechless for the first time in as long as Derek could remember. Finally, he rolled onto his back and opened his arms for Derek. "Well, okay then."

Derek slid next to Scott, forcing thoughts of Tim and responsibility aside, until sleep finally claimed him.

~~~~~

The next evening, Derek threw on a pair of jeans and a simple white t-shirt when he got back to his room from classes. Scott was at wrestling practice and wouldn't return until later in the evening.

He stopped by Tim's room and knocked on the door. When there was no answer, he knocked again. A few seconds later Tim appeared wearing sweats and his hair disheveled. "Derek. What's up?"

With access to his room unbarred by a door, the scent of weed filtered into the hallway. Derek glanced to see if anyone was there. *Nope.* "Did you forget about the meeting?"

Tim scratched his head. "Oh yeah. You said there was one tonight. Listen, I think I'm gonna stay in. But I'll go to the next one with you."

Derek forced a smile. "Sure. No problem."

Tim closed the door. On the way to the Student Center, Derek chastised himself for not saying anything to Tim about his pot smoking. If Tim kept that up, he'd either get caught and face disciplinary action or he'd turn into a slug and fail his courses, earning him academic probation.

Scott's voice rang in his head. *And that's your problem because?*

It's not. Why did he feel the need to save every stray dog that crossed his path? The question would need to remain unanswered for the moment. Derek had other concerns on his mind.

Elections. If he won, he'd be one of the youngest officers the club had elected in several years. As much as he enjoyed the new friends he'd made, no one was above jealousy and competition. He'd practiced blending in, but winning would put him in the spotlight. He took a deep breath, grounding himself against the sense of panic rumbling in his gut.

Jared called the meeting to order as soon as there were about thirty members in attendance. "Everyone, if you could please take your seats, I'll outline the night's agenda."

Students took their time finding a place to sit, clumping together as they had at the last meeting. "Tonight we'll be holding elections. Ballots will be handed out, and you'll check off one candidate for each of the three offices. I'll collect the ballots in this box here." He held up a shoe box with a slit carved into its top. "We'll take a ten minute break while I tally results. After that, we'll meet with the head of the Psychology Department to discuss the peer counseling project."

He handed out piles of paper to two members sitting near the front. "Would you mind handing these out?" When Derek received his, a mixture of excitement and dread filled him once again. He couldn't deny the pride of seeing his name. Just two years earlier, he'd been hiding who he was. Now, others recognized him as a leader.

He shouldn't have been surprised when Jared announced the results. Jared's recommendations stood. The group applauded and a few students sitting next to Derek offered congratulations. Despite the vote of confidence, doubt curled its cold fingers around Derek's neck, leaving him slightly jittery. To accept this responsibility was equal to claiming himself as one of the figureheads for gay students across the campus, whether they were part of The Alliance or not. He'd only just found his own peace and comfort. It seemed an unwise temptation of fate to push his luck.

Jared cleared his voice, drawing attention back to him. "And now, I'd like to introduce you to Professor Hunter. He's agreed to support our efforts to start up the peer counseling initiative by bringing in some of his colleagues to train us. It will take a few weeks for us to learn how to handle the various scenarios we're likely to face, and members will receive certifications to memorialize their participation in the training."

Derek restrained himself from shaking his head. Jared needed to loosen up. All those lofty words and his stiff posture made him look uptight. This initiative was important. The most meaningful way Derek could imagine to provide support to his fellow students.

Jared continued in his businesslike fashion. "These aren't official certifications enabling you to claim the ability to provide psychological counsel, but you'll be well equipped to field basic issues and to redirect the more serious ones to the appropriate agencies in and around Boston."

It looked like Jared was about to continue, but Professor Hunter stepped forward and placed his hand on Jared's shoulder. Jared stepped aside, sitting in one of the seats in the front row. "Thank you, Jared, for inviting me and for initiating such an important resource to our community of students here at Boston University."

He acknowledged the round of applause with a tight smile and a nod, and waited for the appreciation to die down before continuing. "First of all, I'd like to commend you for embracing such a huge and important undertaking. Even in today's age of openness and acceptance, young people in the gay community still suffer debilitating emotional issues which often lead to self-destructive behaviors. You see it in the news all the time.

"I'm not here to preach, however. I'm here to lend my expertise and support. Over the next month, a select group of you will undergo training to learn about effective communication, reflective listening, different interaction styles, and developing a menu of skills to draw from depending on the circumstances you encounter."

Derek hung on every word, desperate to learn each of these skills. Helping others ran through his veins, as essential to him as air or water.

"We'll start by giving applications to those of you interested in learning how to become peer counselors. It's difficult work. It requires certain personality traits. And not all of you who apply will be accepted into the program. This isn't to say your interest isn't appreciated, but what you're trying to accomplish is important and can do as much harm as good."

Derek glanced around the room, pleased to note most people were nodding. Jared stood after the professor finished his speech and faced the group. "Thank you,

Professor Hunter, for joining us tonight and agreeing to support the initiation of a peer counseling program."

The group applauded once again and Professor Hunter smiled.

Jared held his hands up, and the members settled down. "We're going to break up into teams now, one led by Jeff, one by Charlie, and one by Derek. Charlie needs help preparing for the mid-winter dance, so please join his group if you're interested. If you don't have any specific ideas about what you'd like to work on, Jeff and Derek will brainstorm ideas with you."

He clasped his hands in front of him. "Professor Hunter and I will remain at the front of the room for any of you who have questions about peer counseling."

A few people immediately crowded around Charlie. Derek shook his head, glad he hadn't been roped into being the Events Coordinator. That job would be more than he could handle along with everything else.

For the next half hour, he fielded ideas ranging from a school fair to community service in the local schools and youth organizations. He kept notes on who made which suggestion, asking each person to include their e-mail and phone number so he could follow up with them.

At the end of the meeting Jared made a few closing remarks then returned his attention to Professor Hunter. Derek thanked his group for their participation and joined Jared and the professor.

"Derek. I figured you'd want to talk to Professor Hunter." Jared placed a hand on Derek's shoulder, giving him a gentle squeeze. "Congratulations on the election." His smile spread wide. "Let me introduce you personally to the professor here."

Derek took Hunter's hand, his grip firm. "Nice to meet you. Thanks for coming tonight. I'm very interested in the peer counseling initiative."

"Funny you should say that. Jared mentioned you'd be an excellent candidate." The professor released Derek's hand. "He also filled me in on what happened last year with that student who attacked you. I'd heard about it of course. So sorry that happened."

Derek glanced at Jared, surprised he would share such personal information with a stranger, then returned his attention to the professor. "He's got a higher opinion of me than perhaps he ought to." He'd have to make sure to talk to Jared about bringing up the challenges of Derek's freshman year. Especially when Scott was around.

"I highly doubt that." He nodded at Jared. "We'll be in touch to set up the training sessions." He picked up his things and left.

Alone with Jared, Derek searched for the right words to bring up his concerns about Tim. "Can I talk to you for a second?"

"Sure." Jared guided them to two seats in the front row and sat in one of them. "Listen, sorry if that made you uncomfortable. I mentioned you to the professor, and he inquired why I thought you'd be such a good candidate."

Derek nodded. "Yeah. I'd appreciate it if you'd let the past be the past. I'm still catching shit from my family and Scott about my involvement with Tyrell. They think I get too involved with people. Which is why I wanted to talk to you."

The weight of Tim's behavior was a distraction he couldn't take on. Not with Scott so worried. Better to hand Tim off to someone with more experience dealing with wayward freshmen. Still, Derek didn't want to get Tim in trouble. Hopefully Jared wouldn't ask too many questions. "It's about the guy I brought to the last meeting."

"His name was Tim, right?"

"Yeah. Good memory." Derek slung his arm over the back of his seat so he faced Jared, trying to make his demeanor seem casual despite the racing of his heart. "I feel like he's growing a bit attached to me and was wondering if you could maybe take him under your wing."

Jared cocked his head to the side. "Why wouldn't *you* do that?" A moment later it was as if a light switched on. "Wait. When you say attached, you don't mean like last year, do you?"

"No." He sounded more sure than he actually felt.

Tension seeped out of Jared's body instantly. "Thank God. So what's the problem?"

He didn't know how to share that Tim used drugs and that Scott didn't want him to spend time with the kid. "It's just Scott doesn't get a good vibe from him and I promised him I'd watch myself this year."

He knew he'd made a mistake the moment the words were out of his mouth. Jared sat taller in his seat. "If Scott has doubts, I think you should listen to him."

"That's what I'm trying to do." He hadn't meant to sound petulant, but the idea of turning someone away who needed or wanted his help was like chopping off his own leg. He'd survive, but suffer. "I think he needs someone to be his mentor. You know, to get him started and guide him in the right direction."

Jared nodded. "This worries me, Derek. But I'm happy to help you."

Relief flooded through him like a calming salve. "That would be great. Thank you."

Jared held up a hand. "I'm not finished." He leveled Derek with a knowing gaze, the same one he'd used the previous year when Derek came to him about Tyrell. "I'll help, but I'm going to keep an eye on him as well. I don't want any more *problems* like we had."

"That's fine." Derek sounded confident, although his stomach sank to his feet. Tim hadn't demonstrated any reservations about smoking pot, and Scott had mentioned he thought he used other stuff as well that night of the dorm party. If Jared sensed anything close to that, he'd probably have no issue filing a complaint. *Not your problem.* He seemed to have to constantly remind himself of that lately. "I appreciate it."

Jared placed a hand on his leg. "I like you, Derek. Always have from the beginning. You've got a heart of gold and an innate ability to see the good in people and situations." He stood and glanced around the emptied room. "Looks like we closed the meeting out."

Derek stood as well, following Jared to the door. Once outside, they said their goodbyes, Jared strolling off in one direction and Derek in the other. On his way back to the dorm, he started planning what he'd say to Tim. He'd definitely give him Jared's number and let him know of the party planning committee. That would probably be the best place for him since he'd be surrounded by some of the more rambunctious members of the group.

Still, Derek's heart tugged at him. He was essentially turning his back on Tim, which was all sorts of wrong, but he'd made a promise to Scott and that had to be more important than helping a stranger. No, prioritizing Scott wasn't the problem. The fact he had to make a choice was.

Chapter Eleven

By the time Scott arrived back at their room, Derek was already asleep. He glanced at his watch. *Ten-thirty.* He considered waking him. It was unusual for Derek to go to sleep so early, but he seemed so peaceful, Scott didn't have the heart to disturb him.

He stripped out of his clothes and slid into bed as carefully as possible. Derek rolled over, a short snore escaping him, and fell back into deep, rhythmic breathing. Derek's scent surrounded him as he closed his eyes. In just two years, Scott's life had blossomed and he had the beautiful man next to him to thank for it.

Scott stared at his sleeping lover, the pale skin, unblemished and smooth. Drawing his gaze down Derek's body, Scott admired the gentle contours of inactive muscles beneath the skin. Even at rest, his pecs sloped, meeting to form a distinct crevice in the middle of his chest, continuing down his abdomen. While not cut with a six-pack, his abdomen sported indents along both sides, framing his torso. Scott followed the visual trail from Derek's stomach along the vee of his navel angling toward his groin until his skin disappeared beneath boxer briefs. And his cock pressed at the fabric, not hard, yet filling the front pouch nicely, his Scott's own cock sparking to life.

So trusting. So innocent and kind. Scott wiped at the sudden sting in his eyes. Never, in his whole life, had he experienced love like he felt for Derek. The kind of love that filled him to the point of overflowing. The kind of love that poured out of him and influenced his interactions with others.

He leaned over Derek, savoring the minty scent of toothpaste, fresh and clean, as it filtered into his nose. He brushed his lips against Derek's, tender and light, not wanting to wake him. The warmth of Derek's lips radiated along Scott's mouth, penetrating his skin and filtering through him. He'd never know what he'd done to deserve Derek.

Scott rested his head on the pillow, placing his hand on Derek's chest. The easy thump-thump-thump of Derek's heart pulsed against his palm.

Closing his eyes, sleep crept upon him, unnoticed and easy.

~~~~~

The next morning, when he woke up, Derek was still asleep. Resting his hand on his lover's shoulder, Scott gave a gentle shake. "Hey, we've got class in half an hour."

Derek groaned and pulled his pillow over his head. "Five more minutes."

Chuckling, Scott got out of bed and took a quick shower. By the time he returned, Derek was sitting on the edge of the bed, his elbows resting on his knees, his head supported in his palms. "You okay?"

"Yeah. Just super tired. I don't think I've been working out enough. I should start running in the mornings to re-energize." He pushed himself into an upright position and crossed the room to plant a gentle kiss on Scott's neck. "I'll be ready in a few."

When did he take off his boxers? Scott couldn't help but admire Derek's lean body. Fuck but Derek's ass had rounded out with muscle. *When did that happen?* Had he stopped paying attention to those details? "If it'll help you to have more energy, cool. But you look awesome."

Derek wrapped a towel around his waist and trudged out of the room, giving Scott a thumbs up as he left.

Scott rifled through his clothes, picking up and putting down the same shirt several times. Something was off with Derek. What could have happened to make him so sleepy and lethargic? A tightening in his chest accompanied the likely answer. He'd pushed too hard on the Tim issue.

A discomfort settled in his gut. He'd challenged Derek plenty of times, but had never forced him to go against his conscience. If he was the cause of Derek's unease, he'd back off no matter how worried he might be. That didn't mean he wouldn't keep careful watch, but from a distance. If he sensed trouble, he'd step in no matter how pissed off Derek got.

Derek seemed more himself when he returned to the room. "Jesus. I slept like a rock."

"Yeah. You barely even budged when I got into bed last night." Clothes he hadn't even realized he'd picked out were in his hands. "How'd the meeting go last night?" He was about to ask whether Derek had talked to Jared, but swallowed the question back.

"I was elected."

"*Great!* Congrats." Scott strode to Derek's side and kissed his cheek.

"A professor from the psych department came in and spoke to us about the peer counseling program The Alliance will be starting."

"That's cool. You mentioned something about that last week." The peer counseling might be just the thing the both of them needed. Derek could continue to help others, but with limits on how deeply he'd get involved with their problems. Maybe Scott could stop worrying about all the strays that seemed to flock to his lover.

He sat on the couch and watched Derek dry himself. Derek pulled on his pants without putting on underwear, and Scott took note. The image would make concentration more difficult in their music class.

Derek cleared his throat, forcing Scott to snap out of his own head and return his attention to Derek's face. "And I talked to Jared about Tim. He shares your concerns."

There was no anger in the statement, but Scott decided to tread lightly anyway. "Listen. Maybe I'm not giving you enough credit. If you really think you can keep a boundary with Tim, I should be supporting you."

Derek stopped weaving his arms through his shirt sleeves and stared at Scott.

Trapped like that, several ideas popped into Scott's head about how he could take advantage.

"I appreciate that, but I think you guys are right. I have to figure out how to put some distance between my bleeding heart and the people who latch onto it."

If Derek only knew how soothing those few words were. Scott slipped across the room and pulled Derek's shirt down his torso, then dragged him into a hug. "I won't lie. It relieves me to hear you say that. But I want to make sure you know I'll support whatever choice you make."

Derek cupped Scott's cheek, his palm warm and soft. "Have I told you I love you lately?"

Scott captured the hand on his face and felt the smooth metal of the promise ring. His heart beat faster, and his vision tunneled in on Derek's face. "You don't have to say it for me to know. But yeah, you've said it plenty."

They basically jogged to the music building, stopping at Java's for a morning coffee and a bagel. When they arrived at the classroom, there was a message on the board instructing students to keep their bags packed and listing a different room for their class.

He and Derek traversed the stairs and hallways until they reached a room that looked like a recording studio. The professor stood by a Smartboard at the front and fiddled with his laptop and the connection cords. Finally, his desktop screen appeared on the display.

"Good morning. My name is Professor Jordan. Today I'll be introducing you to the art of mixology."

Scott had only connected that term with alcohol and suspected the professor had made up his own word. He squirmed in his seat. Was this guy going to be one of those arrogant fucks who liked to make themselves seem more important than they really were?

Whatever. Scott cut off his own judgments. Derek was going to be in his element, and the clouds casting shadows over his lover's mood would evaporate as soon as he had music and machines at his fingertips. If Derek was happy, that was good enough for him.

The studio was nothing like Scott expected. The room contained approximately thirty computers set on long tables. He and Derek hustled to one close to the front of the room and claimed their spot. Other students found seats until duos and trios speckled the room.

"I'm going to train you how to use a computerized mixing program. These stations are loaded with several different styles of music. Over the course of the next few weeks, you'll need to learn how to isolate the sounds and place them onto tracks." He puffed his chest out, as if he thought he was presenting an early Christmas present to the class.

This was the reason he'd taken the class. He'd finally be able to develop the skills to put music together the way Derek did. Maybe he wouldn't need Derek's assistance to mix after all. If he could figure out the program, he could make his project serve double duty as a piece of classwork and a gift to Derek.

"Before we begin, has anyone ever performed the art of mixology?" The professor surveyed the room. No one raised their hands.

Derek also glanced around the room and then, tentatively lifted his hand into the air.

"Ah, and your name?" The question seemed more like a challenge.

"I'm Derek Thompson, sir." He lowered his hand and remained silent.

"What sorts of things have you mixed?" Again with a superior tone. Scott suppressed the sudden urge to rush the pompous man like a bull.

"Mostly dance stuff. Overlaying various beats and musical sounds with popular songs." He maintained a demure tone as he spoke.

"He's being modest, sir." Scott hadn't planned on talking, but words were coming out of his mouth anyway. From the corner of his eye he could see Derek staring at him. "He deejayed the school dance last year, mixing original music for the entire party."

The professor lowered his glasses from their perch on his pointy nose and stared at Scott. "I see. Very well. Since no one else has experience, we'll start with the basics. Perhaps our young celebrity will become my assistant."

It amazed Scott that the man had turned the word assistant into the sound of a hissing snake. "You'd be lucky to have him assist." He used the same tone the professor had.

Derek kicked him under the table, but Scott ignored him.

Professor Jordan continued with his lecture, walking the class through the various features of the program. Derek seemed to already know everything, but he took notes and remained silent like a good student should.

Scott's temper continued to flare with each new comment from the front of the room. He clenched his hands as images of Tim, melded with the professor's arrogance and Derek's passive behavior. Where did all the anger come from?

By the end of class, his head was full, although he hadn't actually picked up much information about the mixing program at all. Instead, he stood on unsure legs, examining his odd reactions. He'd certainly overreacted to the professor.

Since they started school, it seemed anything that threatened Derek set Scott off, even if the attacks came in the form of attitude. Protecting Derek was nothing new to him, but losing his temper left him unbalanced. Calm, cool, and collected ruled his temperament. At least it always *had.* Besides, from the little he said, Scott knew Derek would give him an earful as soon as they got outside.

Derek didn't disappoint. "What the hell was that back there? Were you *trying* to antagonize the professor?"

Scott stared at Derek, even opened his mouth, but nothing came out. He had no explanation for his behavior, not understanding it himself.

Shaking his head, Derek trudged in the direction of their dorm. After a few steps he stopped, facing Scott who hadn't moved. "Come on."

He followed Derek, putting one foot in front of the other, although his thoughts were somewhere else altogether. Once they were in their room, the weight he'd been carrying finally loosened. Even though he was still unsure why he'd reacted so strongly in class, he could at least form words. "I'm so sorry, Derek. I don't know what came over me. When that bastard started talking like he was better than you, I just wanted to smash his head in."

Derek remained silent. At least his facial expression was relaxed. Finally, his shoulders sagged, and he closed the distance between them. "You've got to stop worrying about me so much. I can take care of myself. You have to believe it, otherwise you're going to spend the rest of our lives tense and paranoid."

Derek was right. Deep down, his faith in Derek was as strong as it had been back in high school. Derek had embraced their relationship with ease, had accepted Scott when his own father wouldn't. "I think I'm going for a run to clear my head. Maybe I can figure some of this out."

Derek nodded and hugged Scott close. The tightness anchored Scott, safety and love pouring into him from a simple touch. "I think that's a great idea." He stepped away from Scott and perched on his desk. "I don't have class until this afternoon, so I think I'll get some work done while you're out."

Scott stripped out of his clothes, put on a pair of shorts and running shoes, kissed Derek goodbye, and exited the dormitory.

The landscape by BU was all cement and buildings, nothing like the green and blue river scenery of Cambridge.

Scott waited on the sidewalk as a rush of cars spewed exhaust into his face, all in a hurry, honking horns and switching lanes in a mad rush to get wherever they had to be. The moment they passed, he hustled across the street, working his way down to the Hatch Shell where the Boston Pops performed on the Fourth of July. There he'd find long stretches of running paths. No cars. No horns. Clean air.

A half hour of dodging four-wheeled missiles and he'd reached the basin where the paths began. His body was warmed up and itching to expend pent up energy. He took off at a quick clip once he hit the grassy area, his footfalls *pat-pat*-patting a steady cadence on the worn dirt path down by the water's edge.

Picnickers outnumbered runners, most likely enjoying the remnants of summer heat this late in September. Soon enough people would crowd the gyms as the months wore on, which suited Scott just fine. He preferred isolation when running unless Derek ran alongside him.

Sweat formed at his temples and the back of his neck. Thank God he hadn't worn a shirt to hamper the breeze cooling his heated skin.

His shoes pounding against the ground lulled his racing mind until his only focus became the mechanics of his body. Arms pumping. Legs propelling him forward. Steady breathing. Each part of his body falling into line.

The path wound through a patch of tall brush, isolating him even further. He entered his own world, full of trails, trees and shrubs. No people. Just him.

Shadows and sunlight painted the ground in a web of light and shadow, adding to the sense of nature and peacefulness. Sunbeams pierced the shade through overhanging branches. Dust motes floated in the air, weightless and shimmering, the sun reflected off their surfaces. His own private fairyland, where *he* made the rules.

About a mile into his run, the brush opened and he ran along familiar ground toward the area where the Charles narrowed from the wide basin into the winding stretch of river. If he kept running, he'd be home in a couple of hours, all rubbery muscles. Of course, he'd have to take public transportation or a cab back to school if he did, and he hadn't brought his wallet with him.

He'd just barely arrived at school, and already the tranquility of his summer faded to a dream. A couple short weeks was all it took for a possible threat to muscle it's way into Derek's life. Tyrell's sneer forced its way into Scott's head, alongside the picture of Tim.

Why does Derek attract the nut jobs? It wasn't a fair question. Pure-hearted Derek always saw the best in people and situations and couldn't stop himself from helping others any more than he could stop breathing.

Fear gripped Scott by the throat and tried to strangle the wind out of him. Derek's choices didn't create Scott's issues. No, those were buried deep within himself. Derek only helped identify what they were, but Scott's demons were his own to battle.

His nomadic childhood and cold, unloving prick of a father weren't Derek's fault. And it wasn't his responsibility to provide reassurances whenever Scott felt insecure.

He's hidden nothing from me. I have no reason to doubt his ability to protect himself. Ah, the root of the problem. It wasn't Derek he doubted. Every risk, every crazy person who might harm the man he loved was a threat to his new-found stability. Security, companionship, these were his only because Derek had brought them into his life.

But you shouldn't need to have Derek in order to feel those things. A stitch in his side blossomed into full pain. Fuck. Scott stopped, sucking in air. He fell to his knees, hands on the ground, digging his fingers into the dirt and then lifting them, watching the powdery soil sift through his fingers.

Breathe in, breathe out. Trees, shrubs, chirping birds, clear, sweet air. No harm here.

The earth beneath him remained firm, holding him in place. If gravity failed, he'd lose his sanity. He'd lose Derek. *Hold steady. Get a grip.*

He pushed himself onto his haunches. Sweat poured freely down his sides, chest, and back. The sun beat down on his head, fingers of warmth working into his tender muscles and easing frayed nerves. His course was clear. Derek's helping others wasn't the problem.

The truth, each new realization, pressed at Scott's skull, struggling to escape. He rubbed his palms against his temples yet couldn't ease the steady throbbing. If only he possessed the energy to keep the phantoms at bay.

All his life he'd sought something to count on. Damn, but he'd scored big, with more than he'd hoped or dreamed for.

Fear was the enemy, an opponent living within him, not an external threat. What defenses could he build against an adversary immune to physical strength and intellectual wit?

Tired. So tired. With a lead weight for a heart, Scott scrambled to his feet and brushed himself off. He couldn't summon the strength to run. Walking might be out of the question too. All of his energy channeled into the one thing he'd never been able to count on…faith. And there was only one thing he had faith in: his love for Derek.

Derek came first, in all things. Scott's needs? Well, they didn't even run a close second. Faith. Trust. Derek would take care of himself. And if he didn't? Pity the man who crossed him.

You've got to stop worrying about me so much. Otherwise you're going to spend the rest of our lives tense and paranoid, Derek had said. Plain and simple, Scott's boyfriend was a genius. Which didn't really help him figure out *how* to accomplish the massive task of not worrying.

Chapter Twelve

Derek's acceptance into the peer counseling group kept him busy for the next few weeks. The selected group of five met with the two psychiatrists enlisted to train them.

He'd kept his word and connected Tim with Jared and Charlie. Bittersweet failure warred with his sense of loyalty to Scott, but...he had no intention of completely cutting Tim off.

In the weeks since the election meeting, Tim had become scarce. The few times he *did* see Tim, the kid was all kinds of fucked up. Frustration prickled along Derek's skin, as if the little no-see-ums that swarmed the campus each evening nipped at his skin. But distancing himself from Tim, fighting the instinct to get help him, had been necessary, out of his love for Scott.

Even so, Scott had retreated into himself, no longer badgering Derek about where he was going or what he was doing.

Scott wasn't distancing himself physically, proven by Derek's aching ass and swollen lips. The tender *I love yous* and tight squeezes each morning when Derek awoke denied any emotional distancing. Yet a shadow clouded their relationship, an elusive *something* Derek couldn't quite put his finger on. Unease settled like a rock in his stomach.

He had another training session for peer counseling that evening, the third of four, and then the core group would begin their work.

Grabbing his binder, Derek trekked across the campus, the weight of his confusion about Scott churning in his stomach. The cool air of early fall filled his lungs. Revitalizing. The sweatshirt he'd tied around his waist hugged him, providing some additional comfort as he left the campus grounds and approached the downtown clinic where his training took place.

The psychiatrists, John and Sam, short for Samantha, jointly led the sessions. Sam's enthusiastic voice chirped a sweet "Hello!" when he arrived, lifting his spirits. John's smile grew as Derek entered, blanketing him in acceptance and confidence.

Once all five students arrived, Sam addressed the group. "Good evening, everyone. We're officially halfway through with the training. So far we've learned about barriers to effective communication, when to use *I*-messages, and the three types of behavior you might exhibit as a peer counselor. Tonight we're going to engage in some role playing, and then we'll focus specifically on the behaviors you'll want to use in your work. Any questions?"

Derek glanced around the room. The other participants remained as silent as him.

Sam waited a few seconds before continuing. "Okay. I'm going to present a scenario where I'll be someone who's coming in for counseling. One of you will be the peer counselor. John will facilitate." She positioned two chairs in the middle of a circle of five others. "Who'd like to go first?"

Amanda, a junior who'd been in the Alliance since her freshman year, raised her hand, although it seemed like she was lifting a weight to do so.

"Wonderful. Take a seat in the middle of the circle."

Amanda went to a center chair and sat without saying a word.

Sam smiled. "Relax. This is for practice. No one expects any of you to get this perfect on the first try. We all learn from our mistakes." Grateful for Sam's reassurance, Derek relaxed, his breath coming easier and tension seeping out of his muscles. These people were here to help.

Sam reached into her pocket and withdrew a stack of index cards. Flipping the top one, she read the contents silently to herself then placed it on the bottom of the deck. She gripped the edge of her seat, her eyes glued to her lap. "I'm having some difficulty with my boyfriend."

Amanda's silence filled the room. John nudged her into action. "If someone states a problem and offers no more information, what should you do?"

Derek flipped through his notes, although he already knew the answer. "Use the assertive practice of probing. Say something like, *Could you tell me more about that?* or *What kinds of problems are you having?*"

"Good." John faced the other observers. "When someone is reluctant to provide information, asking open-ended questions to prompt them is an effective assertive strategy. Go on, Amanda."

Amanda crossed her feet one over the other and tucked them beneath her seat. "What seems to be troubling you about your boyfriend?"

Sam bit her nail. "He wants to have sex and I don't feel I'm ready. I'm afraid if I don't, he might leave me to find someone who will."

"You should do what makes you comfortable." Amanda leaned forward in her seat, placing her hand on Sam's knee. Sam jerked at the touch.

"Stop. Okay, who can tell us what just happened?" John's voice, smooth as velvet, carried no criticism.

Kevin, a sophomore like Derek, spoke. "First, she gave advice. Then she made physical contact before determining whether Sam was comfortable with that."

"Right. One of the barriers to effective communication is giving advice. This sends the message you don't have confidence in Sam's decision-making ability. Physical contact, especially when the subject matter involves physicality, runs the risk of shutting Sam down."

Amanda continued. "I'm sorry. I didn't mean to make you uncomfortable."

Sam leaned back in her seat. "It's okay. I just don't know what to do."

Amanda maintained an upright posture and responded with a soothing cadence to her voice. "When I'm in situations like this, I ask myself what *I* feel. Sometimes that helps me to get a little closer to a decision."

Sam pursed her lips, then folded her hands in her lap. "I feel it's my choice when to have sex, and if he can't accept that, maybe he's not the right person for me."

"Have you said that to him?"

Sam smiled, but quickly schooled her expression to match the emotion expected of her role-playing identity. "No. Like I said, I'm afraid if I don't have sex with him, he'll find someone else."

John interrupted once again. "There were some excellent moves there. Who can identify them?" William, a senior, raised his hand. John chuckled. "No need to raise your hand. Just speak. We're not in a formal class setting here."

William nodded. "She used an *I*-message to prompt Sam toward a decision-making strategy without giving advice, and then she asked an assertive question."

"Very good. Amanda, please take a seat. Who'd like to replace her and continue with the session?"

Derek stood, taking Amanda's spot in the center of the circle. Once settled, he took over where Amanda left off. "What I'm hearing you say is you feel you shouldn't have to sleep with your boyfriend until you're ready and you're afraid of the consequences if you don't have sex. Is that correct?"

Sam nodded.

Several responses flipped like pages of a book through Derek's head. All of them seemed to fall into a category of barriers to effective communication. Recommendations, judgments of the boyfriend, of her, all of which had the potential to shut her down. Since Sam was still relatively silent, another question was in order. *Ask open-ended questions.* "How would you feel if you spoke to your boyfriend about your concerns and his response matched your fears?"

Sam closed her eyes. "I'd die."

"I understand it would be painful, but I'm wondering if you can examine how it would make you feel." The strategies he'd used unfurled like a list in his head. *Reflective listening. Use persistence to get the other person to delve into the problem. Get the person to name a worst-case scenario so it loses its power.*

"Well, I suppose I'd feel hurt and sad. But I'd also feel angry and disappointed. I know I shouldn't be with someone who can't respect my decisions or who wants to make me do something I'm not ready to do." Sam's tongue had finally unleashed.

"What do all of the things you just said tell you about how you feel about this situation with your boyfriend?" Butterflies flitted in Derek's stomach, the good kind, tickling him from the inside, worries about failing Tim, Scott's sudden change in behavior, sliding to the background. For the first time all day he felt like he fit in his own skin.

Sam sat a bit straighter. "It tells me that even though it might be painful, I shouldn't be with someone who doesn't respect me."

Derek nodded. "What's your next step going to be, and when are you going to do it?"

"I'm going to confront him. Tonight. We have a dinner date."

"Are you sure you want to do this in a public place like a restaurant or dining hall?" Derek sat taller in his chair, puffing his chest out and giving himself a mental high-five.

Then John's voice cut in. "Stop. Derek was on a roll there, but he made one error at the end. Can anyone tell me what it was?"

"He made a judgment when he asked her if she thought it was a good idea to talk in a public place." Amanda smiled at Derek as she made her contribution, her eyes kind.

Derek replayed the question, pinpointing the phrasing and how he could have changed it. "What if I used an *I*-message and said something like, 'I might choose to have a conversation like that in private since I'd be concerned about how my boyfriend would react and wouldn't want to be in a public place if he reacted badly'."

John opened his arms toward the group in an inviting gesture.

Bill, the one person who hadn't spoken yet, chimed in. "That *I*-message works because it avoids giving advice or making a judgment. It also shares what Derek is thinking without imposing his opinion on Sam. Sam is still able to make her own decisions without being influenced by an implied suggestion."

"Excellent." John's smile broadened. "Textbook explanation."

Sam stood, turned to the group, and applauded them. "That was fantastic. I'm truly impressed with the way you were able to name the strategies, critiquing each other's choices without passing judgment."

Derek stood, his head floating with echoes of the scenario. Warmth raced along his skin, raising the fine hairs along his arms and neck, as he reflected on his first counseling session. Sure, he'd made some mistakes, but in the end, the co-ed Sam portrayed would be walking out with a sound plan that would likely result in a positive outcome for her.

Sam faced the group. "For the remainder of the session, we'll be focusing on strategies for assertive counseling. Remember, passive counseling is where you hold back for fear of making the kinds of mistakes you made tonight. Failing to make adequate contributions in a counseling session can shut people down. I can tell this group isn't at risk of being passive. We'll concentrate on identifying that nearly invisible line separating assertive counseling techniques from aggressive ones."

The group took their seats and John handed out an article they'd be using for the evening. Derek glanced over the sheet, his heart beating with an extra staccato as he recognized each strategy as common sense to him. He settled into his seat, wanting to absorb as much as possible but salivating to get to the real work of being a peer counselor.

When Derek left the clinic an hour later, cool wisps of air licked at his arms, the chill penetrating his skin. Slipping his sweatshirt over his head was akin to wrapping himself in a warm blanket, offering protection and security, something which seemed to be slipping away from him with Scott.

And just like that, the euphoria of his training session liquefied and seeped out of him, leaving him hollow. He could pinpoint the exact moment Scott changed. He'd gone for that run after their music class, and when he returned, it was like a light had extinguished. The typical warnings and overprotectiveness had vanished, replaced by a stranger who questioned nothing.

Derek's shoes tapped on the hard surface of the paved sidewalk, cityscape giving way to college scenery. As he crossed the grassy quad leading to his dormitory, his feet seemed to take on a life of their own. His watch indicated it was eight. Scott wouldn't be back from practice for another hour at least, and only then if he didn't go out with his teammates afterwards.

The thought of entering an empty room clutched at Derek's heart, the muscle thudding in protest. No, he didn't want to be alone so he could wallow in his misery.

Instead, he trailed through the maze of walkways making up the inner campus until he reached the Student Center. Scanning the packed room, isolation wrapped around him. The groups of laughing and smiling students, playing pool, eating, simply hanging out, served as a slap in the face, reminding him he'd not enjoyed this kind of easiness with Scott for the better part of a month.

Shards of ice raced through his veins, stabbing at him from the inside. His muscles trembled, taut and burning. The mixture of fire and ice stormed inside him, and his vision blurred. To make matters worse, he'd squashed his urges to confront Scott. After all, he'd given Scott plenty of reasons to stress and worry over the past year. The least he could do was give his boyfriend the time he needed to work through whatever it was that troubled him.

Still, why the complete turnaround? Did Scott no longer care? Had he pushed Scott past his threshold of tolerance? Derek sucked in a breath as his heart skipped a beat. No way could he lose Scott.

A hand on his shoulder snapped him from the internal hurricane of emotion. "Derek!"

Wheeling on the spot, he glared at the person who'd touched him. "What!"

"Whoa. You okay?" Jared stood before him, his eyes wide.

His muscles collapsed, releasing all the tension at once. The fuzziness in his eyes intensified then cleared as hot tears streamed down his cheeks. "I don't think so."

Jared caught his lower lip between his teeth, sliding his arm around Derek's shoulder and glancing around the room. "C'mon. Let's go for a walk." He led Derek toward the Student Center entrance and outside.

The breeze whipped around Derek, his cheeks growing chill as his moistened skin caught each gust of wind. "It's Scott." Jared hadn't asked what was wrong. He hadn't said anything, but the unspoken question flailed in the air like a live wire.

"Just talk." Jared's tone was easy, soothing, like hot cocoa on a cold winter night. He kept his arm firmly planted around Derek's shoulders, the heat seeping through his armor of ice.

"Something's changed. Ever since he told me to stay away from Tim, ever since I pawned the guy off on you and Charlie, Scott's become distant. And I don't understand it. I did what he wanted me to do." Putting words to the problem made the change in Scott's behavior real. With no clue about what the problem was, Derek couldn't *do* anything to make things better.

Invisible fingers tightened around his throat, a painful lump blocking his airway. "I thought by backing off from Tim, by taking steps to distance myself from his erratic behavior, it would settle things for Scott. Give him the peace of mind he seemed to need. But he's been wrestling more. Coming back to the room later. And worst of all, he's stopped hounding me about the things that typically worry him. It's like he doesn't care anymore."

"I seriously doubt that's true, the part about him not caring, I mean." Jared's words latched on to Derek's waning sense of hope buried deep inside, nudging it to grow and blossom. "When people change, it's usually something that's going on with them."

"Then why isn't he talking to me about it?" He winced at the whiny tone of his own voice.

"I don't know." Jared stopped their progress and positioned Derek so they stood eye to eye. Placing one hand on each shoulder, he captured Derek in a steady gaze. "And there's only one way to find out."

Derek's head seemed to grow ten pounds heavier. His lungs ceased to pull air in and out. Even his heart clenched as the truth smashed into him. "You're right."

"Then get to it." Jared released Derek, giving him a gentle shove in the direction of his dorm.

What started as trudging turned to speed walking, and then a jog. When his dorm came into view, he started running, his breathing labored. Blood coursed through him, melting the ice, pushing the chill away, easing the tension which lived in his muscles. He leapt up the stairs, taking two at a time, and rushed to their door. Opening it with more force than he'd expected, he found Scott sitting on the couch reading.

He snapped his head up at Derek's arrival.

For seconds that stretched out over what felt like minutes, Derek's breath heaved. His heart pounded. The rush of blood thundered in his ears. Sweat licked at the back of his neck and forehead. Once the initial adrenaline rush subsided, he took a step inside the room.

He stared into Scott's widened green eyes, noted the book which was folded in his lap, sensed Scott's intensity when he leaned forward in his seat. Time hung, as if suspended. What came next could change everything between them, good or bad.

And then strings that had puppeted Derek's behavior for nearly a month snipped away, one by one, freeing him to let go of the control he'd been harboring. Words flew through his head first, then rushed out his mouth just as quickly. "Why have you changed with me? You don't criticize. You don't nag. You just agree with everything and let me do whatever I want." He gripped a bed post, digging his fingers into the wood. "Ever since you went on that run, you've been like a different person. Did I do something? Did your feelings change toward me?"

Each muscle in his body froze as he stood, rooted to the spot, waiting for a response.

Scott stared at the floor. When he lifted his gaze to meet Derek's, his cheeks had taken on a crimson hue. He stood and closed the distance between them. Each move, each expression, sent rays of heat toward Derek, licking at his skin, trying to gain entrance through the wall he'd built. "No, Derek. You didn't do anything, and my feelings for you haven't changed."

They were the words he wanted to hear, but Derek held fast, forcing himself to remain glued to the spot. His arms twitched to reach out for Scott. He wanted to taste Scott's mouth. Feel his hands as they ran along his body. But he needed an answer.

Scott stopped just short of touching him. How had Derek missed the dwindling of simple touches? "All right. I can see you need a full explanation. Can we sit?"

Derek longed to rush into Scott's embrace, but one tenuous step and he'd probably crumple to the ground. "I'm good here."

Shaking his head, Scott remained where he was. "Long version or get right to the point?"

"Why don't we start with getting to the point and take it from there." His voice remained steady, although the rest of his body trembled.

"Okay." Scott took a tentative step closer. "When we were in class and the music professor started verbally attacking you, something inside me snapped. I wanted to kick his ass so bad I had to grip my seat to keep from getting up. And watching you with Tim when we got back from playing pool, crouching by his side and inviting him into our room, I wanted to wring the little fucker's neck." He paused for a second. When Derek said nothing he continued. "And I realized I'm not trusting you. I'm so afraid of stifling you, and the only way I know how to prevent that is to keep my concerns to myself."

Derek's heart beat slower, although it still pounded at an increased rate. His feet gripped the ground with greater stability. Taking a hesitant step, he found he was able to support his own weight. "*That's* what's been going on?"

Scott nodded, but said nothing.

The invisible vise clutching at Derek's throat released, as if snapped like a rubber band. "Scott, I've been so worried about us. I wish you'd told me about this before."

"I didn't want to put my burden on you. It's not anything you've done. It's something inside me that needs fixing." His arms hung at his sides, dangling limply, and his eyes shimmered.

Without making a decision to do so, Derek stepped forward and swept Scott into his arms. "Baby, I *love* the fact you watch out for me. You and I both know I've got a tendency to let helping others overshadow my better judgment. You're the rock that keeps me safely anchored."

"When I went for that run…" Scott's voice wavered, but he wasn't crying. "I realized something about myself…about us." He wrapped his arms around Derek, leaning his head on Derek's shoulder. "I'd been blaming you for all my stress. You *do* show poor judgment when it comes to your own personal safety. But that's you."

"Scott, I—"

"No let me finish." Scott's resolve was firm, but there was undeniable gentleness beneath the bite of his tone. "The problem lies inside me. I never had anything resembling a stable life until I met you. *You're* the anchor. Not me. And I'm terrified of losing the one person that grounds me in this world."

Derek squeezed Scott. "I should have been able to put this together."

Scott chuckled, although there was no mirth to it. "Maybe. But even if you did, it still wouldn't be your problem to solve. You've done nothing but be there for me. If my sense of stability is unsteady, that's something *I* have to work through."

Stepping out of Scott's embrace, Derek glanced at his hand then Scott's. He ran his fingers over the shining band of silver on his own finger, the metal warm and solid. "Look at this, Scott. You gave this to me because you wanted me to make a promise to you. You wanted to know I was as committed to our future as you are. This ring binds us together. It's unending, like us, going on forever."

He took Scott's hand and spun his ring in a circle, tracing the Celtic pattern with his eyes. "As we travel around this circle, we're going to face challenges, but when we face them together, we'll end up okay."

Scott stared at the ring Derek handled. "You just have to give me some time to reach your level of confidence. I've lived a life that taught me a different lesson."

"I know you have. Which is why I've chosen to help you out by pushing Tim away." He released Scott's hand, sliding his fingers along Scott's arm, along his neck, and cupping his cheek. The stubble massaged the pads of his fingers, reminding him how masculine this fragile man really was. "You're far stronger than you give yourself credit for."

"When you say it, I believe it. I have to figure out how to believe it on my own." Scott placed his hand over Derek's, the warmth radiating along Derek's skin, his arm, and sinking into his flesh, melting away the ice.

Derek drew in a deep breath and closed his eyes. Scott's scent surrounded him, his breath a gentle breeze, floating between them. Deep in his chest, Derek's heart swelled, longing to kiss Scott, to wrap him up in love and safety, the same love and safety Scott had offered him ever since they met.

Sliding his fingers from Scott's cheek to the nape of his neck, he pulled Scott toward him, sealing their lips together.

Scott opened his mouth and Derek slid his tongue inside. Soft lips pressed against his own, melding in a perfect play of pressure and tenderness.

Withdrawing, Derek cupped Scott's face. "Talk to me when you're worried about something. Don't leave me in the dark."

Scott nodded, a single tear finally slipping from one eye, running a trail down his cheek until it disappeared behind Derek's palm. "I promise."

With the conversation over and the stress he'd been harboring gone, Derek's body suddenly seemed weighted as if all his energy had flowed out of him. His eyelids felt leaden. His muscles rubber. Derek stripped out of his clothes, helped Scott do the same, and led them to their bed. Usually, Scott cradled him, but tonight Derek wanted to reverse their roles.

As Scott's warmth seeped into him, drawing him closer and closer to sleep, he savored the slight hint of musk surrounding them. Scott's rugged odor, the slow and even sound of Scott's breathing, lulled Derek into peaceful contentedness.

Hugging Scott close, Derek rested his head on the pillow. He should have thought about Scott's history. If he could have punched himself without disturbing Scott, he would have. As if love alone could purge Scott of his demons. Love might be the key, but time was the cure. As hard as suppressing his own nature might be, he'd do it for Scott. He just hoped the price he'd pay for denying a part of himself, even for a while, wouldn't cost either of them too much.

Chapter Thirteen

Scott circled his teammate, Marcus, muscles relaxed but poised. One step to the left and Marcus gave him his opening. Springing, Scott captured the leg in one sweep and had Marcus on the mat.

Working his arms through Marcus's, Scott forced his opponent off balance. He pressed his feet into the spongy mat, gaining purchase, and used his shoulder as leverage, bringing Marcus first to his side, and then to his back. A simple half-nelson was all it took to finish the job.

Sweating, muscles tingling, Scott released his partner and sat on his heels. Breath heaved in and out, bringing revitalizing oxygen into his body. Marcus remained prone, his eyes closed. "Dude, you suck so bad."

Scott laughed, hopped to his feet, and offered his hand. He was tempted to make a comment about how Derek would refute such a claim, but managed to restrain himself. "If I suck, what does that say about you?"

Marcus took Scott's hand and allowed himself to be hoisted to his feet. "Fuck you." His smile lingered for a few seconds, then his lips flattened together in an expression of grim determination. "Again."

For the next half hour, Scott sparred, practicing takedowns, escapes, different methods for exposing Marcus's back to the mat. The scent of sweat fueled him. The internal furnace of heat that caused his skin to sheen from moisture was cooled by the constant breeze of the overhead fan circulating stale air. His muscles swelled from exertion, yet remained limber and pliable, obeying his every command. Yeah, here on the mat he had total control. In this place, nothing could get him down. Not even his own doubts and insecurities. They simply didn't exist inside the wrestling circle.

Everywhere else was a different story. The moment he stepped outside the practice room, thoughts of Derek, their relationship, Tim, his father, moving around so much, crowded for space in his already saturated mind. He'd thought his talk with Derek would've eased his stress. Old wounds took time to heal apparently, even when the most understanding boyfriend in the world stood by his side.

"Why hasn't Derek come to any of the practices lately?" Marcus's question pulled Scott from his internal storm.

"I dunno. He's pretty busy with his new peer counseling gig." He stripped off his shirt and wiped the back of his neck and chest, drawing the attention of several girls who stood by the water bubbler. "Plus, he's been working on a project for our music class. We have to put together a mix, choosing a particular genre."

Marcus clapped Scott's shoulder, the sound echoing in the room as his hand made contact with damp skin. "Derek is fuckin' awesome at mixing. I remember the slammin' music at last year's dance."

"Yeah. He's awesome all right." Scott started toward the exit, Marcus tagging behind him. They stepped into the locker room in silence.

At the lockers, Marcus stripped out of his clothes. Funny how Scott never felt aroused when wrestling or in the locker room. Sure, he understood the ribbing about wrestling being a *gay* sport from guys who played on other teams, but the intensity of focus and drive when on the wrestling mat was anything but arousing. Marcus wrapped a towel around his waist. "If my girl went through what Derek went through last year, someone attacking her, I wouldn't let her out of my sight. I don't know how you do it."

The comment hit way too close to home. If Marcus only knew how poorly he was handling his fears, he would've kept his mouth shut. But like any move on the mat, forming new habits took practice. Trusting Derek to take care of himself and to ask for help when and if he needed it was a habit he was determined to form. "He can take care of himself." Scott wasn't sure whether he was reassuring Marcus or himself.

He took time in the showers, allowing the heat and wetness to soothe his muscles. Warmth pelted against his arms and legs, massaged his chest and back, soaked his hair, cocooning him in a blanket of safety and isolation.

Stepping outside helped clear his head. Long gone was the lingering warmth of summer. Halloween would be upon them in no time, and in another month after that, wrestling season would begin. Practice five days a week, finals to prepare for. It all seemed to be rushing past him, too fast.

Derek was having the time of his life. Funny how just one year ago, Scott had been simply living his life, and Derek was the one on a mission, wanting to live out loud and proud, stressing, fretting, and figuring himself out. Now, he fit into his skin as if his life were just where he wanted it to be.

Scott, on the other hand, could understand what crustaceans who'd outgrown their shell must feel like. He lived in that raw and dangerous stage, where his flesh was exposed, vulnerable to the elements and to prey that could swoop in at any time. What he wouldn't give to find his new shell.

Derek was his safety. So was wrestling. But every day, when he and Derek were apart, he couldn't stop his racing mind from wandering down forbidden paths. *What if some new head case latches onto him? What if he changes his mind and decides to help Tim after all? What if—*

He clenched his fists, digging his nails into his palms. He had to stop asking those questions. Just thinking them evoked Derek's warning: *You'll live your life with tension and paranoia.*

The battle between his head and his heart was his undoing. His heart swelled whenever he thought of Derek, but his head would insinuate itself, pushing love and security to the side, taunting him with his past. *But your dad didn't love you. Anyone could take Derek away from you in one act of hatred or craziness.*

"Damn!" Scott glanced around to see if anyone stood nearby to witness him cursing at himself. It was like a body snatcher had taken permanent residence inside him lately. Every time he began to feel a sense of stability or happiness it slipped away like he was Teflon. For two years he'd managed to remain calm and to enjoy Derek. He'd accepted his new friends, the welcoming embrace of Derek's family, his mother's newfound backbone. No longer under the controlling scrutiny of his father, he'd managed to believe things would work out, that he'd found what he'd always longed for. So why the change? What was so different now that his past struggles prohibited him from happiness in his present?

He quickened his pace, physical exertion placing errant thoughts at bay. Within ten minutes, he stood outside his dorm room. A soft beat emanated from within, accompanied by music. He tried to place the song, but it wasn't one he'd heard before.

When he entered the room, he found Derek totally engrossed in whatever he had on his desktop. He faced

Scott, then quickly shut the laptop lid, cutting off the source of the music. "Hey. I didn't expect you back so early."

Scott took inventory. Derek's clothes were on, so he hadn't been jacking off. No one else was in the room, so he hadn't been entertaining. But the flush in his cheeks definitely spoke to something he was hiding. "Uh, did I interrupt something?" The lilt in his voice carried playfulness, as he'd intended it to.

Derek shook his head. "Nope. Just working on the project for music class."

That caught his interest. "Really? Let me hear."

"No!" Derek snapped. "I mean. I don't want you to hear it until it's done."

Suspicion skittered through Scott's head. Scott blocked his doubt, forcing himself to accept Derek's words for what they were. *You only break old habits and form new ones by practicing.* The internal chant had become his personal mantra.

"Okay. Well, maybe you can help me with mine." Scott pulled up a chair and took a seat next to Derek.

"Yeah. Let's do it." Derek angled the laptop away from Scott, opened the lid, and clicked on something. He then shifted it back so Scott could see the screen, the blank homepage of the mixing program on display.

Scott kissed Derek's neck. "You're such a tease."

Derek sucked in a sharp breath, painting an expression of false shock on his face. "You kiss me on the neck like that and call *me* a tease?"

Cords of tension snapped, releasing Scott from his worries and concerns. A simple inflection, a gentle flirtation, easy banter. That's all it took to bring him back to himself. If only he could figure out how to generate those feelings on his own, maybe he'd be able to finally trust that everything would work out okay.

"Let's start up a file." A few clicks and Derek had the screen ready. "The code the professor gave us allows access to all the stored music from the lab, but I have a shit ton of other beats, sounds, and music if you want better variety."

"Why don't I start easy and work up to the big-boy stuff you do?" Scott slid his chair closer to Derek, the warmth of Derek's skin reaching out to him. "How do I start?"

"Well, you could start with a beat or you could start with a sound. Depends on what moves you." Derek opened a file which had two subfolders in it, one labeled *Percussion* and the other labeled *Music*.

"You're what moves me." He'd intended it as a flirtatious comment, but once he'd said it, the hairs on his arms stood on end, and a rush of tingles raced along his spine, his longing anything but playful. Scott nuzzled against Derek's neck, inhaling deeply through his nose. "Mmmm. You smell good."

Derek leaned against him. "I love you."

"Love you more." Scott slid an arm around Derek's waist. "Let's start with music…or a blowjob. Up to you."

Derek elbowed Scott's side. "Music first. Blowjob later." He clicked on the file which opened to a lengthy list of even more sub-folders. These had titles organized by genre. "Shall we start with love songs?"

Scott released Derek and took control of the mouse, scrolling through the options. The list went on and on. "There's so much. How do you even begin?"

"I just do. I pick something and see where it takes me." He leaned back, giving Scott more room to explore.

He just picks something and sees where it takes him. That's how it had been from the beginning. He'd picked Scott right from the first day they met. And he'd stuck with him, weathering the shit storm Scott's father put them through.

Scott forced himself to concentrate on the music, thoughts of rejection and pain slipping away.

He clicked on the folder labeled *Ambient* and a new list of files filled the screen. Each one had a numerical title, so there was no way to identify the music by looking. He opened the first one. A French horn played a regal tune, subdued yet majestic. Scott closed his eyes as he listened, gold and blue and green filling his mind, like a summer day with a cool breeze. Tranquil. Hopeful.

The next file contained what sounded like monks singing hymns, mystic and gentle. He closed his eyes once again, a series of images forming in his mind. Churches and mountains. Lakes with floating wafts of steam hovering over the surface like ghosts. Twilight and twinkling stars. The depth and wonder of endless space.

He opened his eyes. "It's like each sound creates a world." Scott swallowed back the lump in his throat as the images the music had evoked dissipated like mist. "It's cathartic."

Derek ran his fingers along Scott's arm, a gentle caress, sliding up until they cupped his cheek. "You always get it. Whenever I introduce you to something new, you understand exactly what it is that moves me about it."

Scott smiled, his breath flowing easily, muscles loose and relaxed. "Do you mind if I listen to these for a while on my own? There's too much here for me to make a decision right now."

Derek got out of his seat. "That, my sexy boyfriend, is the hottest request you've made all week."

"Hey, what about last night when you had me twisted me into a pretzel?" Scott's ass twitched at the thought.

Derek's playful shove let Scott know he'd taken the jab as intended. "Take your time and get lost in the music. I have to go to the Student Center anyway. I'm scheduled for peer counseling."

"That's right. I forgot." Scott kicked himself for getting so wrapped up in his own head. Derek started toward the door. "Derek, wait."

Derek stopped and faced Scott.

"Let's go on a date sometime this week. We haven't been out just the two of us in a long time."

Derek returned to Scott and sat on his lap. "Sounds like an awesome plan." He kissed Scott, then headed out, closing the door behind him.

Scott continued listening to the music files. Sounds from nature, like rushing water and chirping birds were mixed in with the lofty melodies of vocals and instruments.

He backed out of the *Ambient* folder and opened a new one called *Lyrics*. All the files were labeled numerically like the previous folder. He clicked on the first one. The words *"I'm the one you want,"* repeated over and over. Scott shook his head and clicked on the next. *"Nothin' matters but you."* He laughed at this one. *Cheesy much?*

The third file caught his attention. *"You got to fight for what's right."* He leaned back in his seat as he listened.

His whole life had been one long battle after another. The pace was too fast. His own battle was slow, internal. Not simple and plain like the words surrounding him.

The menu bar contained controls to modulate the timbre of the voice as well as the tempo. He slowed the pace, separating each word with a second of silence. Hypnotic, as if each word were demanding to be heard before the whole message could sink in. He lowered the timbre so the voice resonated with a deep baritone, a soft but strong whisper.

He sank deeper into the chair. His heart rate slowed, his thoughts becoming fluid, almost dreamlike. When he glanced at the time on the bottom right corner of the screen, minutes had passed without him even realizing it.

Trippy. Using the tools he'd been taught in class, he started recording the words onto a track, separating them into two distinct phrases. *"You got to fight"* as one track and *"for what's right"* for a second. He let it run for about a minute, then saved the file in the mixing board labeling it *Baritone Whisper.* Already he could picture using those words to build a message of endurance. After all, he'd had to persevere through several trials.

Returning to the *Ambient* sound file, he clicked on the French horn once again and started recording a new track. Stately music filled the room. He sat up straighter, his body naturally leaning forward. As the muffled blare rose and fell, images of armies from the past formed in his head. Dressed in reds and gold, charging forward into war, fighting for some noble cause. The fact they might die only added to the nobility of their commitment. Funny how a simple sound could touch him so completely. In his own life he'd fought, holding his head high, through change and rejection, clinging to the belief that the goal of happiness was worth the pain and disappointment.

After another minute he stopped recording the track, but allowed the music to continue. His chest puffed out. His legs itched to carry him outside so he could run. Energy seemed to rise from somewhere deep inside his body.

The second file had been the one with the monks singing. Mellow, sad voices, surrounded him, cutting through his exterior and sinking into his marrow. The interplay of the various vocals blended together, swirling and wafting like a gentle wave, caressing his heart. He sank back into the chair, muscles melting, turning elastic.

He could picture men, bald and dressed in brown woolen cloaks, standing along a cliff, overlooking the sea, soulful incantations rising into the air toward God. His sense of the seat beneath him, the soft buzz of the light overhead, faded, as he floated to someplace else. Trees swayed, water crashed along rocks, wind swept through his hair, as he was transported to the spot where the monks communed with nature.

An odd combination of isolation and connectedness dueled in a perfectly choreographed dance, at once tying him to the sounds while centering him within himself. And through the sadness, light found its way into his heart, spearing outwards, licking through his veins until his body felt aglow with the hope of newness and possibility.

After what seemed like several minutes, he forced himself to open his eyes. He'd only been recording for two.

Scott stopped the recording and saved the file, calling it *Monks Song*. He then closed the program and slipped into bed. It was early, but the ache from his practice throbbed in his muscles.

Derek's scent clung to the fabric, perfuming the air around him, and his mind drifted even further away. No wonder Derek loved mixing if it could evoke such powerful emotions and sensations. Scott had always loved listening to Derek's music, appreciating his creations. To truly feel the music, to unite with its message, brought the experience to a whole new level.

His music project would not only be a grade, it would be a tribute. To Derek. To himself. To their relationship. And maybe, through the process, he'd figure out why he couldn't let go of the past and accept the future which lay before him. A future Derek affirmed each and every day.

Old habits die hard. Practice makes perfect. Scott rolled onto his side, not wanting to admit the idioms of his youth were in fact true.

Chapter Fourteen

The crisp air of late October had no effect in chilling the glow of warmth burning in Derek's heart. Simple things gave him great pleasure like Scott's interest in music, living it, rather than just hearing it. To witness the expression of awe, plucked at every cord attached to Derek's heart, reminding him why Scott was, and forever would be, his one true love.

The Student Center bustled with activity, old friends, new people to meet, gathered by the food court and pool tables in the main lounge. Bypassing them all, Derek hopped up the stairs two at a time, the spring in his step matching the buoyant melodies of his own mix, the one he'd been working on before Scott entered their room. Soon enough, he'd have his project completed, not only an assignment for a course, but a gift to Scott, to let him know through music and beat, he'd always be there.

The room Jared had booked for peer counseling was at the end of the second floor hallway. Far enough from the main gathering area, where sessions could take place in quiet privacy.

He took a seat on the brown leather couch set up for meetings. He never knew whether anyone would show or if there'd be hours of nothing to do, but he had his thoughts, and the memory of Scott's smile to keep him company. That and a backpack filled with his course books.

Within minutes, the sound of footsteps approached the session room. Tentative clicks of shoes on linoleum drew closer, stopped, and then continued again, growing louder. When the source of the noise appeared in the doorway,

Derek's heart skipped a beat, before rumbling into overdrive.

Tim.

A flush of pink adorned Tim's cheeks, whether from embarrassment or the weather outside, Derek had no idea. Tim stepped through the open door, closing it behind him and crossing the room slowly. "I knew it was your night, and I wanted to talk."

Surprise rose within Derek's body along with bile from his stomach, but he swallowed it down, stood, and closed the distance between them. "Come on in."

Tim settled into his seat and stared at his hands for a few seconds. "I know I've been a disappointment to you."

"Why don't you tell me why you're here?" Derek's voice, steady and warm, should have come out weak based on the constriction of his lungs and his inability to draw in a strong breath.

"I have a problem. Several problems. And I'm getting worse." Tim dug his fingers into his lap, gripping tightly enough for the whites of his knuckles to show.

"What kinds of problems do you have?" *Drugs. Drinking. Pursuing older men who could take advantage of you.* Derek forced himself to maintain eye contact and sat straight, leaning slightly forward, inviting conversation.

"Well, you already know one of them. I've got a problem with drugs. Pot." Tim's gaze fell somewhere on the floor between them. "And a few others."

"Tell me more." Derek leaned forward, biting the inside of his cheek to stave off the judgments itching to escape his mouth.

Tim lifted his chin and made eye contact. Moisture shimmered, brimming along his lower lids. An urge to pull

Tim closer swept through Derek, but he managed to maintain his position.

"I smoke all the time. Before class, after class. When I'm going out. When I'm alone. It's like I can't stand to be by myself." The tears welled up, threatening to overflow.

Derek drew a tissue from the box on the table next to the couch. "Here."

Tim accepted the offering and dabbed at his eyes. "I know I've been fucking up. I'm failing my classes. I'm failing you. Did you know I quit The Alliance?"

"I haven't seen you at the meetings so I assumed you'd decided against joining." Derek's chest constricted. He'd wanted to confront Tim about this very issue, but hadn't out of loyalty to Scott. "But let's focus on the pot and the classes. Those are more important than Alliance meetings right now."

Tim nodded. "True. I'm just so upset that I'm disappointing *you*. You're the only person who's been nice to me, and I'm screwing up."

If words could have killed… "I don't understand."

"It's like everything else in my life. The second someone tries to help me, I find a way to push them away. It starts with pot. Sometimes other stuff, and then I ditch my responsibilities. I don't want to be this way. I want to change, but I always fall back on the things which have worked for me."

"By *things* are you referring to the pot?" He mentally checked off the rules from his training. *Ask questions to clarify meaning when meaning isn't obvious. Don't make assumptions.*

"That. And also…" Tim shifted in his seat. "I started go-go dancing at Ecstasy. Have you heard of it?"

Derek did know of the place, although he'd never been there. It was notorious for backroom hookups. He decided to pretend he didn't, hoping Tim might share more details. "No. Tell me about it." *Don't make judgments.*

"It's a dance club. All types go there, but it's kind of sleazy, and guys pay good money to watch hot young twinks strip down to almost nothing." Tim blew his nose before continuing. "They like me there. They say I'm cute. It makes me feel good."

Derek sat on his hands, fighting the urge to slide closer to Tim and comfort him. *Remain objective. Don't give reassurances.* "Based on what you just said, it sounds like you question your worth. Would that be a fair statement to make?"

Tim nodded, a new round of tears spilling down his cheeks. "I wish I could be more like you. You're so confident and happy. Everyone loves you. You have the hottest boyfriend in the school. Well, except for you. I guess Scott has the hottest boyfriend in the school. If someone like you wanted to go out with me I bet I wouldn't have any problems at all."

A sharp tug yanked at Derek's heart, forcing him to draw in a breath. Instinct urged him to cross the divide and pull Tim into a hug. Derek closed his eyes. He'd heard these kinds of things before, from someone who professed to care about him, and he'd nearly lost everything. Tim was another Tyrell, and here Derek was, alone with him, no one else around.

A shiver raced up his spine, raising bumps on his flesh. "Tim, I think we should keep the focus on you. Whenever I feel insecure or doubt myself, it's always because something's going on inside me. And I don't solve the problem until I figure out what's going on internally."

Tim nodded. "You're right. I didn't mean to make you uncomfortable. Sorry."

Derek settled back onto the couch, thankful he'd recalled the use of *I*-Messages. "Tell me an example of something that happens to make you choose to smoke pot or go to Ecstasy."

Tim wouldn't meet his eyes. "You're not going to like my response."

"I'm not here to judge you. I'm here to help." He meant it, although he believed Tim's warning.

"I started going there after you wouldn't spend time with me anymore." Tim raised the tissue to capture new tears, but stopped as the crumpled and used material started to shred.

Derek handed him a new tissue. Acid burned a painful trail along his esophagus. He'd never turned his back on someone before, and Tim had sought him out for help. Instead of following his gut, he'd honored Scott's request, and now the kid was heading down a bad path, one that could've been avoided.

"Tim. I'm sorry if you feel I've somehow let you down. That wasn't my intention. With my work for The Alliance, mixing, Scott, classes, I just don't have a lot of time." Blood pumped faster through his veins, roaring behind his ears. He picked up his binder and flipped through the pages. He needed a few seconds to collect himself, to remember his training.

Reflective listening. When the other person has a problem or tries to focus on you, reflective listening can redirect the conversation back to the purpose of the meeting. Derek drew in a deep breath of air, releasing it slowly. Starting at his head, he scanned his body, identifying areas where he carried tension, forcing himself to relax. This all took place over the course of a few seconds, and then he continued. "What I'm hearing is you believe your choices are connected to how others treat you."

Tim nodded, but said nothing.

"And when you feel insecure or upset, you turn to the things that give you a sense of comfort. Like pot or the bar." He knew his comment was dangerously close to a judgment, but objective enough to be a reflective statement.

Another nod. Still no words.

"Okay. So now we've identified a possible trigger." Derek's heart rate slowed. His muscles unclenched. "I have resources for supports to help you with this. Based on what you're saying, it sounds like you would benefit from some counseling. The school offers it for free. Or, if you'd prefer to meet with someone not associated with the school, there are other agencies around the city available to you as well."

"Couldn't I just keep coming back to you?" Tim's voice squeaked with a high-pitch, his eyes wide and peering directly at Derek for the first time since he'd entered the room.

The word *yes* was at the tip of Derek's tongue, but he swallowed it back. Not only would it go against the training, but he wasn't qualified to provide the kind of help Tim needed. Not to mention he'd be breaking his promise to Scott.

Right now Scott needed him to keep his distance from people like Tim. Scott had to be his priority. He was going through something and needed Derek to be his rock, not another source of stress.

The words stuck in his throat, but he somehow managed to force them out. "I'm not trained to provide the support you need, Tim. I'm sorry. We're here to help students identify problems and to point them in the right direction to get help."

Tim nodded. "I understand. I just..." He stood and turned toward the door.

Derek shot out of his seat. "Wait. You just what?"

"I'm afraid to see a counselor. If any of this got back to my family, I don't know what they'd do. Like I told you before, they don't know anything about me. I'm afraid they'd make me go home. Or worse, maybe they'd cut me off altogether." Tim trembled as he stood like a wounded animal in the middle of the room.

"It doesn't work like that, Tim. Counseling is confidential. Unless you threaten to hurt yourself or someone else, nothing you say will be shared with anyone." He took a step toward Tim, but stopped. If he closed the gap between them, he wouldn't be able to stop from helping Tim himself. "Let me give you the information. Go to at least one appointment. They'll help you decide the best thing to do."

Tim nodded and returned to his seat.

Derek rifled through his materials, trying to hide the shaking of his hands. When he found the brochure for campus counseling, he handed it over. "They have office hours and a hotline for you. I'll even walk you to your first meeting."

Tim smiled, although barely, then stood and headed toward the door once again. Before he exited, he turned and faced Derek. "Thanks for listening. You really are an awesome guy. Scott's lucky to have you."

Derek nodded, unable to speak. He waited until Tim had left the room and the sound of his footfalls disappeared. Once he was sure Tim was gone, he fell back onto the couch and drew in a ragged breath.

He rubbed his face with his hands. How could he possibly summon the energy to concentrate after *that* interaction? The hollow space in his chest answered his question. He couldn't. Hopefully no one else would show up.

He fidgeted with his hands, then got up and paced the room. Tim needed help, and every cell in Derek's body yearned to go after him. To hold himself back was like driving bamboo shoots under his nails. Excruciating. Wrong.

Scott would be happy. That much Derek knew. And he'd make sure to let Scott know what he'd done.

He leaned back against the unyielding cushions. Even the damn couch gave him push-back when all he wanted was to sink into soft comfort. Scott hadn't lived the same life Derek had. But fuck if it didn't kill Derek when he had to go against his own nature while Scott sorted things out.

He owed Scott that much. However long it took, he'd wait. After all, Scott had put up with Derek's shit the previous year, and he hadn't complained…much. If only there were a way to speed the process along.

Derek pictured Tim's watery eyes. Replayed his concerns. The kid was in crisis. No question about it. And he'd latched onto Derek for some reason. If the guy was smart, he'd call the counselors and schedule an appointment. They were the ones who could help him dig himself out of his hole. Derek knew enough to acknowledge he wasn't equipped for the task. But at least he could have scheduled a time to make the call with him. But Scott wouldn't want him to do that.

His checks heated. Damn. What harm could possibly come from ensuring Tim got the help he needed?

Derek swallowed past the lump in his throat. He had no right to get frustrated with Scott, even if the reaction was natural.

Luckily, there were no more visitors for counseling, although the two hours he'd sat in the small room seemed to stretch out for an eternity. Bypassing the main lounge, Derek headed outside. The taunting laughter and chatting of his peers filtered through the Student Center, a stark contrast to his own dour mood.

He took a few steps into the late October night, spreading his arms, reveling in the sensation of freedom and openness. Facing the sky, he stared at the shining moon, nearly full. Beautiful, but nothing like the sky in New Hampshire on Mount Washington with the millions of stars.

Had it really been two months since he and Scott had camped together? He glanced at the ring on his finger, touched it. He'd promised himself to Scott...yet Scott still doubted. At least that's how he was acting.

Propelling himself toward the dorm, Derek mapped out a confrontation. The image of Tim's tears still freshly burned in his memory. Scott had already told him to go ahead and help Tim, but then Scott would be the one compromising for Derek, as he always had. No, picking a fight wasn't the answer.

If Scott was to heal, he needed to focus on himself, and Derek owed it to both of them to let their relationship take precedence. Scott was his present and his future. Tim was a kid in need, yet someone he barely knew. There was no contest if he had to make a choice.

And that's exactly what he was doing, wasn't it? Choosing one person over another? Why did it have to be either-or? Couldn't it be both-and? Derek quickened his pace. Maybe he *should* confront Scott.

Shit. He knew how the conversation would go. When had he become so indecisive? He'd made a choice to put Scott's needs first. Now he needed to live with his decision.

He arrived at his dorm faster than he would've imagined. Drawing in a deep breath, he checked himself for tension, then entered the building. When he arrived at their room and opened the door, Scott was in bed, asleep, the only light in the room the bright glare of the desk lamp, muted by an earth-toned shade. Kind of like the glow of the campfire from their summer trip.

He padded into the room, closing the door gently behind him, and crossed the room. Scott's chest rose and fell. Up. Down. Up. Down. Hypnotic. His breath barely audible.

Toeing off his shoes, Derek couldn't drag his eyes from Scott. It'd been a long time since he'd had the opportunity to simply watch the man he loved peacefully sleeping. Scott had pulled the covers down and lay in the middle of the bed, only in his boxers, his bulky muscles relaxed as he slept, yet still displaying his powerful form. So damn sexy.

Derek absently ran his fingers along his own groin, probing the hardening length beneath the fabric. Stripping, he took a seat at the desk and flipped open the laptop. The mixing program filled the screen. Clicking on recent documents, he read the top item on the menu. *Derek's song.*

His breath caught in his throat and his vision blurred. Scott was mixing a song for him. Just as he'd suspected when he'd left earlier, Scott was beginning to understand another aspect of Derek's world. Hopefully he hadn't gone scouting to find the file Derek had started. Funny how they both had the same idea to make mixes for each other, but not surprising.

He closed the program and shut down the laptop. If Scott wanted him to know about this project, he'd tell him.

No sense in ruining a surprise if that's what this was intended to be.

For several minutes, he stood by the bed, observing Scott's sleeping form. His expression was serene, a hint of a smile adorning his lips. Scott had one arm draped over his head, his bicep bulging in a relaxed manner, loose, yet still defined. Sliding his gaze down Scott's body, he took in similar images. Pectorals mounded, but not tense. Abdominals framed by indentations along each side, the six-pack visible but not in sharp contrast since Scott's core was at rest.

The bulge at Scott's groin tented his boxers, pushing the fabric away from his body. The temptation to slip the impeding article of clothing away and taste Scott swept through Derek, but to interfere with the peacefulness of Scott's sleep seemed cruel. Instead, he slipped into bed, the weight of his stressful evening finally catching up with him.

Scott sighed, turning onto his side, and wrapped his arm around Derek, pulling him close, an automatic action. Hard flesh pressed against his backside, although even breaths gently brushed along the nape of Derek's neck.

Derek closed his eyes, breathing in Scott's scent. If his choice to put Scott's needs before his own resulted in this kind of tranquility, it was worth whatever stress Derek might endure for the time being.

Knowing he was making the right choice battled with a sense of helplessness as Tim's words echoed in his head. The image of Tim's retreating form played like a movie in his head. Even the heat of Scott's body couldn't thaw the ice forming around Derek's heart. *Tim's not your responsibility. Scott needs you.* Derek closed his eyes hoping he'd be able to hold on to that belief without starting to resent Scott.

Chapter Fifteen

Scott floated through the next few days, only half paying attention to his surroundings. The mix he'd begun took center focus as he considered the various messages he wanted to convey. Love, tenderness, heat, strength, vulnerability, pride. They all defined how he saw himself and how he saw Derek.

Who knew fractured sounds and beats could coalesce into one powerful message? Up until the other night when Derek launched the mixing program, music had been entertainment, but now, Scott realized the power it held to convey more than simple words or actions ever could.

A floodgate had opened. He found he couldn't drag his thoughts from his father and rejection. Angry, hard beats, blaring sounds, and harshness accompanied these images. Nor could he ignore the familiar ache in his heart. A furious snare drumbeat accentuated the pain.

Trumpets, the long kind he'd seen in movies, used to announce the entrance of someone important, called their uplifting song. Scott found himself standing taller, the image of his father withered, lifeless, no longer imbued with any form of power. No. He'd not been the reason his father rejected him. His father was an ass.

Later, at practice, different melodies fueled his movements. The trill of a piccolo as he circled lightly on his feet. The dance of competition lit from within him as he searched for an opening to take his opponent down. More limber, faster reflexes, and he scooped Marcus's leg effortlessly into his arms and brought him to the matt.

Piccolo shifted to the metallic crank of chains, hoisting through a pulley, mechanical, sturdy, as he drove his weight into Marcus and turned him to his back.

Did Derek experience music this way? Was every act in his life accompanied by an orchestra of the sounds he mixed for others?

Scott's heart beat faster, not only from the exertion, but from the wonder of his new discovery. He'd have to ask Derek about his music. Find out what played in his head when they had sex. It would tell him more of what the act meant than if he asked the mundane question, like "*What do you think about when we're having sex?*"

He released Marcus, hitting an invisible "off" button in his head.

Marcus rolled from his back and sat up. "Damn, Thayer. Something's different in you today. You're like a machine or something."

"Thanks." Scott's muscles should have been tired. The compliment should have evoked pride. Instead, he hopped to his feet, energized, ready for more.

"Seriously man, what's your secret?" Marcus stood, veins distended along his arms.

"I could tell ya, but then...you know how the saying goes." He clapped Marcus on the shoulder. "Again?"

Marcus laughed and started circling him. Within seconds, Scott had him on the mat once more.

After practice he changed without showering. He'd clean himself back at the dorm. He trekked across the campus barely taking note of the students gathered in clumps under the lamps illuminating the walkways.

Marcus was right. Something *had* changed in him. Searching to describe that *something* proved a bit more difficult. He couldn't identify a word or phrase to describe the foreign sensations, but music was at the core, plucking at strings in his center he'd never known existed.

The thought of plucking strings brought the image of a guitar to mind, and he quickened his pace, anxious to shower and dress for his date.

He'd made reservations at Fire and Ice, the same restaurant where they'd celebrated their first anniversary. He kept the chain Derek bought them as a first anniversary gift, two half hearts to make up one whole, tucked away in a box of other important items. Their anniversary wasn't for another couple weeks, but tonight was for them, and he wanted to wear the necklace.

The wind picked up, cold air rushing along his neck and torso. Pulling his coat around him, he caught a glint from his hand. The ring. His heart beat faster, warming him from the inside out.

He approached their dorm with a stronger gait. Derek wasn't in their room. Odd, since they had to leave in about thirty minutes. He stripped, grabbed a towel, and bounded toward the bathroom. A quick shower and he returned to find Derek dressed and ready to go.

Derek faced him when he entered, his eyes widening as he regarded Scott's body. He licked his lips suggestively, then swallowed, his Adam's apple bobbing noticeably. "Damn. I know we have to go, but with you looking like that, I think I might just have to strip back down to nothing."

Scott laughed, allowing his towel to drop. "Whoops."

Derek gasped, but held his ground. "Seriously. If you want to make it out of this room, you better get dressed. And fast."

Scott sauntered to his dresser, wagging his ass in the process. Derek was behind him in one second, hands on his hips and pressing his erection into the groove of his ass. Scott backed into him, reveling in his lover's panting. "Someone's glad to see me."

"Scott. I'm about to strip out of this outfit and fuck you senseless. I mean it." Derek released Scott's hips and started unbuckling his pants.

Swiveling on his feet, Scott grabbed Derek's hands. "No. Wait. I'm sorry. That was mean of me. We really do have dinner reservations, and then we're going to the Lizard Lounge. I shouldn't have teased you like that."

Derek's eyes widened. "The Lizard Lounge?" He captured his bottom lip between his teeth, then let out a sigh. "I still think me getting naked is a better idea."

Scott placed his hand on Derek's cheek, which had flushed red and radiated heat into his palm. "After."

Derek pouted, but withdrew so Scott could dress.

He made quick work of it, Derek watching his every move. His hands trembled as he pulled on a pair of jeans. He threw on a white Polo then led Derek from their room. "C'mon. Let's go before I change my mind."

Derek growled in response, but followed, clutching his hand.

They rushed to the sidewalk and hailed a cab, arriving in Harvard Square several minutes later. "You remember this place, right?"

"How could I forget?" Derek cupped Scott's face and drew him in for a kiss. His breath smelled of mint. The flavor burst along Scott's tongue as he opened his mouth to deepen the kiss. His cock lengthened, pressing against his jeans, as their tongues tumbled in wild abandon. Far too much time had passed since they'd done anything, just the two of them away from school.

The sweet cat-calls of a few girls passing by distracted Scott from the stormy lust raging through him. He withdrew from the kiss, leaning forward so his forehead rested against Derek's. "Damn."

"You can say that again." Derek reached between his legs to readjust himself.

"Damn." Scott nipped at Derek's lip, then took his hand as they entered the restaurant.

The scent of garlic and grilling spices surrounded them, and Scott breathed the aroma in, just realizing the extent of his hunger. They were seated, and after a few minutes, a waiter took their drink orders and deposited bread at their table.

Fire and Ice specialized in build-your-own meals, so they meandered to the multiple food stations, deciding what to eat. Scott chose chicken in a lemon garlic sauce with broccoli and a baked potato. Derek opted for filet mignon, basted in a Jack Daniel's glaze, with asparagus and homemade balsamic noodles.

Once back at their table, Scott's hunger made itself known in the form of a stomach grumble. He broke off a piece of sourdough bread, lathered it with butter, and took a ravenous bite. With his mouth full, he announced, "I'm fuckin' starving."

Derek shook his head. "You and me both, baby." He dipped a piece of the bread into the pesto-infused olive oil and popped it into his mouth.

By the time their meal arrived, Scott had eaten most of the bread, abating the intensity of his hunger.

He stared across the table, the candle flickering in such a way that the light danced in Derek's eyes. The amber mixed with golden flecks, pulsing with life and earthiness. Derek's skin glowed with remnants of the summer-tinged hues. His smile swept Scott skyward, yet here they were, together, orbiting around one another with their own gravitational pull keeping them together.

Such confidence. Such love washing over him from the man sitting across the table. Scott swallowed against the lump forming in his throat, uprisings of emotion seeming to occur with greater frequency lately. "I stayed up for a while longer after you left. I totally get the mixing thing. Each sound and beat connected to something inside me. Like I could use the music to express more than I ever could with words. Scott blinked, staving off the wetness threatening to spill down his cheeks. For so long he'd learned to bottle his feelings inside, coming to expect change. Living with lasting connections was a luxury he'd never learned to trust. "You've always been so good at conveying feelings."

Derek leaned forward, his smile broadening. "Tell me more about the mix."

Scott started to speak, but forced himself to stop. "Not yet. I'm working on something. But soon."

"Okay." Derek accepted the cryptic explanation easily. Too easily.

Scott changed the topic, diverting attention away from mixing. "Sorry I was asleep when you got back from peer counseling. How'd it go?"

Derek's brow creased, and some of the shimmering life drained from his eyes. "It was rough." He held Scott's gaze for a few seconds, then spoke. "Tim showed up."

Breath failed him, but only momentarily. He'd told Derek to help Tim if he wanted to, and he'd meant it. He fisted his pants to control the rising tide of anxiety at the idea of the two of them alone, but maintained what he hoped was a tranquil expression. "How was that?"

Derek's eyes widened just for a second, then relaxed, but not before Scott noticed. "Really awkward, actually. I'm not supposed to talk about this stuff. Do you mind if I don't?"

Scott suppressed the urge to grip Derek and shake him. *Tell me everything. I can't stand the idea of you being alone with that kid.* "Of course. I understand."

"I will ask you a question, though. Were you serious when you said I could help him if I wanted to?" The way Derek leaned forward in his chair, the innocence in his eyes, washed over Scott. "Because if you aren't comfortable with it I'll back off."

Ouch! Scott's gut clenched, although he made every effort to keep his discomfort from showing. "Of course I meant it."

Derek released a long sigh then picked up his fork and knife. He cut a piece of his filet and took a bite. A dreamy expression crossed his face. "Oh, my God. This is so good. You have to try it." He cut off another piece, added a bit of the balsamic noodles, and held the fork out to Scott.

Scott leaned forward and accepted the offering, although Derek moved the fork about, making a sticky mess on Scott's face and nearly dropping the morsel into his lap. Better to enjoy the meal and Derek's company. He'd spent too much time underestimating Derek.

Maybe his doubts stemmed from the nightmare of Tyrell the previous year. Then again, a year ago he would never have kissed Derek in public. People changed, and he seemed slow to grant himself or Derek the credit either of them deserved. "Maybe you should go with him to the university counseling center. That way you'll know he's seen someone. Once he gets started, you can step back again…if you want to."

Derek blinked. "Really? You wouldn't have a problem with me escorting him? Because that's what I thought about doing. I just know how you—"

"Think you get too involved? Don't know how to distinguish between someone who needs help and someone who can be dangerous to you?" Even a week earlier, the answers to both questions had been *yes*. But now, experiencing the way Derek viewed the world, feeling how the music could ground him, purging tension and confusion, it became clear Derek had grown and learned whereas Scott had remained stagnant, viewing his lover as someone who needed protection.

Without even realizing it, he and Derek had switched roles. Scott had once been the voice of reason grounding Derek. Now?

"I really would feel better if I could bring him." The way Derek lifted up in his seat, sitting taller, sent shivers up Scott's spine. How could he have pressured Derek into any other choice?

"Of course you would. And you should." The sense of dread Scott expected never came.

"Wow. Okay. I will." Derek forked another bite into his mouth, his momentary survey of Scott interrupted as he closed his eyes, savoring the food. After a few seconds, he continued. "I'm impressed."

"With what?" Scott certainly didn't deserve accolades.

"At how far you've come. I never would've guessed you'd encourage me like this."

Well shit. Scott supposed he'd earned the comment, but the fact Derek doubted him still cut deep.

Scott paid for their meal and led Derek down the street to the Lizard Lounge. They were each given a wristband indicating they were underage, but neither of them had come for alcohol.

The lounge boasted one of the few locations featuring live performances. Big name musicians never played there, and only rarely would a mid-range name make an appearance. But that was the appeal of the place.

Derek beelined straight for the stairs, descending to the basement level where the stage was located. Tables dotted the floor, and narrow wall tablebars lined the room so people could stand on the fringe, listen to the music and still have a place to put their drinks.

Derek led them to the side of the room, elbowing his way through the crowded area and choosing a spot close to the stage. Once he secured a place for them, he faced Scott and hugged him. "You amaze me, you know that?" His breath feathered along Scott's neck.

Scott wrapped his arms around Derek and squeezed. "You got that backwards." He dotted several kisses from Derek's ear to his lips, then leaned against the wall, pulling Derek with him. Derek snuggled into him, his lower back brushing against the bulge in Scott's pants. The way he glanced over his shoulder, a sly grin on his face, let him know Derek had felt his arousal. He pressed back, grinding in time to the music coming from the stage.

The performer had shaggy brown hair and a light dusting of stubble, appropriately suited to the rustic sound of his voice. He plucked at guitar strings with his fingers instead of a pick, his hands dancing up and down the neck.

Each movement carried with it the sound of a metallic slide. The performer probably had calluses on calluses.

Scott hugged Derek close, closing his eyes and inhaling his scent, a hint of cologne mixed with the honey sweetness of his lover's skin. The quick tempo of the song matched Scott's rising libido. He should've let Derek strip down in their room. Opening his eyes and observing the expression of euphoric devotion to the musician on stage erased any sense of regret. Well, most of it anyway.

For an hour they listened to the music, not speaking, but comfortable in the silence. Derek leaned his head back onto Scott's shoulder, tilting his head so tendrils of breath caressed Scott's ear. "Thank you for this."

Scott sealed their lips together in answer. He could taste the faint remnant of the Jack Daniel's glaze and garlic from Derek's dinner. He swirled his tongue, exploring the recesses of Derek's mouth, breathing in his scent, gaining purchase with his hands along firm muscles.

A soft hum vibrated in his mouth and Scott squeezed Derek tighter. Derek turned so they stood face to face without breaking the kiss, arching his back and pressing his groin against Scott's thigh. Feeling the rigid cock pressed against him sent shivers along Scott's spine. He withdrew from the kiss, capturing Derek's plump bottom lip between his teeth, then released him, gazing into eyes burning with a desire that rivaled his own. "Wanna get out of here?"

"Yeah." Derek used their bodies as a shield as he readjusted himself, and Scott took advantage of the moment to do the same. Even so, as they climbed the stairs, he glanced at Derek's groin, the evidence of his excitement pressing at his pants.

Scott was in no better shape.

Luck seemed to be on their side. An available cab arrived outside the lounge within minutes, and about ten minutes later, Scott and Derek strode, hand in hand, toward their dorm room.

Scott wasted no time stripping Derek the moment the door closed behind them. Dropping to his knees, he unbuttoned Derek's pants and slid them, along with his underwear, down his legs. He gripped Derek's cock and angled it toward his mouth, flicking his tongue to capture the salty droplet of pre-cum glistening at the tip.

Derek gasped, palming the back of Scott's head and burying his cock into Scott's mouth. He pumped, gently at first, but with increasing speed and force.

Scott steadied himself, gripping Derek's thighs, eager to taste the waterfall of his release.

Derek pulled back, his cock nearly escaping Scott's mouth. "Gonna shoot."

Scott grasped Derek's hips, sucking his way back down the shaft until his lips pressed against Derek's pubic bone. He swallowed several times, gratified by the trembling in Derek's thighs and the grunts escaping his mouth.

After a few more strokes back and forth, Derek pressed at Scott's head. Scott allowed himself to be guided from his ministrations, glancing up with what had to be an expression of frustration.

"Let's move this to the bed." Derek kicked his pants, bunched around his ankles, to the side of the room, and peeled off his shirt, tossing it behind him.

Scrambling to his feet, Scott tore off his clothes as he approached the bed, then collapsed on top of Derek, grinding his erection against its twin beneath him. He kissed a path down Derek's body, but his journey was blocked by Derek's hands, sliding to his armpits.

Derek swiveled until his head was aligned with Scott's cock and captured the head in his mouth. Currents raced along Scott's skin. Tingles rushed through his body. He almost shot his load, which would have brought an unfortunately quick end to the mind-altering blowjob. Damn but he'd have to start beating off on a regular basis if he didn't want a simple thing like shivers to bring about an early orgasm.

Once sure he'd regained some semblance of control, Scott returned his focus to Derek's shaft, diving in and reveling in the sweet taste once again. Hard flesh filled his mouth as hot wetness surrounded his cock, the double sensation of pleasure intoxicating.

Scott's saliva mixed with the pre-cum flowing freely into his mouth. The sharp flavor of Derek's arousal coated his tongue and slipped down his throat. He placed his hand around Derek's shaft, pumping in time with his suction. Derek did the same, forcing sparks of light to flash behind Scott's eyelids.

Heat turned to fire in the pit of his belly. His legs trembled. His jaw stretched, accommodating the increasing thickness as Derek's cock became even harder and more unyielding.

Just as Scott felt the stirring of his own release, Derek thrust all the way into his mouth, a hot stream of cum coating his tongue. The scent of arousal and semen perfumed the air.

The fire in his belly exploded outward, and his body released. His hips bucked helplessly as Derek sucked Scott's orgasm out of him.

Ropes of thick fluid continued to fill his mouth in concert with his own release firing into Derek. No longer focused on any specific point of pleasure, he succumbed to the raw energy ripping through him.

After several pulses, his muscles finally relaxed. Derek's cock remained hard, as did his own.

Using what strength he could muster from his rubbery limbs, he withdrew himself from Derek's mouth and pushed himself into a seated position, panting. A sheen of sweat covered his shoulders and back.

Derek rolled onto his back, flinging one arm across his face. "That was fucking amazing."

Scott lay next to him, unable to speak. No words were needed. Derek curled into him, slipping an arm across his chest, and Scott could feel the rapid pounding of Derek's heart.

For several minutes the sound of their panting filled the room, and then Derek's breathing eased into a steady rhythm.

Scott closed his eyes, his lids like weights he couldn't hold open any longer. The night had been fucking amazing. Dinner, music, sex, holding his lover.

Maybe he was finally learning to accept that his life had stabilized. After twenty years, maybe he'd finally found his spot in the world, next to the magnificent man in his arms.

It was Derek's gentle snoring that drew Scott from his thoughts. No matter how content he felt, Derek still needed to help others. He needed to help Tim.

Every time Derek reached out to others, he put himself at risk. And in doing so, he put Scott's tenuous sense of balance at risk as well. Still, he couldn't impose his own fears on Derek. All he could do was trust that Derek would honor his promise to maintain distance from those who'd take advantage of him...or worse. The only other option was for Scott to impose his own needs on his lover and that wasn't an option. Not if he wanted to ensure Derek's happiness.

As they lay there, the distinct scent of pot laced the air. The stale herby smell seemed a too regular part of their life in the dorm courtesy of the very kid Derek so badly wanted to help. Tightness pulled in Scott's chest, and that magical night ended with a dose of reality and what may lie in wait for them in days to come.

Chapter Sixteen

In spite of the concern over Tim, life settled into a routine over the next couple of weeks. Derek enjoyed his classes, his Alliance committee had contacted several youth organizations and schools and rallied a few volunteer programs, and he was getting better and better at peer counseling.

The only thing he hadn't managed to accomplish was getting Tim to the school counseling center. Each day he knocked on his neighbor's door, and each night he returned to his dorm. The distinctive scent of pot filled the air. Why Elizabeth turned a blind eye, Derek had no idea, but he had no intention of reporting students to the deans unless they were a danger to themselves or to others. As far as he could tell, Tim was running full speed toward failing out of college or at least landing on academic probation. But he didn't seem to be a physical threat to himself or to anyone else.

For the past couple of nights he hadn't seen Tim at all. He didn't know which worried him more…the pot smoking or not knowing where Tim was. Maybe he'd met someone and was staying with them, although he would've had to come back to his room to change clothes. At least Derek hoped he would. Just imagining a week wearing the same outfit made his skin crawl.

Fate seemed to hear his concerns because he found Tim at the Student Center after class the next day. He decided to put pleasantries aside. Marching right up to the booth where Tim sat with two other people, Derek plopped himself down in the one empty space. "Hey. What's up?"

Tim nearly choked on the burger he was chewing. "Derek. What're you doing here?"

Derek glanced at the other two guys at the table. One had bloodshot eyes and the other, shaggy hair sprouting from underneath a woolen winter cap. "I haven't seen you around and was worried about you. I thought we agreed to go to that appointment together." It wasn't his most subtle moment, but he didn't know when he'd see Tim again.

"Yeah. Uh. I've been hanging out with Jerry and Lance." Tim stared at the table.

Derek ignored Tim's tablemates who seemed too invested in shoveling food into their mouths to take any notice of Derek's rude behavior. "I'm free for the rest of the day. I'll grab a bite and we can go today."

Jerry and Lance barely even lifted their heads to acknowledge Derek's presence. One inhaled his fries as if he might die without them, and the other seemed to find a knot in the wooden table particularly fascinating.

"Sure. I guess." Tim slumped in his chair.

That caught Dumb and Dumber's attention. "Dude, we were gonna head to the room and, ya know."

Derek had a pretty good idea of what they might be referring to. The choices would fall into the category of sex or drugs, probably a combination of both. But he wasn't particularly interested in the strange idiots at the table. There was only one idiot who he cared about, and Derek was damn sure he'd get the kid to the counseling center before he let him out of his sight again.

He ordered himself a tuna sandwich and a bottled water. A few minutes later, with his food in one hand and Tim's arm in the other, he tugged his reluctant captive toward the entrance of the Student Center. Tim's friends didn't say anything when they left. Probably hadn't even noticed.

"All right. I'm coming with you. You don't have to yank my arm off." Tim wrenched his arm free, but didn't run.

Derek hadn't realized his grip had been tight, but wasn't about to take any chances. "Where've you been?" All of his tension carried in his voice.

"I told you. Hanging out with Jer and Lance. They live in another dorm and have a killer set up." He kicked at a rock on the sidewalk. "They're a couple, so the extra bed in their room isn't being used."

"Where'd you meet them?" Derek wasn't sure he really wanted to know.

"They came into Ecstasy and were hanging out by my platform. When I had a break, they—" Tim bit his lower lip and continued walking in silence.

"They…" Derek was right, he didn't want to know how Tim had met them, but he *did* want to get Tim to the counseling center.

"They were rolling and offered me some." Tim shared the information like it was common knowledge what he was talking about.

"I'm sorry. Rolling?"

Tim's cheeks flamed. "You're not gonna like it."

"I already don't like it, but tell me anyways."

"Rolling is when you get high on E. Ecstasy. A lot of guys use it at the clubs. It makes you feel like you're in love with the world." Tim stopped, his eyes trained on the ground. "So, now that you know, what're you gonna do about it?"

Derek wasn't sure whether Tim's challenging tone meant, *mind your own business* or was bravado covering his fear that Derek might actually do something. "Dude, I'm not your parents, and I'm not responsible for your choices. I just want to make sure you see someone and get help. I don't know anything about this ecstasy drug you're talking about, but it doesn't sound very good."

Tim's eyes lit up. "Are you kidding? It's the best. The only thing better is meth."

Derek placed his hand on Tim's shoulder. "Do you use meth? Isn't that the drug that makes you want to have sex and not care with who, or whether you use protection?" Every cell in his body screamed at him to get involved. A million *What if* scenarios ticked away in his head, each one leading to the same end result…something bad.

Tim didn't respond, which gave Derek the answer to his first question. If Tim hadn't used, he would've said so.

"Tim, have you screwed around while on meth?"

"No." His answer would've inspired some confidence in Derek if Tim had chosen to make eye contact. For the first time, faced with a person in crisis, he was glad someone else would handle the problem. Derek shook his head and continued in the direction of the counseling center.

Tim came rushing up behind him. "Hey. Don't you have anything to say?"

Derek whipped around, forcing Tim to stop short. "What do you want me to say? Don't use meth?" He practically spit the words. "All right. Don't fucking use meth!"

Tim took a step back but didn't make a move to run. "Why're you so angry?"

"Because you're gonna get yourself killed. Because you'll catch a disease, like HIV." Derek clenched his fists, trying to calm the rush of blood pounding behind his ears. "For Christ's sake. Don't you have any self-respect?"

Once he'd finished his tirade, Derek let out his breath in a huff. Maybe he was good at counseling in the Student Center, but over the past ten minutes he'd abandoned each and every one of the lessons he'd learned. Why'd he let people get underneath his skin so easily?

Tim stared at him, eyes wide, visibly shaking. "I know. I'm so stupid. I'm sorry I'm such a disappointment to you."

The words were like a jolt of electricity, firing Derek back up. He closed his eyes and counted to five, fighting the desire to grab Tim by the arms and shake him. "Shit, Tim. You didn't do anything to *me*. It's *you* you're hurting." And for Christ's sake why did he care so much? The only thing Derek knew was if he did nothing he'd regret it. If he stepped in to provide support he'd be prioritizing Tim over Scott. Once again, he found himself stuck in a position where he had to make a choice. If only he could help Tim *and* honor Scott's need for time to work things out then maybe he wouldn't feel like he was crawling inside his own skin. "Let's get you some help. You need to find someone you're comfortable talking to, and in three months I highly suggest you get yourself tested for a whole range of diseases. Hopefully you'll be lucky and won't have any." Fuck if he wasn't being harsh. Tears welled in Tim's eyes. "You really think I might...you think I—" He couldn't finish his sentence. Instead, tears welled up in his eyes then spilled down his cheeks.

Derek pulled him into a hug, glancing around them and waving off the few people staring. At least he'd found the supportive version of himself, even if it took someone's tears to jerk the kindness out of him. He rubbed circles on Tim's back, hoping it would calm him down. "I don't know. Only one way to find out."

After Tim's misery eased to silent tears and Derek thought they could continue, he shifted his position so his arm slung across Tim's shoulders. The contact helped to ground Derek. Walking the thin line between support and over-involvement was exhausting.

Tim leaned into him and allowed Derek to guide their progress.

A few minutes later they entered the Boston University Medical Center, which also housed the Psychiatry Department. As they passed through the doors, Derek tightened his grip around Tim's trembling shoulders.

"It'll be okay, Tim. You're here, and you'll get the help you need. You just have to talk to someone, on a regular basis, to work through all the shit you've been through. They'll educate you about the drugs you've done and will let you know about any medical concerns you might have to consider." Derek wasn't completely sure of anything he was saying, but babbling helped to ease his own frayed nerves. Certainly, idle words drowned the distinct sensation he was shirking an important responsibility by handing Tim off to someone else.

"Will you come in with me?" Tim sounded more like a ten-year-old kid than a freshman in college. Derek waited for his instincts to kick in. Whenever someone made a request of him, especially when the request came from someone so desperately in need, he offered himself freely. Instead, Derek remained coldly detached. He'd done the right thing by bringing Tim there. Anything more would be a betrayal to Scott.

"I need to get back to the dorm. Thanksgiving break is in a couple of days and I need to pack, write a few papers, work on my mix for the music class." There were other reasons he didn't want to stay, but saying them out loud wouldn't make Tim feel any better. Like, *Scott would kill me,* *You're an idiot,* and *I won't get dragged into your nightmare.* "Here, let me program my number into your phone in case you need to call me."

His head whirled. What the hell was happening to him? Who was this person who responded in cold, blunt statements and withheld help when asked? A chill originated in his chest, his heart turning to a block of ice, sending freezing blood through his veins.

A few stray tears ran down Tim's cheeks, but he nodded and handed over his phone. "I understand."

Having something to do snapped Derek's attention away from his troubled thoughts. He programmed his number into the phone and handed it back. Leading Tim to the counter, he stuck around until the receptionist knew why they'd come. He even waited with Tim until he was called in to meet with the psychiatrist. As soon as Tim passed through the reception doors, Derek gathered himself together and left.

~~~~~

Back in his room, Derek tried to focus on his mixing, but couldn't manage to keep his attention on anything for longer than a few minutes at a time. He'd denied someone help when they'd explicitly asked for it.

Not only that, but Tim had begged, tears in his eyes, for Derek to come in with him. Just a few months earlier, he would have given Tim whatever he wanted. Not Tim specifically, but anyone who asked for his help. And he couldn't blame Scott because he hadn't even thought about him the entire walk to the Medical Center. No, Derek had made his own decision to leave Tim to someone else's care.

He leaned back in his chair and closed his eyes. Where was the guilt he should be experiencing? Where was the headache accompanying his worries over someone else's troubles?

Helping others defined him. What had changed? Maybe, in trying to provide Scott the time and space he needed, something had broken inside him. Could this cold, empty shell, someone he didn't even recognize, be Scott's doing? Was Scott to blame?

He pushed himself off the couch and started pacing the room. Too many questions, all without answers. Should he step in to help Tim despite Scott's needs? Should he speak to a counselor and get advice on what to do? Rather than stew, he'd go for a run. That always helped clear his mind.

Throwing on his shoes, a pair of shorts and Scott's long-sleeved shirt with the Tasmanian Devil on it, the same shirt Scott wore the first day they met senior year at Brampton High, Derek stepped out into the brisk fall evening.

He took off at a quick jog, heading directly for the athletic complex where the track was located. It was too cold to run by the river and he didn't want to fight traffic. Maybe running around an oval was boring, but it beat the shit out of the circles his thoughts were running inside his head.

Ten minutes later he arrived at the track, and he picked up his pace. Sweat coated his body. Pumping his arms and pounding his feet in a steady rhythm, he ran, loop after loop, pushing himself, not worrying about pace or stamina.

The sky shifted from blue to a pinkish purple. The fence lining the field became a mere blur as he pushed himself harder and harder. Why hadn't he stuck around to support Tim?

Birds streaked across the sky, like black lightning bolts. The lights in the athletic building dotted the large cement wall, emitting a soft yellow glow. Their inviting warmth cast a stark contrast to the biting chill as the wind cut against Derek's chest and back where the cotton cloth of his shirt was pasted to his skin.

What happened to the person who couldn't say no to the stray dogs? Had his bleeding heart finally bled out?

That last thought stuck, and Derek fumbled, his legs rubbery. He slowed to a jog, and finally to a brisk walk. Sweat poured freely down his neck, into his already soaked shirt, and down into the waistband of his shorts.

After a few more minutes he dropped to the ground, supporting himself on his hands and knees. He didn't care that his teeth chattered or that his nipples had hardened to tiny concrete nubs. He didn't even care about the cold he'd likely get from his ill-chosen workout gear.

He needed answers. And they weren't coming.

Movement in his peripheral vision caught his attention. All light had faded from the sky. No one should be out on the field. The only passersby would be athletes going to or coming from their practices.

A figure crossed onto the lawn and headed toward the track ring, coming slowly into focus.

Scott.

"What're you doing out here?" Scott rushed to Derek's side. "Why are you on the ground?"

"How'd you know it was me?" Derek mopped his forehead with a sweat-slicked arm, accomplishing nothing.

"How could I *not* recognize you? We've been together for two years." He removed his jacket, placing it over Derek's shoulders. "You're shivering. Here, put this on."

Derek accepted the covering gratefully, savoring Scott's lingering scent in the material. Staring into Scott's eyes, answers to the millions of questions he'd been asking himself started to form.

Scott put his arms around Derek, rubbing his hands vigorously over Derek's back and generating heat. "You stink."

Derek chuckled, trying to pull out of Scott's embrace.

Scott tightened his grip and helped Derek to his feet. "I like it." He held Derek for another minute before speaking again. "So, wanna tell me what's up?"

"I brought Tim to the Medical Center." Derek pulled back from Scott's embrace enough to look at his face. Scott's expression radiated nothing but love and understanding. "And I left him there even though he begged me to go in with him."

Scott didn't flinch. Not a quiver of his lip. Not a squint of his eye. He did nothing but keep his hands on Derek, rubbing him.

"I don't get it. I've never denied anyone like that before. He was crying. He needed me to go in with him, and I said no." Derek's legs wobbled.

Scott squeezed him close, the warmth of his body penetrating Derek's cold exterior. He didn't know whether the actual heat radiating from Scott helped to thaw Derek's frozen heart or if it was Scott's love which sunk through his pores and into his bloodstream. All he knew was Scott was his home. For the first time since he'd left Tim, Derek could recognize himself.

"I couldn't go in with him. He needs to take care of himself. I got him there. That was all I needed to do. I waited with him until he went in. I didn't *need* to do that, but I did."

A gentle brush of lips grazed the top of Derek's head, and warm breath flitted along his neck. *Yes.* The world spun on its axis once again. The whirling dust storm of doubt and insecurity settled. He could think.

"If I do all the work, he'll never have to do any of it. And then I'm not really helping him at all." Sudden clarity seemed to shed light on all the questions he'd been asking and couldn't answer. In Scott's arms, he could see, really see.

"I agree." They were the first words Scott had said since Derek began talking.

Derek pulled out of Scott's embrace so he could face him. Despite the cold, heat flooded his cheeks. How could he have thought Scott had broken him? If anything, Scott had fixed him. Just staring at those worried eyes grounded Derek in a way nothing else could.

His heart clenched, pain throbbing in his chest and thrumming outwards along his limbs. Guilt. This is what guilt felt like. Or maybe betrayal. He'd allowed himself to think the worst of himself and pinned his own failures on Scott.

"I have a confession to make." Derek stared at Scott who remained silent, stoic in his strength, his blue-green eyes as soothing as a gentle sea. "I thought your demands for me to hold back from helping Tim had somehow broken me. Made me less capable of being there for others."

Scott stared at Derek for a few seconds before speaking. "I guess I deserve that, but I won't lie. It hurts."

Derek pulled Scott close. "I was wrong though. Back in the room, I couldn't sit in my own skin. Everything I tried to do to distract myself wouldn't work. So I came out here to run, hoping the exercise would stop me from thinking at all. Instead, I just asked myself even more questions. Ones I couldn't answer."

Scott wrapped his arms around Derek, squeezing with comforting pressure. Derek squeezed back. "But I was wrong. You've allowed me to grow. I can breathe when I'm in your arms."

"So what now?" Scott didn't let go. He held tight.

"Now we go back to the room. In a couple of days we go home for Thanksgiving. We keep living." The answer was so simple he almost laughed. In all his worrying, he'd missed such an obvious truth about himself. "I'll help people, but I won't lose myself in the process. People have to help themselves."

Scott released Derek, holding him at arm's length. "Do you have any idea how amazing you are?"

Derek fought back a smile. He didn't deserve praise. Not after he'd considered himself broken and blamed Scott for it. "It's not *me* who's amazing."

"Yes. It is." Scott leveled Derek in a gaze he couldn't have turned away from even if he wanted to. "Because you're so alive. Everything you do propels you forward, and I'm the lucky son of a bitch who gets to come along for the ride."

For the first time all day a smile tugged at Derek's lips. "Don't talk about your mother that way."

Scott shoved Derek, then took his hand. "C'mon. You're gonna catch pneumonia. Let's get you back to the dorm and into warm clothes."

They walked in silence for a few minutes. Once their dorm came into view, Derek stopped them. "I really am sorry I doubted you."

Scott placed his hand against Derek's cheek, the warmth penetrating his chilled skin. "I know. It's okay."

Of course Scott would show compassion and understanding, even though Derek didn't deserve it. Guilt crept through him like an army of ants. He'd given Scott the space to figure shit out, and Scott had done exactly that. It was time to give credit where it was due.

Chapter Seventeen

Scott lay on his bed staring at the ceiling. Although days had passed, Derek's admission wore heavily on his heart. He knew right away it was Derek running on the track when he saw him. He would've known even if Derek hadn't been wearing that shirt. No one ran like Derek when they were burning off frustration. Scott swallowed back the painful lump in his throat. Lately, it seemed, he was the cause of that frustration.

He'd worked hard to cushion Derek from the inner workings of his erratic thoughts. Apparently not hard enough. His need for Derek to step back from Tim had come at a cost.

Sliding out of bed, Scott flipped open his laptop. He'd been working on the mix for his music class, his gift to Derek, every chance he got. Now, with Derek at class for the next couple hours, he could get some work done without looking over his shoulder. The least he could do was put together something Derek wouldn't forget. Maybe through music he could show Derek how much love and faith he inspired.

Scott clicked open his file. The mix was split into three sections labeled "past," "present," and "future." The first part included the monk's song. The mournful chanting resonated in Scott's heart. How often had his heart sunk when his parents announced they were moving once again? The French horns provided a distinct shift. Uplifting, they represented the moment he set eyes on Derek in English class senior year in high school. Just one look and he'd known something big would happen, something inexplicably good.

From that moment, happiness had begun to take root in his life. Meeting Derek had been the dawn of his belief that he could build something for himself he could keep. Even when his father tried to control every minute of Scott's life, Derek's unwavering love served as a beacon, leading him through the dark.

The final section, the part that would represent his future, had to embody all that happiness. But how? In time, he'd shed the scars of his past and live the healthy future Derek's love promised. What kind of music sent *that* message?

He needed something triumphant.

Derek's confession of blame played in a loop in his head, an echo, taunting. Scott swallowed once again, a damn lump refusing to go away.

He flipped his laptop closed. He wouldn't be able to find the right music to bring this musical journey to an end until he dealt with his own hang-ups. The music wasn't playing in his soul yet, and there was no way anything could resonate within him until it did.

~~~~~

Derek stood by the kitchen sink, a cutting board in front of him, his eyes watering freely as he diced a third onion. His mother stood to his left, hands buried in a gooey mess of breadcrumbs she'd soaked in water. They'd absorbed the liquid, and she now kneaded eggs and spices into the slop. How something so disgusting turned into the amazing stuffing his mother always made was beyond him. Every few seconds she'd turn to face Derek and sigh.

The fifth time she did, Derek turned to face her, eyes bleary. "What?!" He hadn't meant to snap, but he still carried tension from the last few days at school. Guilt plagued him at leaving Tim, but to blame Scott…no amount of reassurances from his overly understanding lover could douse the flames of self-recrimination burning his insides.

"It's just so good to have you home." She smiled, totally unfazed by Derek's ill-tempered tone or the tears running down his cheeks.

"Please, tell me I'm done once I finish with this onion."

"Oh, you're done…with the onions. I still have veggies that need cutting, sweet potatoes that need to be boiled and skinned, and at least two errands you need to run." She returned her attention to the mush in her hands.

"Is that all? And here I thought you were gonna put me to work." Derek shrugged his shoulder toward his eyes, trying to wipe the wetness away.

He continued chopping the onions, his mind drifting to Scott. Once Scott showed up at the track the other night, everything had made sense. The simple act of placing a coat over Derek's shoulders and holding him while Derek spouted off revelations, was exactly why he loved the man. No one got him like Scott did. He knew when to push and when to just be there.

Derek had some making up to do. Scott had brushed off the confession, but he couldn't hide the pain. Derek had no doubt Scott's wide-eyed expression and the shallow gasp of air would haunt his dreams for a while.

"What's on your mind, sweetie?" Leave it to his mom to read him like an open book.

"Nothing. It's just my eyes." The excuse was weak, but he wasn't in the mood to reveal what an ass he'd been.

"Why don't you take the list I made and go to the supermarket. Then you can stop by the bakery and pick up the pies." His mom removed her hands from the goo and squished as much as she could back into the bowl. "Mind turning on the water for me?"

Derek did as requested, then grabbed a dishrag and wiped his eyes. "Where's the list?"

"On the fridge." She turned off the water and picked up the knife Derek left on the counter.

Derek slipped the shopping list from under a magnet and shoved it into his pocket, took the keys from the hook next to the kitchen table and started for the front door.

"Honey!" his mother called from the kitchen. When Derek faced her, he noticed she still faced the sink, knife in hand.

"Yeah?"

"When you see Scott, tell him I said hello and that we'll be eating around four. He and Shannon can come earlier if they like."

"I never said I was—" His mother turned to face him, her expression freezing his words. She didn't have to be a rocket scientist to figure out he'd stop by Scott's. Twenty-four hours of separation and Derek was already experiencing withdrawal. "I will." He rushed out of the house before his mom could say anything else.

Hopping into the car, Derek drove the few blocks to Scott's house. Shannon swung the door open before he even had a chance to knock, pulling him off-balance into a giant hug. "It's so good to *see* you."

"You too." Derek hugged her back, glancing over her shoulder for signs of Scott.

Shannon released him, then stepped aside allowing space for him to enter their home. "He's in his room."

"Thanks." Derek bounded up the stairs but stopped midway. "Oh, my mom says dinner's at four, but you guys can come by early."

"Should we bring anything?" Shannon's eyes shone with affection. "Other than the wine she asked me to pick up?"

"Have you met my mother? The house is stuffed to the gills with food, and she has me grocery shopping."

"I'll just bring the wine then. And some champagne too." Shannon hustled off to the kitchen.

Derek continued to Scott's room. He hesitated outside the closed door, all sorts of devilish thoughts of what he might find on the other side popping into his head. Maybe Scott was rubbing one out. That would be an awesome sight to witness, especially because Scott would likely assume it was his mom barging in.

Without knocking, he opened the door. Scott lay on his bed, definitely *not* in a compromised position. He turned to Derek and his face lit up. "Hey. What're you doing here?"

Derek crossed the room, climbed onto the bed and snuggled into Scott's open embrace. "I missed you."

Scott wrapped his arms around Derek, kissing the top of his head. "It's only been a day." The tight squeeze let Derek know Scott missed him as well. "How's it going over at your place?"

"Mom's in a cooking frenzy. Sent me out to go shopping. Wanna come?"

Without answering, Scott disentangled himself from Derek, hopped out of bed, and shoved his feet into his shoes. "Let's go." Grabbing Derek's hand, he tugged him out of the room, down the stairs and to the front door before calling over his shoulder. "I'm going out with Derek."

Shannon called from the kitchen. "All right, dear. Don't be too long. We've got to be there in a few hours and I want you showered and dressed in nice clothes."

Scott rolled his eyes, but said nothing, opening the door, pulling Derek outside, and closing it behind him. "What! Am I four? She's driving me crazy."

Derek chuckled. "Whatever. Moms are like that."

The supermarket was a hurricane of people rushing about. Shelves were stripped of virtually everything. The cashier lines blocked passage along the entire length of the front end of the aisles. "This is gonna suck."

Shopping wasn't as bad as Derek had anticipated. His mom's list wasn't too long, and they used the self-checkout lane which moved at a fairly quick pace.

Back in the car, Derek keyed the ignition but didn't shift into gear. Words he'd withheld over the past few days danced on the tip of his tongue, but he couldn't seem to force them out.

"What's wrong?" Of course Scott would sense his uneasiness.

When Derek faced him, the telltale signs of concern showed on Scott's face. He'd captured his bottom lip between his teeth, and his brow furrowed, small lines creasing the normally smooth skin. "I just...I feel really bad about the other night at the track." Pushing the words out felt harder than weight lifting, but once he'd said them, he was glad.

Scott's expression softened. "I figured your silence had something to do with that. Listen. Don't beat yourself up. It's not like I'm blameless here. I've been putting a lot of pressure on you. Especially this year. You've had to deal with my baggage, too."

They were words Derek wanted to hear, yet somehow didn't penetrate to his heart. "I was so rotten to assume you were responsible for any of my choices. Tim—"

"Let's not talk about him. You took him to get help, and now it's on him to follow through with whatever supports they have to offer." The words weren't spoken harshly, but Scott rarely cut Derek off. Maybe he'd hurt Scott more than he thought.

"Okay." He didn't know what else to say without pushing an issue Scott clearly didn't want to address. Better to simply enjoy themselves. A shift in topic was definitely in order. "We're gonna have to run for a week to burn off the calories from this meal."

A smile curled Scott's lips. "Don't I know it?"

All too soon, they arrived back at Scott's house. Scott reached for the car door, but hesitated before opening it. He leaned across the console and kissed Derek. Nothing more than a gentle brush of lips, tender and sweet. "Please don't stress about the other day."

Scott stared at him, love and acceptance buried within his eyes. "Okay." The one word response was all he could manage.

He waited until Scott disappeared into his house. Leaning his head back on the seat, he let out a heavy sigh. Hopefully, one day, he'd learn to avoid his idiot tendency to hurt the man he loved.

~~~~~

Scott trudged into the kitchen, falling heavily onto one of the chairs by the table. His mother sat next to him, placing her hand on his shoulder. "What's wrong?"

"I feel like I've fucked up with Derek."

She sucked in a breath. "Trouble in paradise?" Scott winced, but had to give her credit for withholding admonishment at his cursing.

"No. Nothing like that. It's just, I think I pushed him too hard. There's a kid at school who has a problem with drugs, and he's latched onto Derek. I kinda put my foot down saying I wanted Derek to stay away."

Sharon's face relaxed although her brows remained furrowed. "That sounds like a perfectly normal thing for you to request."

"Not when it's in his nature to help people. Tim needed intervening support, and Derek was ready to do whatever he could. He would have, too, if it hadn't been for me." The same pattern seemed to repeat, like a broken record, where Scott imposed his own needs on Derek. The weight of his behavior crushed down on him, constricting his chest and making breathing slightly more difficult.

Shannon slid her arm around Scott's shoulders, pulling him close. "After last year and what that horrid boy did to him, to both of you, Derek could hardly blame you for worrying."

"He doesn't." Of course Derek's admission on the track told a different story. "But because of me, he held back. He didn't do what he normally would have. Just so he could give me what I asked for."

Scott's mother took a seat next to him. "Have the two of you talked about it?"

Scott had committed each word of their conversation to memory. Remembering Derek's words was the only thing preventing him from feeling like a monster. "Yeah. Derek says he figured out that helping people doesn't mean doing all the hard work for them. Like he did with Tyrell. Tim needed someone to make sure he got psychological help.

Derek did that, then stepped back. He said he understands Tim has to do the rest of the work himself if he really wants to get better."

Shannon nodded. "Smart man."

"Tell me something I don't already know."

Shannon swatted the back of Scott's head. "Don't get smart. Maybe you're not giving him enough credit. He's grown up so much. He learns from his mistakes."

The words echoed inside Scott since he'd been thinking the same thing lately. "I know I'm lucky to have him, but sometimes I wonder if he's lucky to have me. You know I don't usually fish for compliments, but mind filling me in on whatever I seem to be missing?"

"Oh honey. It makes me sad that you still bear the scars of your childhood. Your father…" She pressed her lips together. "…was a fucking asshole."

"Mom!" Scott knew his mom wasn't a saint, but he'd never heard her curse.

"I just wish I could've been stronger when you were younger. I tried to shield you from him, but—" Her words trailed off, her eyes hazing over as if she'd gone somewhere else.

Scott took his mother's hand in his own. "You came through when it mattered."

Wiping a tear from her eye, she managed a weak smile. "That's sweet of you to say but I could've done much more much sooner."

"I think I'm gonna take that shower and get changed. We need to leave in like an hour." He pushed himself to his feet.

"Wait. I didn't answer your question." His mother beckoned with her eyes for him to sit back down.

"Know what? I think I need to figure out why I'm doubting everything for myself. It'll mean more that way."

She nodded, a smile replacing the expression of concern and sadness. "You're *already* figuring yourself out. And when you're ready, the answer will come. You won't even be looking and realization will smash into you."

"I hope so." Scott leaned forward and kissed his mother on the cheek.

In the shower, hot water pelted his skin, massaging and punishing at the same time. For a few minutes he simply focused on the sting of water as his screaming nerve endings acclimating to the heat.

Slowly, his mind unwound, easing him from the worries and concerns he'd lived with for the past few days. Derek had said not to worry. Scott owed it to both of them to believe him.

Derek was like sunshine burning through the cloudy world Scott had lived in for most of his life. Hopefully his mom was right and he'd figure himself out before too long. But that wasn't going to happen by dinner.

Chapter Eighteen

By the time his mom placed the final dish on the table, Derek was salivating. This was no dinner. It was a banquet of epic proportions. His father sat at the head of the table, his mother and Shannon on one side, he and Scott on the other. There was no way five people could eat the amount of food before them in one sitting. Maybe not even in a week.

Scents mixed together, turkey taking up dominance and all other smells playing a perfect harmony to the central dish. All fifteen pounds of the first bird lay on a platter, perfectly carved, gravy in two different dispensers. Green bean casserole, sweet potatoes with marshmallows, cranberry sauce, and chestnut stuffing, placed in smaller dishes or bowls, seemed more like garnishes to the main course. The sheer number of calories easily soared into the high five-digits, perhaps creeping toward the six-digit range.

His mom used the good china exactly two times a year: Thanksgiving and Christmas. Same with the crystal glasses, which she'd filled with water. Light filtered through the clear liquid, casting rainbow reflections along the crevices of the notched glass. The three parents also had wine glasses filled with a cabernet, two bottles of red sitting on the table. Derek and Scott also had wine glasses, but theirs were filled with sparkling cider. Just as well. Derek didn't particularly enjoy the taste of wine anyway.

Henry cleared his throat. "I'd like to give thanks before we eat if that's all right with everyone." Derek's mother took Henry's hand, gazing at him like a teenage girl in love. Everyone else took hold of their neighbor's hand until they formed a joined circle.

"We have a lot to be thankful for this year." Henry made eye contact with everyone around the table before continuing. "And they're all sitting here. I'd like to give thanks for this beautiful and loving family surrounding me. For the food on our table. And for the happiness of our children, Derek and Scott. May this year bring even greater joys than the last."

"Hear, hear." Derek watched as his mother raised Henry's hand to her lips and kissed his fingers. "I'd like to give thanks for my darling husband, the love of my life. For good friends." She gave a nod and a smile. "For Scott, who I consider a son. And for Derek, who brightens my life with his infinite goodness."

Shannon went next. "I'd like to give thanks to Henry and Claire who've taken Scott and me in as family. For Derek, who's given love and support to my son through trying times. And most of all I give thanks for my son, for his strength." She stared at him, and Derek sensed a silent message passing between them. She ran her hand along Scott's cheek, and Scott smiled. Then the moment passed.

Scott shifted in his seat, his cheeks flushing slightly. "I'd like to give thanks for our parents who've accepted Derek and me as a couple without question, and continue to support us as we build our lives together. Especially my mom, who stuck up for me even when my dad made it difficult for her to do so. And I'd like to give thanks for Derek, who's given me his love and friendship, without which I'd still be lost."

Derek wished they were alone. He wanted to pull Scott into an embrace and never let him go. Why couldn't Scott see his own strength the same way everyone else at the table so clearly could? The layers of guilt and blame he'd dumped on his boyfriend the other night hadn't helped.

Derek forced himself to stop thinking about his own remorse, and faced the people sitting around him. "I'd like to give thanks to Mom and Dad. I couldn't ask for two more loving or supportive people to call parents." He then leveled his gaze on Shannon. "And to Shannon, who's accepted me as one of her own. You've become like a second mother to me."

Finally he made eye contact with the one he longed to spend the rest of his life with. There were so many reasons he gave thanks for the man sitting next to him. Scott's love completed him in a way he'd never imagined possible. Before Scott, he'd been bits and pieces of his true self. With his man by his side he'd become whole. He wished Scott could see how much he'd given Derek over the past two years. How much better Derek's life was for his presence. "I'd like to give thanks for Scott, because without him, I wouldn't know the meaning of true love. Having you by my side lifts me up so I can be the best version of myself."

There were so many things he wanted to say, but not in front of an audience. Besides, the lump in his throat wouldn't allow more without him breaking down. Soon, maybe even this weekend, he'd find some alone-time for the two of them.

He glanced at everyone sitting around him, each of them staring back, eyes shimmering. After a few seconds of silence, his mom wiped her eyes and cleared her throat. "All right. Who wants white meat and who wants dark?"

For the next few minutes the sound of utensils clinking against plates filled the dining room, dotted with compliments to the chef who, as usual, had outdone herself. Derek couldn't believe how a lavish meal could take days to prepare, only to be devoured over the course of an hour. He rubbed his belly. "I couldn't eat another bite. Everything was great, Mom."

His mother flashed him a bright smile. "I'm glad you enjoyed it, dear. You've been losing weight. You better believe I'm going to stuff you over the next few days like I stuffed that turkey so I can fatten you up."

That earned chuckles from around the table from everyone but Derek, who knew she'd actually stuff him with food if she could. "At least let this settle first before you force me to eat more."

"We'll see," was all his mother offered before she and Shannon started clearing the table.

Henry pushed his chair from the table and groaned as he stood. "Oh boy. I think my belt size just increased by two inches from that meal alone. Better get into the kitchen and help the ladies out." He grabbed a few plates from the table. Derek stood, picking up some dishes as well, but his father stopped him. "Why don't you and Scott go for a walk? You're gonna need to make some space for dessert because I'm not suffering through your mother's complaining if you don't at least try a bit of everything she's made."

Derek suspected his dad was providing an opportunity for him to talk to Scott privately. He didn't doubt, however, that his mother would be very disappointed if he didn't take at least a bite of each dessert. "All right. Thanks."

Derek turned to Scott. "C'mon."

Scott took Derek's hand and accompanied him outside. Darkness had already begun to descend even though it was only just past five. Derek shivered. Earlier sunsets meant winter wasn't far away.

They strolled down the block, hand in hand, silent for a few minutes. Derek had so many things he wanted to say, but each time he glanced at Scott, the firm set of his jaw or the slight crinkle at the corner of his eyes held Derek back. Something was going on inside that handsome head.

Derek didn't have long to wait.

"You amaze me. You know that?" Scott delivered the statement as casually as he might've said, *"Dinner was great."* "Everything about you, your openness, your desire to help, music, wrestling, making friends, figuring yourself out. Everything comes so naturally to you. Sometimes…"

Derek waited for Scott to continue. When silence stretched out, he prodded. "What were you about to say?"

Scott shook his head. "It's stupid. You'd be pissed if I said it."

"And I'll stress out if you don't." He wasn't sure where Scott was going with his line of thinking, but didn't like the seriousness of his tone.

"Fine. But don't tell me I didn't warn you." He stopped walking and stared at Derek.

"Okay. I promise." Whatever Scott had to say, he sure was being dramatic about it.

Scott drew in a deep breath and let it out slowly. Finally, he leveled Derek with a steady gaze. "Sometimes I feel like I hold you back."

Ice prickled at his heart, shivers running along his skin that had nothing to do with the temperature. Derek knew Scott struggled with himself, but he'd never suspected Scott questioned their relationship. "You're right. I don't like hearing you say that. Not only because it's not true, but it means you don't have a very high opinion of yourself." Not to mention the role he'd played in Scott's self-doubt.

"Sometimes I don't." Again with the matter-of-fact intonation. At least he was opening up. Derek had made him promise he'd share whatever was on his mind after those few weeks Scott had pulled away earlier in the year.

"You don't hold me back, Scott. Your pushing me didn't change the decisions I made. Maybe they did at first, but I figured things out on my own." Scott didn't need to know just how big a role his fears had played.

"My worrying made you change your behavior. You said so yourself. I was your priority." Scott barely made eye contact as he spoke.

Derek cupped Scott's cheek, forcing him to focus. "Look at me." With a little coaxing, he got Scott to glance up. "If I'd wanted to make someone else the priority, I would have. I chose you. I'll always choose you. At the track I figured out how selfish I've been, putting you through all that worry. I thought I was helping kids like Tim. But I wasn't. In the end, I was actually hurting them because they didn't have to do the work themselves."

"We've gone over this. I understand you came to these conclusions yourself. Don't you see?" Scott tried to look away but Derek placed his other hand on Scott's cheek, holding his gaze. "You figured that out *despite* my demands and worries. I can't figure a damn thing out about myself, and it's frustrating as hell."

This was not how Thanksgiving was supposed to be. The holiday was about celebrating, having fun, and appreciating things. Scott was beating himself up, and even if Derek *could* stop him he had no idea how. Whatever was going on, Scott had to figure it out himself. No perfect words or magical wave of a hand could fix whatever was broken inside him.

Derek still had the power to do *one* thing. "Scott. I love you. I get that you've got some shit to figure out. I know it's tough and you'll probably doubt yourself along the way. But there's one thing you should *never* doubt." He paused for a second, more for dramatic effect than anything else. "I will be here to support and love you. And when you figure out whatever's going on that has you so down, I'll be here to celebrate with you."

Scott nodded, a hint of a smile curling his lips. Far more than he dared hope for. "Thank you."

Simple words, genuine, yet Derek's heart thudded, each rapid beat pounding like a hammer. "There's nothing to thank me for."

Scott pulled Derek into a hug. "Thank you anyway."

~~~~~

At around eight, Beck showed up, decked out in a floor length dress. She wore a bra based on the way her breasts stood out, but Derek couldn't see any straps. Racing to the door, he pulled her into his arms and twirled in a circle, lifting her off her feet. "Beck." Quietly, he whispered in her ear, "Scott's been beating himself up tonight."

Beck hugged Derek back, her brash laughter filling the room. "Happy Thanksgiving." In Derek's ear she whispered, "We'll talk to him."

Derek set her down, and they exchanged a knowing glance before Beck paraded up the stairs to greet everyone.

Dessert was almost as extravagant as the meal. Pumpkin cheesecake, apple pie, cinnamon spice rolls, allspice infused vanilla custard, an assortment of harvest fruits, and, of course, his mother's famous flourless chocolate cake with raspberry topping. Plates far too small to accommodate the wide range of choices were set in front of each chair. The scent of coffee wafted into the living room from the kitchen, and a wicker basket filled with an assortment of flavored tea sat next to a pot of hot water on the breakfront lining the dining room wall.

Before he even selected the first serving of any of the choices onto his plate, Derek could already feel his arteries clogging. Of course, his mother lorded over him, making sure he tried at least a bit of everything before she finally sat down and enjoyed a small plateful of fruit and a simple green tea.

Once they'd finished dessert, the parents settled on the living room couches. Shannon procured the bottle of champagne, uncorking it ceremoniously.

Derek dragged Scott and Beck up to his attic room before his mother could concoct an excuse for him to eat even more.

Once upstairs, Derek stripped down to his boxers, slipped into a tee and sweats, then collapsed onto his bed. "I'm not eating again for three months."

Beck let out a loud *Ha!* "Yeah right. You'll be the first one in the kitchen tomorrow morning."

"You're probably right." Derek shifted his attention to Scott, who slid onto the bed next to Derek and lay back, resting his head on one of the pillows. "You okay?"

Scott let out a contented hum. "Yeah. Sorry I was such a downer earlier. I just have some shit to work through."

Beck shot a quick glance at Scott, then rifled through Derek's dresser and procured a pair of sweats and a ragged T-shirt. She shimmied out of the dress, unhooked her bra, and stood before the two of them naked but for her panties. Derek was too tired to come up with a witty comment.

Once dressed in the more comfortable clothes, she crawled onto the bed and weaseled her way between Derek and Scott. Luckily, the queen size was large enough to accommodate the three of them. "What's got you so down anyway, Scotty?"

Scott rolled onto his side and glared at her. "I hate that nickname. It makes me feel like I'm three."

Beck rolled her eyes. "Whatever. Spill. What's going on?"

Derek remained silent. Beck was asking the questions he'd asked earlier. Hopefully, coming from a different person, Scott might actually produce an answer.

Scott heaved a sigh and plopped down on his back. "I'm only going to say this once, and then I want us to drop it for tonight. Okay?"

Beck propped herself up on her elbow. Derek sat up. "Okay," they both said in unison.

"The other day, when you came to that realization at the track, the one about giving too much help isn't really helping at all — not the one about me breaking you —I thought a weight would've lifted from my shoulders. I worry about how you put yourself in situations where you could get hurt." He spoke to Derek, talking past Beck as if she wasn't even there.

"I should have felt happy to know you'd be safe and that I could breathe easier whenever we were apart. That didn't happen. I still feel heavy and burdened." Scott's voice was even and calm, odd given the seriousness of his words. Derek bit back the instinct to question him about his strangely docile manner.

"When you say I haven't held you back, I believe you. I know I haven't broken you. And I trust you've truly come to understand there's only so much you can do for other people." Scott's voice remained eerily subdued, as if he'd shut off his emotions. Again, Derek fought an internal battle to keep from interrupting whatever Scott had to say.

"Yet I still feel like I'm lost. Like I'm here on Earth, but gravity doesn't really apply to me. I know that doesn't even make sense, but it's like I don't know where I belong anymore."

"You belong with me." Derek's shuddered hearing all the stress and angst he would've expected from Scott reflected in his own voice.

"I know. I do. I always will." Scott sat up, his energy buzzing in the air, a stark contrast from seconds earlier. His voice, animated and strong, finally carried the emotion Derek had been looking for. "But I need to find myself. I didn't grow up like you did. With two loving parents and staying in one place. My mom does her best to make up for what my dad never could, or would, do. Still, I have a totally different view on what it means to trust that anything, good or bad, lasts."

Derek remained silent, fighting desperately to remain still. More than anything, he wanted to lunge across the bed and wrap Scott in his arms.

Scott's words were choppy as if he were struggling not to cry. "I've never trusted things will remain stable. As soon as my life seems to settle, the bottom falls out, and I crash."

Derek couldn't help the tears. They filled his eyes and dripped down his cheeks. He reached for Scott and pulled him close. "I'll never leave you, Scott. You have to believe me."

"Hey, kind of getting squished here." Beck's interjection was delivered quietly, but served to break the tension and seriousness of the moment.

A rush of annoyance flooded through Derek but melted away as he realized they'd completely shut her out of the conversation.

Scott kissed Derek on the lips, then withdrew from the embrace. "Sorry, Beck." He glanced at Derek. "I know you won't. I just have some things to figure out. Like you did. And it's gonna take some time. You'll just have to be patient with me while I sort through my feelings."

Beck pushed herself into a seated position and draped her arms around Scott's neck. "We'll give you all the time you need, Scotty."

To his credit, Scott let the endearment slide and hugged Beck in return.

Derek wiped his eyes and got off the bed. "I think we need a pick-me-up." He darted over to his bag and dug out his iPod and the portable speaker Scott had bought him for Christmas the previous year. Within seconds, he located the song he wanted.

"Don't Stop Believin'" by Survivor filled the attic, bouncing off the walls. If it were a normal night, his mom would barrel up the stairs yelling at him to turn the volume down. With all the drinking and full bellies, it wasn't likely anyone would disturb them.

Beck was the first to hop off the bed to dance with Derek in the middle of the room. Scott remained on the bed, but at least he smiled. After a minute, he joined Derek and Beck, and by the end of the song all three of them were bouncing around.

The song had served its purpose. For the next hour, Derek played a private deejay show for them. All of the songs were upbeat and danceable.

It wasn't until Shannon was standing in the middle of the room that he realized their privacy had been interrupted. She placed a hand on Scott's shoulder. "I hate to break up the fun, but I'm beat. I think it's time to go home." She waited a few seconds as Scott caught his breath. "If you'd like to stay, you could walk home, but if I don't leave now, I might fall asleep behind the wheel even though it's only a four block drive."

Scott nodded. "I'll be right down, Mom." Shannon left the room and Derek turned off the music. Scott pulled Beck into a hug and kissed her cheek. She hugged him back then eyed Derek and headed out of the room without saying a word.

Alone with Scott, Derek held his breath, hoping he'd succeeded in lightening Scott's mood, but also worried the tension from earlier might creep back in. Scott wrapped strong arms around him and squeezed. "You always did know how to cheer me up."

Derek released the breath he'd been holding. Together, he and Scott returned to the living room where everyone was saying their goodbyes.

Later that night in bed, Derek stared at his ceiling, unable to sleep. Scott had unloaded an awful lot. Impressive, since Scott usually kept things in.

With Tyrell, Scott had been supportive. At least up until Tyrell targeted them with hateful gay-bashing, writing *faggot* on their dorm room door. And even then, he hadn't pushed Derek to do anything he didn't want to do.

This year Scott seemed to be coming apart at the seams. None of Derek's reassurances seemed to have the desired impact. Scott still doubted his worth. That was clear. It was a bitter pill to admit there was nothing he could do to force

Scott to see himself the way everyone else did. All he could do was stand by his lover's side and hope that was enough.

Chapter Nineteen

Scott rolled Marcus onto his back for the third time. Each move seemed to come from an instinctual place inside, as opposed to him making a decision to sweep Marcus's leg to take him down or slide into a half-nelson to wrest him from his belly to his back. On the mat, Scott had everything he needed. He was the best version of himself.

It was their first practice back from Thanksgiving, and Scott had excess energy, especially after the emotional rollercoaster of the holiday weekend. Now, back at school, in the wrestling room where *he* held dominion, all the mental stress faded into the background. No doubt he'd face those demons once again after practice, but for now, he could rely on himself completely. Scott released Marcus and rolled off him.

Marcus lay on his back. "You're the fuckin' bomb, man. I can't get one move past you."

"Ready to go again?" Scott hopped to his feet, extending his hand to Marcus.

"Give me a minute. My muscles feel like rubber." Marcus sat up and spread his legs into a vee. He stretched first toward one foot and then the other.

Scott grabbed a jump rope, whipping the cord as fast as he could in quick arcs. His feet bounced off the mat, feather light. One minute, two. Sweat beaded over his body, dripping freely down his neck, arms, back and legs. Breathing became mechanical, deep, replenishing intakes of air, solid huffs as he exhaled.

The clock read five-forty. Derek would be at the dining hall by now. And then he had peer counseling and wouldn't get back to the room until ten at the earliest. Later, if he stopped by the Student Center.

Thinking of Derek only dredged up thoughts of the holiday weekend. Scott still couldn't believe he'd laid everything out the way he had with Derek and Beck. Definitely out of character for him. Yet naming his problem hadn't been cathartic, since he didn't know how to solve it.

Scott knew in his head and heart Derek would stand by his side. Just as clearly, he knew he'd continue to live in a haze until he came to terms with his own past. Didn't people spend years in therapy to accomplish that…if Scott actually *went* to therapy? And why should Derek have to tag along for that miserable ride? Both questions had haunted him ever since Thanksgiving.

He whipped the rope faster, focusing on the burn in his calves. With lactic acid building up, biology taking charge, he didn't need to dwell on Derek, his own problems, or anything else except for synchronizing his mind and body.

"Dude, you've been going for like five minutes." Marcus stood before him, just out of reach of the rope's arc.

Scott stopped swinging the rope and tossed it nearby on the mat. Panting, he leaned down, bracing himself, hands on knees, sucking in air. Physical exertion. Sweat. Adrenaline. These were things he could understand. He could manage the effects of hard exercise, stretching to influence blood flow and bring oxygen to tired muscles. The pure simplicity of anatomy never failed him. A constant in a life filled with inconsistencies.

For the rest of practice, he continued to spar with Marcus, doling out punishing takedown after takedown, pin after pin. Marcus's extra ten pounds barely even hampered his domination.

In the communal showers, his teammates bantered, talking about their first meet, coming up in a week. Bits and pieces of their conversation registered, but the pelt of hot water along his body drew his attention with a stronger pull.

Encased in liquid heat, he savored the last few minutes before he'd exit the athletic complex and re-enter his other life. The one far less certain and predictable.

The early December evening air cut at his skin with a chilling bite. Scott wrapped his jacket around himself tighter. Step by step, he focused on the ground under his feet, watching the pavement pass beneath him. One foot in front of the other. The blend of small rocks and glinting bits of crushed glass sparkled like stars in a dark night sky. The same glimmering as in New Hampshire when he and Derek had camped before school started.

Too soon, he stood before his dorm. No escaping real life anymore. He stepped through the door into the warm interior, although none of the heat penetrated the cold shell surrounding his heart.

Just three months earlier he'd known happiness unlike any he'd ever experienced. He'd given Derek a ring, a promise of their future together. He'd believed the act and Derek's acceptance would ground him once and for all.

Now, standing before the room he shared with Derek, nothing seemed certain. Nothing except Derek's love. Why couldn't he see himself through Derek's eyes?

He unlocked the door, stepped inside and tossed his bag on the floor. He removed his jacket and hung it on the rack they'd installed along the wall then kicked his shoes off somewhere in the vicinity of the couch.

Trudging to his desk, he flipped open his laptop. The semester was nearly over. Half the school year gone. So fast, yet so much had changed.

Or had it?

He lived with the ghosts of experiences he'd had no part in creating. He bore the emotional scars of other people's choices. Enough. Scott refused to play victim to his troubles. His mother'd said he'd come to his own understanding and acceptance in his own time. Hopefully that time would come sooner rather than later.

He'd avoided starting a paper for his economics course. Opening the file he'd created several weeks earlier, he stared at the blank page. Typing several sentences, he then highlighted all of the words and hit "Delete". The work was shit.

He opened the file of his mix for Derek. For the past few weeks he'd racked his brain, trying to figure out what song would bring the mix to its conclusion. He had music to represent the solemnity of his past and the hope in his present. Without knowing where his future lay, how could he choose a song to represent that final piece?

Closing the laptop, he decided to try reading. He grabbed his weathered copy of *A Separate Peace*. The book was his favorite, although Gene always made him sad. Such a good kid driven to an act which hurt and eventually killed his best friend. Up until this year, he'd seen himself as Finn. Upbeat, living each moment rather than longing for the future.

He'd had to.

Now, for the first time he could understand how Gene must've felt. Gene hadn't consciously decided to hurt Finn. When he'd jostled that branch, he'd been motivated by insecurity. Scott knew he wouldn't do something so detrimental to Derek that it would scar him permanently. At least, he hoped he wouldn't. Still, Scott brought heaviness to their relationship. No matter what Derek said, he had to feel tethered to a sinking rock.

Flipping to the part he wanted to read, the part where Gene visited the hospital once Finn woke up after falling from the tree, he lost himself in the story.

Buzz! Scott looked around the room. *Buzz.* What the hell? He glanced at Derek's desk, surprised to see Derek's phone rattling against the table. The clock read nine-thirty. It wasn't like Derek to leave his phone behind. Maybe he'd borrowed someone else's to call it. Scott did that all the time when he couldn't find his cell.

Curious to see who was calling, Scott placed his book on the coffee table and crossed the room. The name on the screen forced the breath out of his chest.

Tim.

He reached for the phone and pressed "Answer" before thinking about what he was doing. "Hello?"

"Derek, it's Tim. I need your help." Tim's words were rushed, and his voice carried a higher pitch than usual.

"This is Scott. Derek left his phone in the room. What's wrong?" He'd never liked Tim, but the kid sounded desperate.

There was a brief pause before Tim spoke, his voice strained. "I'm at The Paw and there's a guy who's freaking me out. He won't leave me alone, and I'm scared. Can you come get me?"

Scott had only heard about The Paw through an Internet search he'd done on gay nightlife in the Boston area. The place catered to older bear type guys. If Tim was there, he was fresh meat. "Can't you just leave? What's this guy doing?"

Tim didn't respond right away. "He's been buying me drinks, and he grabbed my cock. I'm afraid if I leave he'll follow me out, and...I'm drunk." Tim's high pitch had shifted almost to a whisper.

Scott rubbed his free hand over his face, trying to brush away his mounting frustration. "Did you mention anything to the bartender?"

"See, the thing is, I...I was flirting with the guy. He was so nice. Paying attention to me and buying me drinks. Back home, guys like that made me feel good about myself." Tim sounded so pathetic.

"Are you by the bar right now?"

"Yeah."

"Is the guy with you?"

"No. He went to the bathroom."

Scott heaved a sigh, relief mixing with his agitation. "Can you put the bartender on the line?"

"Wh...Why?" Tim's voice wavered, and for a second Scott feared he might deny the request.

"Please, Tim. I'd just like to speak to the bartender for a second." Maybe if the guy knew what was going on, he'd call Tim a cab and make sure he got safely into it.

"Okay." Tim sounded like a frightened child. A strong impulse to hug him rushed through Scott, and he wished he could reach through the phone and place an arm around his shoulder. *Huh!*

A few seconds later, another man's voice sounded over the line. "Yeah?"

The guy sounded annoyed. Best to get a name. "Hi. My name's Scott and you're with my friend Tim. What's your name?"

"Bob. Get to the point, man. It's busy here." More warmth could be found in an icebox.

"The thing is, Tim's gotten himself into a bit of a situation. It seems there's a patron who's making advances. I was hoping you could call a cab and make sure Tim gets into it. I'll take care of the cost."

"Listen, I don't run a babysitting service here, kid. And from what I've seen, your twink friend knows what he wants."

Scott closed his eyes, rage boiling in his veins. What the hell kind of bartender was this ass wipe anyway? He wanted to question whether The Paw made a habit of allowing underage people into their bar, but if he let the fucker know Tim wasn't of legal age, he'd probably kick him out. Then Tim might be in some real trouble. As much as it killed him, Scott swallowed his anger. "I understand." How he managed to speak through gritted teeth, he had no idea. "Could you put Tim back on the line please?"

Scott waited for Tim to come back. For the first time, Scott's heart went out to Tim. No matter what kind of shitty situations the kid placed himself in, he didn't deserve other men making unwanted advances on him. No one did.

"Scott?" Tim again.

"Listen to me. Stay by the bar. Don't go to the bathroom. Don't leave. Stay in the lightest spot you can find. I'll be there as soon as I can."

"Thanks." A shaky breath sounded over the line. "I'm so sorry for dragging you into this."

"Don't worry about it. Just wait there until I come and get you."

Scott rushed to Derek's desk and scribbled a note. *Tim's in trouble. Went to The Paw. Call me when you get this.* Then he shoved his feet into his sneakers, grabbed his jacket and keys, and rushed out of the room. He'd only just gotten his jacket on by the time he stepped outside. Despite the chill, heat raced through him.

Jogging to the street helped to ease the tension crawling up his spine. Cabs weren't easily found on a Monday night. At least not near the campus this late in the evening. Luckily, he didn't have long to wait and hailed an available taxi five minutes later.

Once in the back seat, he realized he had no idea where The Paw was other than somewhere near Fenway. "Do you know where The Paw is?" He fished his phone out of his pocket and opened his web browser.

"I know the place." The cabbie clicked on the meter and started driving.

Stupid. He should've asked Tim for the address. If Tim tried to leave on his own, Scott wouldn't be able to help him.

Twists and turns. Scott never gave much thought to the configuration of the Boston street system since he lived in Cambridge and used the red line to get wherever he needed. Now, depending on a cab to get him somewhere quickly, he didn't know which to be more pissed at, the red lights or the one way signs. It seemed they encountered both at every intersection.

Minutes passed, ticking at a torturously slow pace. What if Tim went to the bathroom and the guy followed him in? If the scumbag was getting him drunk it was possible he might consider using the john as a place to take what he wanted from the kid. Or maybe the fucker of a bartender let the guy know Tim called someone. Would the dude hustle Tim out of the bar? What would happen then?

He called Derek, hoping he might've returned to their room. If anyone knew how to handle a situation like this,

Derek did. The call went to voicemail after four rings. *Damnit! Must still be out.*

So many questions and no answers. Scott drummed his thighs with his fists. His blood rushed through him, heart beating wildly. Was this how Derek felt every time he rescued one of his strays? How could he stand it?

Minutes continued to pass until finally, the CITGO sign marking Fenway Park came into view. A few seconds later, the cab turned a corner and the driver pulled up next to a small bar with a huge pink neon image of a bear paw cresting the door. Above that were the words *The Paw* written with cursive lettering.

The cab fare was only twelve dollars. Scott grabbed fifteen and tossed it into the front seat. "Sorry man. I gotta bolt. Keep the change." He pushed the door open, hopped out, and slammed the door shut once again.

He ran to the front of the club and took a steadying breath. By now he'd imagined a million possible scenarios, each one worse than the last. *Please be inside and okay!* The silent prayer offered no comfort, but at least it gave him hope.

He tried Derek's number one more time, getting voicemail again. *Fuck!* He shoved his phone back into his pocket, stepped up to the door, and opened it.

The inside was dim, the only good lighting located in the bar area, and even that wasn't enough to make out people's actual faces. No sooner had he stepped through the entrance, a giant of a man, his gray beard surrounding his mouth and hanging six or seven inches below his chin, blocked his progress. Scott stared up at the guy who had to be at least six-foot-three. For all the hair he had on his face, he had none on his head "I.D.?"

"I…I'm just here to pick up a friend." Scott winced as he stammered his response.

"Sorry. No I.D., no entry." The Bald, Bearded Wonder didn't budge.

Scott tried peering around him, but there was no way he'd be able to make anyone out. Especially with the woolly mammoth standing in front of him. Ice rushed up his spine and radiated out toward his limbs. His skin prickled, as if sparked by electric shocks. He *had* to get into The Paw and find Tim. There was no other option.

Tim was the reason he'd rushed across town. Grounded in his purpose, Scott puffed up his chest. While the bouncer had three inches on him and at least a hundred pounds, Scott was one hell of a wrestler if defending himself became necessary. Hopefully it wouldn't come to that. "Listen, I don't know what kind of a place you run here, but are you sure you want someone who's underage in there? I'd hate for the cops to come by and shut the place down." Bravado had a much better effect, especially since he'd managed to deliver his statement with confidence, even though his insides had turned to jelly.

"Everyone here shows I.D." The moving mountain sounded sure of himself, but Scott could read the doubt in his eyes.

"Ever heard of fakes? Last time I checked, bars still get fined or worse if the patrons drink, even if they showed fake identification." Scott wasn't sure whether he was making headway or if he was about to get pummeled. Either way, forcing the issue touched a primal spot deep inside him. If only he'd had someone come to *his* defense when he was younger, he might have escaped years of suffering. He'd be damned if he'd squander this opportunity to be there for Tim the way no one had been there for him…until Derek.

Derek. Was this why he rushed to aid others? The urgency of easing suffering? The sense of pride at putting someone else's needs first? Scott swallowed hard and squared his shoulders in a face off with the towering man in the doorway.

Woolly, the nickname Scott decided to give the guy since Woolly Mammoth fit him so well, called across the bar. "Bob. Where's that kid?"

Scott tried to peer over Woolly's shoulder, but the man's body blocked the view of the entire bar.

A few seconds later, Tim peeked around Woolly's massive trunk. "Scott!" He managed to squeeze through the tiny space between Woolly and the doorframe and rushed to Scott, wrapping his arms tightly around Scott's waist.

Scott hugged him back, shocked by how violently Tim trembled. "It's okay. I've got you. We're going back to the dorm now."

Tim squeezed harder, his breath ragged as he choked out sobs. "I'm sorry...I dragged...you into this."

"It's okay. You're gonna be fine. C'mon. Let's get a cab and get back to campus." Scott gently extricated himself from Tim's vise-like grip and slid his arm over the trembling kid's shoulder.

Once again, it didn't take long to hail a cab and, safely inside the taxi, Tim scooted as close to Scott as possible. He smelled of vodka and sweat, not at all appealing, but Scott simply held him close.

The cab ride back was entirely different than the one over to The Paw. Now that he knew Tim was safe, he could breathe again. From the moment he heard Tim's panic over the phone, he'd responded as if on autopilot. There'd been no other choice but to help. Scott tightened his grip around

Tim's shoulder, knowing what could've happened, how badly things could have turned out.

But they hadn't. He'd acted on impulse, and Tim was safe. Plain and simple. He could understand, more powerfully than ever before, why Derek loved helping others. The rush of excitement and satisfaction coursing through him reminded him of the thrill he experienced when wrestling.

Had he known, he'd never have put pressure on Derek in the first place. Hell, Woolly could have crushed him into the ground if he wanted to. Amazed at how easily he'd disregarded his own safety, Scott closed his eyes, elbowing all the *could haves* aside.

He was safe. Tim was safe. Now he needed to get in touch with Derek.

Scott dug into his pocket, pulled out his cell, and flipped it open. The screen remained black. He pressed the power button. An image of his battery blinked, the thin red line at the base indicating he'd run out of juice. Shit, he'd asked Derek to call him.

Glancing at the time on the radio display in the front of the cab, he saw it was nearly ten-thirty. Only an hour had passed since he left his dorm, yet the world had changed for him. Now he understood what drove Derek to take risks. Knowing, while not relieving the stress, made accepting so much easier.

Tim still trembled in his arms, but all Scott could focus on was getting back to their dorm. He needed to see Derek and tell him all that he'd learned over the course of one short hour.

Chapter Twenty

Derek reached into his pocket, remembering for the twentieth time he didn't have his phone. Hopefully, he'd simply left it in the room. If not, he had no idea where it could be. What a hassle. He didn't wear a watch, but it'd been ten when he left the Center. The dorm was a fifteen minute walk. Scott might be in their room, unless he'd gone out with the wrestling team after practice.

Eagerness to get to his room urged him into a jog. Over the course of the night he'd counseled three people, each of them leaving with firm plans on how to begin the process of healing. Yet he couldn't find the right words or actions to help the one person he most wanted to help.

Scott's problems weren't the sort someone else could fix. All Derek could do was provide love. Love and patience, of which Derek had endless supplies, at least when it came to Scott.

Derek wished he could just get Scott to apply the same confidence he experienced when wrestling to the rest of his life. Maybe then Scott would be able to move forward, letting the past be the past. Easier said than done.

A weight settled in his gut, sapping energy from his muscles. Each step took effort. By the time he arrived at his dorm room, exhaustion invaded every part of his body.

He entered his room, bounding inside.

Empty.

Part of him wanted to climb into bed. He wondered if he even had the energy to undress first. Where was Scott? Maybe he couldn't solve his lover's problems, but a tight embrace was well within Derek's capacity.

Glancing at his desk, relief flowed through him. His phone sat where he'd left it before going to class earlier in the day. He hustled across the room, stopping short when he noticed his cell sat atop a note with Scott's handwriting on it.

Tim's in trouble. Went to The Paw. Call me when you get this.

Derek's throat constricted. Ice raced through him. His heart skipped a beat, then rampaged at a reckless tempo. Hitting speed dial, he paced the room, waiting for the ring which never came. Voicemail. "Damnit!" He scrolled through his recent calls. Scott had tried him twice and…Tim. Derek dialed the number. It rang. It rang again. And then went to voicemail. "Fuck!"

He never knew fear could become a living thing. His stomach clenched. His temples pounded.

He had researched The Paw after Tim mentioned it. The bar catered to older men and contained a back room where discreet, anonymous encounters took place. His searches revealed consistent reviews about the establishment. One guy named Papa Bear loved it, describing all the cute little cubs to be dominated. Another entry by someone named Smooth Stud said it was a great place if you liked rough play. A third, by Timid Twink, complained of aggressive advances, warning that *no* definitely did *not* mean *no* at the The Paw.

When he'd read those posts he'd made a mental note to avoid the place. He'd wanted to warn Tim about going there, but Tim had conveniently disappeared for the past month. Probably still camping out in Dumb and Dumber's room. What was worse, Scott was heading to The Paw. Avoiding the panic creeping along his spine would've been as fruitless as trying not to breathe.

How could Scott be so stupid as to put himself in such a dangerous position? The two of them had experienced a bar like that firsthand when they visited The Boiler Room in the East Village. Older guys lusted after younger guys and became angry by spurned advances. At least that'd been their experience.

Derek's stomach lurched. Luckily there was no food to retch. A painful burn crawled up his esophagus. He couldn't shut out images of Scott and unknown men. What if…?

No, he wouldn't go there. Starting down the *what if* road would only drive him crazy.

He dialed Scott's number again. As before, the call went directly to voicemail. "Fuck!" He tried Tim again. Nothing.

Maybe he should call the bar. Yeah, and say what? You have an underage kid in your bar and another one on the way. Could you let me know if the second one showed up yet? Besides, if he called and Scott wasn't there, whoever picked up the phone could easily kick Tim out. What little he knew of Tim, that scenario wouldn't end well.

Exhaustion was a memory. Adrenaline surged through his body as he paced circles around the room. He couldn't even go out looking for Scott. The only thing he could do was sit and wait, hoping for the best and working as hard as possible to ignore thoughts of the worst.

The clock on his desk provided the time in angry red block numbers. Ten-twenty. He'd been in the room for all of five minutes, yet the emotional whirlwind of fear and panic caused each minute to drag into an eternity.

Had Scott suffered like this each time Derek put himself on the line for someone else? Five minutes and Derek was ready to punch a wall just to deflect his rising panic. He'd put Scott through toe curling fear their entire freshman year and started right back in once they returned to college for their second year.

He glanced at the clock again. 10:22. He swore time seemed to stop. He wouldn't be surprised if it started moving backwards. Hell, if it moved back enough, maybe he could rewind to the beginning of their freshman year. Then he'd be able to undo all the stupid decisions he'd made. Avoid all the unnecessary stress he'd forced on Scott. He'd have avoided Tyrell like the plague.

Twenty-twenty hindsight. What an evil bitch.

10:24. Fuck it. Derek called Scott's phone again with the same results, then dialed Beck's number. The phone rang once, twice, three times. "Fuck it all to hell. Shit. Shit. Shit!" If she didn't pick up he'd probably burst a capillary somewhere deep in his brain. After the fourth ring, the call went to voicemail.

Derek listened to the cheerful message, Beck's chipper voice taunting him in its stark contrast to his own terror-filled internal shouts. Once he heard the beep, he rattled out his message. "Beck, call me. I'm a freakin' mess—"

His call waiting chimed in. Maybe it was Scott. He whipped his phone from his ear, staring at the screen. No such luck. But at least the displayed name offered some comfort.

Beck.

He hit "Accept"'. "I'm freaking out." Derek didn't even wait for Beck to get a word in nor did he begin with a, "Hello."

"What's wrong?" Beck's concern echoed in the hollow space growing in Derek's heart.

"Scott. He went to The Paw. It's a bar where guys like him get eaten as a snack." Saying it out loud only painted his worst nightmare in vivid color, making it real.

"Why'd he go there?" Beck's incredulous tone would've normally grated on Derek's nerves if he hadn't already worn them down to tattered shreds.

"He's there because of fucking Tim. Apparently the kid got himself into some kind of trouble, and Scott had to go off like a knight in shining armor to save him. What if something happens to him?"

Beck remained silent for several seconds. "Now you know how it feels."

The words might as well have been a slap to the face for as much as they stung. "What the fuck, Beck!"

"I'm not trying to be a bitch. But you've spent your whole life making choices that freak everyone out. All through high school I worried about you. I had to watch your back, wondering who might come after you if they suspected you were gay. When you started noticing other guys, I worried you might go out exploring and get yourself into a situation you couldn't handle. There were so many possible things that could've happened to you, and I stressed about it every day.

"Beck, this isn't about you." Derek considered hurling the phone across the room.

"No, this is about *you*, Derek. Think about last year. You took Tyrell under your wing. Scott and I tried to warn you over and over, but you wouldn't listen. Look how *that* turned out? You nearly got stabbed by the freaking nut job." Beck's words slammed into Derek, but nothing she said helped to relieve the terror of wondering whether Scott was okay.

His whole life, he'd made choices that felt right, never worrying about what others thought. He believed he could handle whatever situation might arise. Despite remaining closeted in high school, he let Scott in and had ended up happier than he'd ever been.

Scott. What if someone had him cornered in The Paw? What if—

"You still there?" A light tremor laced Beck's tone.

"Yeah." Derek dragged his errant thoughts back to the conversation, reminding himself not to jump to conclusions. Damn if the task wasn't Sisyphean. Is that what he'd put Scott through all of their freshman year?

"Listen. I'm sure he's fine. I assume you tried calling him."

"Went right to voicemail." Derek kicked the corner of his bed, grabbing his foot as a sharp bolt of pain shot from his toe up his leg. "Shit!"

"I know, honey. You're worried. But it'll be all right."

"No, I just hurt myself by kicking the bed post." Derek hobbled over to the couch and slunk into the soft cushions. "But thanks for finally being compassionate."

"Honey, you know me. Tact has never been my thing." Beck chuckled, but immediately stopped herself. "Sorry. I didn't mean to laugh, but I'm picturing you hopping around your room right now, and I can't help it." After a pause, she continued. "Listen, take this feeling in. Remember it. It's going to help you to understand where Scott's coming from. Remember Thanksgiving and everything he said? This is what he was talking about. Every time you go off to save the world, you rub salt on that wound. Now you know how powerful fear can be."

She was right, damn her. She always had been when it mattered. "I don't think I *can* do any reflecting right now. I'm too—"

Their room door opened and Scott filled the entrance, all in one piece. "Oh, thank God. He's here. I gotta go."

Derek tossed his phone on the couch, rushed across the room, and put his arms around Scott, squeezing him close.

Scott returned Derek's tight embrace, as much to keep from falling over as to offer comfort. Derek shook in his arms, the sound of his crying muffled as he buried his head in Scott's chest. "Hey. What's wrong?"

The response he got was ragged breathing. Not knowing what else to do, he held on tight, riding out Derek's storm.

After a few minutes, Derek lifted his gaze until he stared into Scott's eyes. "You stupid son of a bitch!" Scott fought to hold the smirk off his face, unsuccessfully. "I mean it. This isn't funny. Do you know how worried I've been?"

Scott ushered Derek from the doorway and into the room, then glanced at the clock on Derek's desk. 10:35. "I've only been gone an hour."

"I don't care how long you've been gone. I came back here to that *note*!" Derek spat the word like venom. "And for the last twenty minutes I've been thinking all sorts of really horrible things. I tried calling you, but I kept getting your voicemail."

"I'm sorry. My phone died. Tim called and you weren't here. I just thought, well, I needed to help him." The way Derek trembled evoked all too familiar memories. He'd been on Derek's end of this scenario too many times to count. He stepped forward and placed his hands on Derek's shoulders. "I'm so sorry I worried you. I'm fine. So is Tim."

"Yeah, Scott's my hero. You're so lucky to have him," Tim's mousy voice squeaked.

Derek stepped out of Scott's embrace and charged toward the door. "You! Have you ever heard of cell phones? Why didn't you pick up when I called you?"

Tim's eyes became saucers. He dug his phone out of his pocket and stared at the screen. "Oops."

Luckily Derek hadn't moved out of Scott's reach, and Scott caught him before he could charge at Tim.

"*Oops?*" He struggled against Scott who only tightened his grip. "You...I'm...we're gonna have a *long* talk tomorrow."

"Tim..." A wave of energy flushed through Scott. Emotions were running too high. "Why don't you get some rest?"

Tim didn't need to be asked twice. "Thanks again for you help." And then he was gone, the soft click of his door indicating he'd entered his room.

"Easy." Scott hugged Derek again then went to their door and closed it. Had he ever sounded so irrational and angry when Derek put him in a similar situation? Probably so.

He waited for Scott to return to him then wiped his face on Scott's shirt. "If you ever put yourself in a potentially dangerous situation again, I'm gonna..."

Scott remained silent, waiting to hear what Derek had to say.

After several seconds, Derek shook his head. "I won't do anything. But fuck, I was so scared."

"I know the feeling." Scott cupped Derek's cheek and leaned in, kissing him tenderly on the lips. "But I also learned something as well."

"Yeah?" Derek wiped at his nose with the back of his hand. "What's that?"

"I get why you like to help people so much. When I went to The Paw, the only thing I could think about was making sure Tim was okay. I didn't think of you. Or myself even. Making sure Tim was safe took over everything else, and I couldn't *not* go."

Derek nodded, the corner of one side of his mouth twitching up, not enough for an actual smile, but heading in the right direction. "You're an ass."

Scott smiled, somehow managing to suppress the chuckle pressing for escape. "There's the Derek I know and love."

Derek's mouth pulled up a bit more, this time forming a smirk. Scott released him and slipped over to the couch, plopping onto it. "Tim's fine. I'm fine. Everything's fine."

Scott made space for Derek on the couch. "Come on, sit with me. We should talk."

Derek scooted next to Scott, pressing as close to him as he could manage. Scott hugged him before continuing. "I never got it before. Why you felt the compulsion to put everyone else's needs before your own. Before mine. The way you seemed to look for trouble drove me mad with worry." He kissed Derek's temple.

"But tonight I got a firsthand taste of what your world is like. When Tim called in a panic, something inside me snapped into place. I didn't plan on going. I just kicked into action and went."

Derek took in a deep breath and let it out a sigh. "Yeah. It's like everything else fades when an emergency comes up."

"Exactly." Finally Scott could understand with his heart, not just his head.

Derek sniffled. "I figured something out tonight, too."

Scott was pretty sure he knew what Derek was about to say, but wanted to hear him say the words. "Yeah?"

"When I saw that note and couldn't reach you, I started to imagine the worst case scenarios. I felt so helpless. Sitting here, not knowing if you were okay. Not being able to reach you. I hated not having any control whatsoever." Derek shuddered, and Scott didn't have to guess what was going on inside his lover's head. He'd lived the fear displayed in front of him more times than he cared to remember.

Derek shifted on the couch and stared directly into Scott's eyes. "I made you feel that way. All last year as I fought to live openly, when I tried to help Tyrell, you supported me, but I never realized how much of a sacrifice you made. I had no idea how much I hurt you and how much you held inside."

Scott shook his head. "Trying to stop you would've hurt more. When I got Tim into the cab tonight, I got a real rush, like I'd just done something important. Something I can be proud of."

Derek took Scott's hands in his own. "That's true, but I imagined what those guys might've done to you at The Paw. If they'd been angry enough… If they wanted Tim badly enough… You could've gotten hurt." Derek closed his eyes. "Maybe even worse."

"But I didn't. Now I understand you better. Hopefully I can use this experience to manage my own stress."

Derek stared at Scott and opened his mouth to speak when a muffled sound came from the couch between them. "Ih-duh-ots".

Scott searched the room, trying to figure out where the sound had come from. When his gaze finally landed back on Derek, he witnessed the deep red flush residing on his lover's cheeks. Derek held up his cell. "Um, I didn't disconnect my call."

Scott stared at Derek, unsure what he was talking about. Derek must have understood the unasked question because he hit the speaker button on his phone. "You there?" His voice came out dry.

"You two are such idiots! Fucking kiss and make up."

Scott stared at the phone. "Beck, is that you?"

Beck let out a long sigh. "You two are so wrapped up in blaming yourselves, you're not even paying attention to each other. Tonight you just got a glimpse at what the other one's been going through. For fuck's sake, kiss, fuck, go dancing, but stop acting like morons. You're *both* to blame for stressing each other out. *Deal* with it."

Derek lifted his arm as if he were going to throw the phone across the room. Scott placed his hand on Derek's forearm and gently lowered it back down. "Okay. Point taken. Bye, Beck."

"Don't you hang up on—"

Derek hit "End" and placed the phone on the coffee table. Then he returned his gaze to Scott. "She's right, you know. We're both to blame here."

"All right, I'll make you a deal. We each got a taste of what drives us. Part of the problem was we didn't talk enough." Scott took both Derek's hands in his own. "Let's promise to talk more. Nothing's off limits. And we'll take it from there."

Derek nodded, and a smirk spread across his face. But the flare in his eyes shot tingling shivers through Scott's chest. He'd seen that expression enough to know Derek had inappropriate thoughts floating inside his gorgeous head. "And what happens if one or the other of us fails to communicate?"

Scott felt his lips pull up into what must have been a devilish grin, based on the way Derek's eyes widened. "Then the offending partner gets punished."

Derek kissed along Scott's jaw until his lips rested next to Scott's ear. "Yeah. What kind of punishment are we talking about?"

Scott slid his hand behind Derek's neck, dragging him into a fierce kiss. He licked at the seal of plump lips and slid his tongue into a welcoming mouth once Derek granted access. He pulled away from the kiss, eyes sultry and pointed to the bed. "Get over there, on your back, and I'll show you."

Chapter Twenty-One

Derek allowed Scott to guide him to the bed, although hauling would've been a better description. A semi-forceful shove had him on his back. Scott ripped off his shirt, kicking his shoes across the room at the same time. He unbuttoned his pants and stripped them off, along with underwear, until he stood before Derek in nothing but socks. A towering erection jutted proudly from his groin.

Derek reached to grip Scott's member, only to have his hand swatted away. "Let me get you undressed first." Scott stepped forward and gripped the hem of Derek's shirt, yanking it up and over his head in one smooth motion.

He then dropped to his knees and lifted one of Derek's feet, slipping the shoe off, then peeling away his sock. He did the same for Derek's other foot, then rose up onto his knees and slid his hands up Derek's legs, along his thighs, until they rested at his waist.

Scott leaned forward, pressing his lips against Derek's, a gentle breath of minty air washing along his cheek and into his mouth. Gentle caresses of tongue deepened into heated tumbling. Teeth grazed along his gums, creating a slight sting, but not hurting.

Lost in tongue play, Derek struggled to assist Scott in unbuckling his belt. Scott withdrew from the kiss, although Derek tried to maintain contact. He placed a hand on Scott's cheek and began to slip his fingers around the curve, drawing himself closer.

"Put your hands on the bed." Scott's sharp command halted Derek's movement, and he obediently placed his hands on the mattress by his sides.

"What the—?"

"You asked what the punishment would be. I said I'd show you. Only do what I tell you to do."

Derek's heart skipped a beat, then pattered at an accelerated rate. Scott had never been commanding in their love-making. Assertive, yes, but never directing Derek's actions. His cock, already hard, pulsed, forming a visible tube in his pants.

A smile curved Scott's mouth, his gleaming blue-green eyes enchanting Derek, transmitting lust and desire. The trance broke when Scott shifted his attention back to Derek's waist.

Peeling open Derek's pants, each button popped from its slot. Scott rubbed his hands up Derek's abdomen to his chest, pinching both nipples at once, using just enough force to draw a hiss, then twisted them.

"Holy Mother of Fuck!" A sheen of sweat broke out all over Derek's body. The air in the room wisped along his skin, a rippling chill dancing over him, raising goose bumps in its wake.

When Scott released Derek's nipples, warmth rushed to the center of his chest, the flesh throbbing in time with his heart. Derek chanced a peek at his chest, sucking in a short breath as he viewed the swollen marks dotting each pectoral muscle.

"Lift your hips for me." Scott dug his fingers beneath the band of Derek's underwear. Derek shifted his weight, and Scott slid the clothes past Derek's ass and down his legs.

Taking one of Derek's feet, Scott kissed his ankle and trailed his lips along the calf muscle, inner thigh, then along one hip, bypassing Derek's groin. Once he reached Derek's midsection, he continued his journey along Derek's abs, crawling up onto the bed and pushing Derek into a prone position.

"You're such a tease." Derek's muscles quivered, his cock pulsing. Damn.

When Scott reached Derek's neck, he nipped at the skin, then licked on the spot and blew on it. Derek drew in a shuddering breath just before Scott dropped his full weight on top of Derek, driving him into the mattress.

"Oh yeah." Derek wrapped his legs around Scott's waist.

With a slow grind of hips, Scott pressed his hard cock against Derek's, the heated skin sliding along Derek's equally firm member. "I thought you said this was a punishment." Derek sighed as he wrapped his arms around Scott's broad torso.

Scott rolled them so Derek lay atop him and chuckled. He swatted Derek's ass, the sharp burn tearing a yelp out of him. "Did I say you could talk?"

He opened his mouth to make a retort, but the way Scott narrowed his eyes forced his mouth shut.

"That's better." Scott cupped Derek's face, weaving his hands through Derek's hair, and guided their mouths together.

A simple tongue flick urged Derek's mouth open as Scott pulled them together, lolling his tongue in circles.

Unable to contain his rising need, Derek shifted his hips, trying to generate friction along his shaft. His cock head wept pre-cum, creating slickness and sealing their skin together.

Another harsh swat to his ass forced Derek to yank his head back. "Ouch!"

Scott shot him a devilish grin before painting on a serious expression again. "No grinding. You wanted to see what your punishment would feel like."

Derek began to understand how Scott's methods served as an effective punitive measure. Not allowed to speak or move without permission, Derek became a slave to his yearnings and needs with no outlet to satisfy either.

Scott captured Derek's mouth in another heated kiss. At the same time, he rolled them once again so he lay on top. After several seconds, Scott lifted his head, panting, eyes glazed over. He supported himself on his hands and crawled up Derek's body, wedging his knees between Derek's sides and arms, until his cock head hovered at Derek's lips. "Suck my dick."

A live wire of excitement shot along Derek's spine. With his hands free, he gripped Scott's cock and guided it to his own eager mouth. The tip glistened with a clear droplet of pre-cum.

He plunged his tongue into the fluid, exploring the salty flavor. Probing, he glided against the slit, forcing it open. Scott's leg's trembled and his body rocked as a shuttering breath heaved out of him. "Shit."

Encouraged, Derek repeated the action, rewarded each time with the same helpless bucking of his lover. The torture fed his need to satisfy Scott. Never before had the craving for Scott's hard flesh flooded him in gushing waves.

Closing his lips around the crown, Derek savored the pungent flavor. Surrounded by Scott's musky scent, fingers of pleasure raced along his skin. His own cock bobbed, pre-cum tickling a path along the inside of his shaft. Cold liquid settled on his navel, no doubt his own semen creating a pearlescent string connecting his cock head to his belly.

Intense need made him reach for his own cock, but Scott captured the offending hand and trapped it by Derek's head. "Nope. I said suck me. I didn't give you permission to stroke yourself."

Another rush of electricity whipped along his nerve endings, creating a web of tingles that exploded just under the surface of his skin. He tilted his head up and took more of Scott into his mouth, the angle uncomfortable, but the shuddering sigh from above making the strain altogether worth the tension in his own neck muscles.

Scott gently rocked his hips, sliding more of his length into Derek's mouth until they found a pattern of motion that enabled Scott to face fuck him. Derek loosened his throat muscles and focused on the silken skin caressing the flat of his tongue.

With each press forward, pre-cum coated the back of Derek's throat, the tangy flavor sluicing down his esophagus, leaving a trail of Scott's flavor in its path. His own cock continued to pulse, the fluid on his belly sliding toward one hip and threatening to spill over his side onto the sheets. His mouth full, one hand trapped by his head, the other gripping Scott's shaft, Derek thought he might go mad from the rising tide of unattended pleasure surging through him.

He locked gazes with Scott, who stared down at him, the blue and green in his eyes seeming to swirl like a stormy sea. Scott licked his lips, the moisture capturing light and causing them to shimmer. Muscles along his abdomen rippled under his skin as he continued to rock forward and slide back, his cock entering Derek and withdrawing at a steady pace.

Scott's breathing became shallow. He buried his cock until about two-thirds of his length pressed down Derek's throat. "I'm gonna try something, but you have to tap me if it gets uncomfortable." He released Derek's trapped hand and waited for a response.

Since Derek's mouth was stretched wide by Scott's massive girth, all he could manage was a small nod.

Scott grinned. "Okay. Slide down so you're entirely flat." Derek obeyed and Scott moved with him, keeping himself lodged in Derek's mouth. Once Derek lay completely prone, Scott leaned forward and placed his hands on the wall above the headboard. Slowly, he arched his hips, pushing more of his length into Derek's mouth.

Derek placed his newly freed hand on Scott's ass, fearing what repercussions he might suffer if he tried to grasp his own cock again.

The head of Scott's cock pressed at the back of Derek's throat. His lips stretched taut, and tears formed in his eyes from the strain. Scott continued to apply pressure, sliding bit by bit. Derek maintained his grip on Scott's ass, ready to let Scott know when he'd had too much, but he wanted to see if he could finally take all of Scott.

Scott thrust forward, his glans breaching the back of Derek's throat, then withdrew slightly, allowing him to draw in much-needed air. "You okay?"

Asking a question with Derek's mouth stuffed with cock was a fairly pointless thing to do, but Derek managed a muffled, "Yah."

Scott caressed Derek's cheek, his palm warm and soothing. "Let me know if I go too far."

Derek reached his other hand around to grab Scott's ass and tugged him forward in answer. Scott arched his hips once again, sliding his length deeper into Derek's mouth. The head slipped past his throat once more. Derek concentrated on relaxing his muscles, waiting for his gag reflex to kick in and pleased when it didn't.

Back and forth, Scott swayed, entering and exiting Derek's mouth. Saliva pooled on Derek's lips, mixed with Scott's pre-cum, lubricating Derek's throat and making it easier for him to adjust to Scott's invasion.

Derek lost track of how much time had passed, all his focus on receiving as much as Scott had to give. His jaw ached, almost as if it might come unhinged, but he wasn't willing to stray from his goal. Not now, not when he was so close to taking Scott's whole length into his mouth.

When he felt the tickle of Scott's pubic hair along his upper lip, Derek's eyes shot open. Scott's pelvis was directly in front of him, his skin nearly pressed to Derek's forehead. Whether from sheer excitement at having all of Scott inside his mouth or from pure exhaustion, Derek's gag reflex activated. He gripped Scott's hips and shoved with a bit more pressure than he'd intended. Scott scrambled to Derek's side. "Did I hurt you? I told you to stop me if I went too far."

Derek gasped for air, then slid into a seated position, draping his arms over his legs and curving his back. He stretched his muscles and drew in deep breaths. After a few moments, he relaxed and the burn in his throat calmed. "No. It wasn't that. I just got overexcited when I finally got all of you into my mouth."

Scott stared at him, then shook his head. "You scared the shit out of me."

Derek wiped his eyes, which still had a few tears streaking out of the corners, then gripped his chin and moved it from side to side, trying to work tension out of his jaw muscles. "Damn. You were right about that being a punishment. Although I'll take that kind of torture anytime you want to dole it out."

Scott sat cross legged in front of Derek. "So you got excited that you took all of me in?"

Derek met Scott's gaze and almost laughed at the sight of his pride and the shit-eating grin. "Yeah. I'll give you one thing. You've got a monster cock!"

Scott blushed, his smile spreading even further across his face. "C'mere." He didn't wait for Derek to move. Instead, he slid his hand behind Derek's neck and pulled him forward, crushing their lips together. He devoured Derek, licking at the crevices of his cheeks and along his jaw lines. Derek simply relaxed and allowed Scott to guide the kiss.

Once he withdrew, he wiped his chin, slick with saliva. "Damn, you taste just like my cum. And I didn't even blow my load."

Derek chuckled. "I'd like to say I'm ready to finish you off the way we started, but I don't think my jaw can take it. There *is* another part of me that would have no problem at all."

Scott raised his eyebrow. "Yeah?"

"Throw me down and fuck me already."

Scott gripped Derek by the shoulders and shoved him onto his back. He kissed Derek's neck, nipped at his shoulders, then licked down the line in the center of his abdomen. He hovered over Derek's cock, gripping it at the base and tilting it up so it stood at a right angle from Derek's body, then dove down on it, taking the full length into his mouth in one motion.

Fluid heat surrounded Derek. His head fell back against the pillow, and he released a contented sigh. Scott bobbed on his cock, up and down a few times, then released it from his mouth. Stroking gently with his hand, Scott lowered his mouth to Derek's balls, sucking one in and running his tongue in circles around each nut.

The gentle tug, combined with the slide of Scott's hand along his shaft, had Derek moaning. His breath cut short when Scott reached behind his knees and bent them up to his chest. Sliding the tip of his tongue along Derek's perineum, he alternated licks and gentle breaths, tickling the skin. Derek could feel the fine hairs on his balls stand on end.

Scott continued his erotic journey until he reached Derek's opening. One lick and shock waves of pleasure fanned throughout Derek's body. "Holy damn!"

Scott peeked up at Derek, his eyes brimming with mischief. He winked, then slipped back out of sight, returning his attention to Derek's ass. After a minute of teasing Derek's hole, Scott stopped and lifted his head once again. "I want you to hold your legs in position for me. Spread them as far apart as you can."

Derek slid his hands behind his knees, replacing Scott's, and pulled his legs closer to his chest. Scott disappeared once again beneath the bulge of Derek's cock and balls and returned to laving his hole.

Along with tongue-bathing Derek's sweet hole, Scott slid a finger along Derek's entrance. Alternating between tongue and finger, Scott probed him, breaching his entrance. While Derek expected a burning sensation, the blissful stretch as Scott speared him with tongue and fingers left him panting. He spread his legs wider, desperate for more. "Scott. Please."

Scott lodged two fingers deep inside Derek's ass. "What do you want, Derek? Tell me."

Derek closed his eyes as Scott inserted a third finger. A hint of the burn he'd expected finally came, radiating through his ass and forcing small tremors to quiver through his passage and along his stomach. "I want you to stick your cock in me. I want to feel you stretch me wide and milk the cum out of me."

Scott froze for a moment, his breath hitching in his chest. When he lifted his head so Derek could see him, his expression carried equal parts shock and lust. "What did you just say?"

He didn't give Derek a chance to repeat himself. Raising himself to his knees, he took over the job of spreading Derek's legs apart. "Don't you dare jerk yourself until I tell you to."

Derek nodded, unable to speak. Scott's demands compelled him. When Scott positioned the head of his cock against Derek's hole, Derek's instinct was to buck his hips. Forcing himself to remain still added to the thrill. His heart raced. Sweat beaded in the center of his chest and along his stomach. God but he needed to feel Scott's hard shaft stretching him open. "Fuck...me." The words came out between heaving breaths.

A smile curved Scott's lips. With a steady glide, he pressed forward, slipping his cock into Derek's opening. Derek arched his body, giving Scott better access. The sound of his own measured breathing filled the room as Derek struggled to release his muscles and accommodate Scott's girth. Burn turned to a stinging torture then eased into warmth.

When Scott finished his journey, pubic hair brushing against sensitized skin, Derek sucked in a breath and held it. Filled by Scott, grounded by the weight pressing him into the mattress, any lingering fear and tension from earlier fell away, leaving him wrapped in safety. This connection, him and Scott, joined as one, was home. As long as they had each other, they could overcome anything.

Scott began a steady rhythm, pulling out until only the head of his cock remained inside Derek, leaving him craving to be filled once again. With each plunge forward, Derek moaned, somehow more whole with Scott filling him deeper than before.

Derek reached for his own cock, but stopped himself when he caught the narrowing of Scott's eyes. The crinkles at the corners smoothed, and Scott continued his onslaught.

Stroke after deliciously punishing stroke, Scott picked up speed and force until his skin glowed with a sheen of sweat. His hair was plastered to his forehead and his teeth gritted in an expression of determination, similar to how he appeared when on the wrestling mat.

"Scott. So good." Circuits of electricity sparked inside Derek's core, rushing through him. His skin pricked. The slide of sheets against his back tormented his nerve endings. Still, he managed to keep his hands away from his straining member, which now leaked pre-cum freely onto his navel. "Fuck me harder."

Sweat dripped down Scott's cheeks and neck, stray droplets running down his bare chest and splashing onto Derek.

Derek stared at the contour of Scott's naked form. His muscles bunched and relaxed, bulges pushing at the skin and casting shadows along his body. His chest heaved with ragged gasps. The sheer power of the visual image matched the physical storm of pleasure as Scott pounded deeper and deeper into Derek.

Derek clenched and unclenched the bed sheet in his fists. Heat built upon heat, and he was sure the room would explode in flames at any moment.

"Getting so close." Scott's words were forced through clenched teeth.

"Fucking come in me." Derek reached for his own cock, but the first wave of his orgasm hit before he had a chance to touch himself. His muscles spasmed, shaking his body. "God. Oh God."

Scott smiled down at him, although the smile was more of a grimace as he sucked in one final breath then let it out on a long groan. Heat flooded Derek's insides. Scott's cock pulsed, growing even thicker. Each contraction of his body forced his cock to rub against Derek's prostate, and blinding lights veiled Derek's vision as a new round of shuddering release swept through him.

Once Scott collapsed on top of him, his sweat-slicked body sticking to Derek's soaked skin, Derek was able to breathe once again. For several seconds, the sound of their panting filled the room.

Scott was the first to speak. "I didn't really give you much motivation to communicate with me, did I?"

Derek racked his brain to figure out what the hell Scott could possibly mean.

Scott chuckled in Derek's ear. "I told you if one or the other of us didn't communicate with the other, they'd have to be punished."

"Right." Derek had forgotten, still shocked that he'd come without even touching himself, and too spent to form coherent thoughts. "Yeah, if that's my punishment, I may never speak to you again."

Scott lay flush against him, the warmth of his body better than any blanket.

Derek closed his eyes, sated and perfectly happy. Scott was safe and now understood why he felt the need to help others, and Scott had fucked him to within an inch of his life.

If twenty minutes of fear had led to this kind of connection, he couldn't really complain. Blackness settled in and his breathing came slower and easier. He was just about to fade to sleep when Scott nudged him.

"Derek?"

"Mmm." He couldn't even form words.

"Just because I *understand* why you do what you do, doesn't change the fact that it *scares* me." Scott's voice was no more than a whisper, but he may as well have screamed in Derek's ear.

Derek rolled over. "I know. I got a taste of it myself tonight."

Scott nodded, then closed his eyes. Within minutes his breathing became slow and even.

Derek closed his eyes as well, but sleep eluded him. Now that he'd experienced how deeply the terror ripped, the way it had made his skin crawl, he simply couldn't knowingly put Scott through that again. But the alternative was just as bad. How could he abandon his basic need to connect with others? Why did he always find himself having to make a choice?

There seemed to be two choices: follow his own needs and continue to pursue counseling or take a break and focus on Scott. Either choice would satisfy one part of his heart, but would leave the other part empty.

Chapter Twenty-Two

Scott stared at his open laptop. With the end of the semester a month away, he had a lot of work to complete for his courses, and that didn't count preparing for finals.

Logging into the mixing program, he played his song. He'd completed most of it. Opening with an ambient beat, he created a sense of slow movement. Including the monks' voices gave the beat character, soulful and sad. He'd found lyrics to weave in, single words at regular intervals. "Work. Hard. Lone. Self." And a slew of others, each painting a sense of isolation and sadness. The combination of words, beat and melody, while abstract independently, created a concrete sense of struggle and pain.

About a minute into the mix, he quickened the beat, cutting the word tracks and dimming the monks' song. Infusing the French horns presented a bit of a challenge since he wanted to phase in the regal blare seamlessly while fading out the sonorous hymns. It took him an hour of listening to clips, searching for harmonious tones between the voices and the instrument, until he discovered the pitch function in the program.

Once he discovered that, the work of shifting from the sadness of his past into the hopefulness of his present became far easier. He dimmed the thudding beat, adding the trill of a snare drum. The louder the vibrating percussion became, the more he faded out the slow beat until the tempo had tripled in speed.

The phrase he'd originally found, "You've got to fight for what's right," no longer held the same kind of meaning for him. He'd been fighting his whole life. Up until the point when he'd met Derek. It seemed more appropriate to choose words which symbolized the acceptance that good things could happen.

Once the French horn and snare drums replaced the previous sounds completely, he integrated small phrases. "Receive what is. Enjoy now. Simply be." These were the words representing his present, and he worked them in at each point when the French horn reached a crescendo, then let the sound settle back into a calmer melody.

He wished he could've included imagery with the mix. His present required orange and pink and rose hues. All colors of a dawning morning or a day fading to evening. These were the most reflective times for him. How would he spend his day? Had he taken advantage of every opportunity? He'd lived the past two years learning to appreciate the goodness of others. Of Derek.

Security had proven a fleeting companion, but he worked to trust its permanence in his life.

The mix worked, yet he still couldn't figure out how to represent his future. Thanksgiving, and then saving Tim, had given him insight into Derek. At least he now understood what drove Derek, and, he couldn't deny, drove him as well. But understanding didn't equal acceptance.

A knock at the door provided the excuse to avoid the rising frustration of not knowing how to proceed. After a month he should've been able to find *something* to finish his mix.

He crossed the room and opened the door to find Tim standing there, hands behind his back and eyes glued to the floor.

A week had passed since he'd saved Tim from The Paw, and this was the first he was seeing of him. "C'mon in." When Tim continued to hover by the entrance, Scott slid an arm around his shoulder and guided him into the room.

Once they sat next to one another on the couch, Tim looked at him. "I've been too embarrassed to come by before now. But I wanted to thank you for the other night." He finally lifted his gaze to meet Scott's. "And I'm so sorry."

In the days since he'd rushed to The Paw, Scott had been lost in life-altering sexual exploration with Derek. Neither he nor Derek left the room other than to go to class, eat, or shower.

Derek seemed uneasy letting Scott out of his sight, having experienced the heart-stopping fear of possible loss. Scott had Tim to thank for that. "Those are words, Tim. What are you going to *do* to help yourself? The best apology you could give me would be action. You need to get help, and neither Derek nor I are equipped to give it."

"The deans called me in to meet with them yesterday. Apparently I'm failing all but one of my courses. They offered me two options." Tim leaned back on the couch and tilted his head back so he stared at the ceiling.

Scott had predicted Tim would find himself in a situation like this. After screwing off for an entire semester, using drugs, and not taking his classes seriously, it was only a matter of time before his choices caught up with him. "What happened?"

"I can take a semester off and defer my admission to college until next fall, or I can continue for the spring semester on academic probation. If I don't maintain a 2.0 grade point average I'll get expelled." Tim rubbed his hands along his thighs. "Either way I have to seek counseling as a condition of continuing as a student."

The options seemed fair enough, especially the counseling part. "What are you going to do?"

Tim dropped his head into his hands. "I'm accepting academic probation. Whichever choice I make, the deans have to contact my parents. I can't even think of what it would be like to go home after everything I've done to fuck myself over this year. Besides, I've already found a therapist."

"That's really good." Scott knew all too well how much a parent's disapproval hurt. Had Tim faced this situation even a week earlier, Scott would've felt no pity. He might not have even let the kid in his room. Amazing how a few days and one experience could change everything. "It might not be so bad. If your parents know about everything anyway, maybe this is a good time for you to tell them you're gay as well."

Tim shook his head. "I'm not ready for that. What if they freak? What if they pull my tuition? What if they reject me altogether?"

Reasonable concerns. Even with a hateful father, Scott had his mom, who loved him no matter what. "Tim, I gotta believe that things work out how they're supposed to. The way you're talking now makes a lot of sense. Whether you get a degree or support yourself building a career without a college degree, that kind of level thinking will get you a long way."

"That's easy for *you* to say." Tim closed his eyes, drew in a deep breath, and let it out slowly. "Sorry. I didn't mean to snap. What I mean is, you've got Derek. You've got parents who love you. Your future is set. Mine?" Tim gazed at the floor, his question hanging in the air.

"Tim. I'm not as well off as you think. My dad made my life a living hell. My entire childhood I moved around, never staying in one place for more than two years at a time. My mom didn't stand up for me until my senior year of high school. If she hadn't, my dad might still be in the picture. If he'd known I was gay, he might've kicked me to the curb as well.

"You can't live your life wondering what *could* happen. Planning for multiple outcomes, yes. That's just smart living to make sure you're prepared for whatever may come. But you can't spend your life trying to shape your future without enjoying right now. I learned that the hard way."

Scott replayed the moment he'd walked into his and Derek's shared English class senior year at Brampton High. The second their eyes connected. That was the defining moment that had changed his life. But only because he'd been pushed to accept a new way of living. Had he allowed his past to dictate how he reacted back then, his life could've unfolded entirely differently.

Snapping his attention back to Tim, Scott continued. "When I met Derek, a whole new world opened up. His parents accepted me and my mom. They're probably why my mom had the strength to finally tell my dad to go to hell." He'd never considered what goaded his mother to find the strength to stand up to his dad. He'd assumed it was because she saw how unhappy he'd become. At least that's what she told him. But it stood to reason that she would've needed her own support system as well.

Scott rubbed Tim's knee. "Hey, look at me." He waited for Tim to raise his head. "If I've learned anything over the past couple years, it's that things work out if you have faith in yourself and let others in. My mom and I, we let Derek and his family help us. They never stopped believing in us and gave us all the support we could've wanted. They didn't have to. It's because they had faith and believed in doing the right thing."

"Sounds like you were lucky." Tim sighed but didn't break eye contact.

Scott considered his comment. Was it luck that his mom had finally found the courage to stand up to his dad? Or that he had met Derek? He certainly counted himself as lucky, but there had to be more than random circumstances or serendipity at play. "Maybe I *am* lucky. But you need to take responsibility for your life. You control your destiny. Figure out what you want, and make it happen." Again, he'd never put all of his experiences together and looked at them from the outside in. Tim's needs were the perfect mirror to help Scott see where he'd been and how far he'd come.

"You really believe that, don't you?" A hint of a smile lifted the edges of Tim's mouth.

"I do. I really do." The urge to hug Tim swept through Scott, but he remained still. While he'd lost his aversion to the kid, he hadn't forgiven all that Tim had put them through. In time, maybe he would be able to look past the fear and pain stemming from the fucked up choices Tim made. But not yet.

Tim stared into his eyes, and for the first time Scott saw the person buried deep beneath the outer shell. "I wish I had your optimism."

Scott draped his arm across Tim's shoulders. "Just take it a day at a time. Take advantage of having a counselor. Talk to them about all your fears. They'll help you to figure out what's best for you, and they'll help you plan whatever you choose to do."

"I don't know why you're being so nice to me. I mean, I've been nothing but trouble to you and Derek since the beginning of school." Tim resumed chewing his fingernail.

Scott pulled Tim's hand from his mouth. "You'll get an infection." He chuckled, marveling at how much he sounded like his mother.

Tim pushed himself to his feet. "Well, I gotta go to my appointment with the therapist. Thanks for listening. Hopefully, some day, I can make it up to you and Derek."

"Just get better." Scott stood, escorted Tim to the door, and let him out. He then crossed the room back to his desk and sat in his chair, staring at his computer screen.

Maybe Tim would pull it together. As much as his stubborn mind resisted, Scott could see himself liking the kid once he stopped being such a complete fuck up. Plus, Tim came to apologize. Always a good first step in making reparations.

Leaning back in his chair, Scott thought about the conversation. He'd come to a few realizations of his own about luck and faith. Since when had either played a role in his life? The answer was simple. The moment he met Derek.

Scott's life had trained him to hope for the best and expect the worst. Derek was the one with the positive attitude. He believed that things worked out in the end. His conviction that people could be helped drove him to extend himself even when Scott would've preferred he back off. Hell, Derek never gave up on the two of them. Even when Scott's father effectively wedged himself between the two of them, Derek never stopped believing in the two of them. If he'd lost faith, they might not be together.

Scott shook the thought away, not willing to allow even the idea of a life without Derek to take hold. Not an option. He and Derek belonged together. He knew it down to his bones.

What a journey. All semester his emotions had been on a roller coaster, reaching a terrifying and awe-inspiring pinnacle during Thanksgiving. Even then, Derek knew how to soothe Scott's dour mood. The music and lyrics he'd played in the attic lifted Scott instantly. All the burden and doubt slid away for a few minutes as he, Derek, and Beck danced around Derek's room. What song had he played?

He racked his brain, trying to remember.

"Don't Stop Believin'". Right! The perfect song for that evening. Thinking of the things he'd said to Tim, Scott almost laughed. Maybe Journey's top hit struck a chord in his heart without him even realizing it. The sole message lived in the title. Derek lived by those words each and every day. Scott too, was slowly beginning to accept that the hope in his present would lead to happiness in his future.

"That's it!" He clapped his hands and bounced in his seat, then glanced around the room to make sure he was alone, even though he'd just let Tim out of the room and Derek had a class.

He scoured through the files of music. For ten minutes he searched file after file. Pop, rock, retro, eighties. None of them contained the song. Fuck it. He logged onto Google to look for both a radio and an instrumental version of the hit. He'd be damned if he was going to let the perfect song elude him.

Minutes later, he'd uploaded the music to his computer and filed it into the rock folder. Once he'd uploaded the music onto a track, he recorded the main line of the song. "Don't Stop Believin'" by Journey. The opening lines said enough. There was no question of the beat he'd choose. It had to be fast, techno, and danceable. He wanted people rocking in their seats when they listened to it. Just as he, Beck, and Derek had danced on Thanksgiving.

He selected several different beats. One a steady *thump, thump, thump*. He'd use that to raise the tempo of the song. There were a few other sounds with patterns of intermittent fast and slow beats. Combined, they'd create a rich background. His idea was to add a new percussive track each time the phrases repeated.

With all the sounds locked into tracks, he began to mix the final portion of his song...Derek's gift. He ended the French horn track by extending a blare which carried the same key as Journey's song. He started the track for "Don't Stop Believin'," keeping the volume of that track very low as the French horn blared.

Slowly, he lowered the volume of the French horn while increasing the volume of the cued song until the horns faded out completely and the first few bars of the new melody repeated.

Adding the steady percussion, he quickened the pace of the music. The rise in tempo revved his heart. He found himself rocking in his seat, excitement curling into a vibrant ball inside his chest. Then he added the vocals. The line sounded, then he added a second percussive track, this one with three quick thumps, a pause, and then a final thump. He let that new beat play for about ten seconds, then repeated the vocals.

After he'd added three more beats to the mix, he let it run for another twenty seconds. The combination of the words, the music, and the thudding techno evoked energy. The ball in his chest exploded, filling his entire being with light. The urge to jump out of his seat and dance around the room was difficult to resist, but he wanted to finish the mix.

His mother'd been right when she said he'd figure things out when he was ready. The song was a perfect representation of his future. While he still carried doubt and fear, he believed time would ease those emotions. His mother's love would be there. Derek would be there. Even if they ended up moving somewhere new after college, the plans for their lives would include each other. Despite the uncertainties in his life, Derek ignited confidence.

After twenty seconds, he began a slow fade, allowing the mix to dwindle until it fell silent.

Finally he'd found the way to express his future. Hope. Faith. Optimism. Belief in happy endings. These were the pillars supporting him as he worked to erase the scars of his past. So simple, yet more powerfully true than anything he'd ever known. Except for his love for Derek. Nothing was truer than that.

Scott saved the file and gave it the title *Journey*. The perfect title to represent his life's path. He opened a Word document and settled in to write his explanation of his mix and what he'd learned through the process. He'd leave out some of the more personal details about his father and about his love for Derek. His professor and classmates didn't need to know everything about him.

But he'd tell Derek. Finally, knowing that his future, a happy future, lay ahead of him, he could let go of some of his fear. And in doing so, he could free Derek to be himself without restriction. He had held Derek back long enough. It was time to let him fly and become whatever man he chose to be. And hopefully the music would explain how he felt better than words ever could.

Chapter Twenty-Three

Derek arrived early at his Rocks for Jocks class. Calling this course *boring* would be giving it too much credit. At least his lab requirement for graduation would be completed.

He took a seat at his lab table, hissing at the soreness from his over-used ass. If Scott fucked him one more time, semen might become the predominant fluid in his body. Not that he minded, but the ache reminded him of the singularity of their connection over the past week. So engrossed in touching, they'd not done a lot of talking.

More than anything, he wanted to explore Scott's comment from that night a week earlier. *Just because I understand doesn't change the fact it scares me.* What did that mean? He knew, on a literal level, what Scott meant, but the implications beneath the surface remained elusive. Was Scott giving him permission to pursue his passion, helping others, even if it placed him in precarious situations? Or was Scott pleading for him to slow down so neither one of them would have to suffer the sharp panic of fear?

Just thinking about those twenty minutes when he couldn't reach Scott sent shivers up his spine. He never wanted to worry like that again. Beck had been right, Scott was fine. But what if he hadn't been? If something had happened to Scott...

He couldn't even finish the thought. A world without Scott wasn't a possibility.

He'd heard the platitudes about the random nature of fate. *You could get hit by a bus tomorrow. Live your life fully today.* He'd heard the message time and again growing up, and dismissed the warning as parents doing their job to impart wisdom. He'd never really considered what the words meant until coming home to an empty room and a note.

He wondered how Scott didn't have a bleeding ulcer from the number of times Derek put himself on the line. Yet to withhold from extending himself to others seemed like cutting off an arm. He could survive, but with limitations. And was that really a bad thing?

Derek flipped his book shut with a bit more force than necessary. As a kid, he'd questioned everything his parents told him, especially when they restricted him from doing what he wanted. More often than not, they'd provided an explanation. But sometimes they'd simply said, "You'll understand when you're older."

The comment had infuriated him back then, more because he wasn't getting what he wanted. But now even stubborn resistance couldn't stop him from understanding the words. Somewhere deep in his core he knew they'd been right all along. Maybe limitations weren't a bad thing when they were set for legitimate protection. If he intended on living a long happy life with Scott, he had to prioritize his choices. He couldn't do everything without sacrificing something along the way. He wasn't, as he'd always assumed, Superman.

"Did the book bite you or something?" A voice shocked Derek from his thoughts. Someone had managed to enter the room and sidle up behind him without him even noticing.

He whipped around in his seat to find Tim standing a few feet away. "Jesus. You scared me."

Tim sat next to Derek. "Sorry." He took out his text book and placed it on the table, then slid his bag next to the table leg. "I just came from your dorm room."

"Oh?" After Tim involved Scott in his problems a week earlier, Derek wasn't too happy about the idea of the two of them spending any time around each other. "How come?"

Tim stared at his hands which rested on the tabletop. "I was hoping you'd be there so we could walk to class together." He lifted his gaze. "I also wanted to apologize to Scott for everything that happened."

Derek opened his mouth, but stopped himself. He hadn't expected Tim to admit he'd been wrong, let alone take responsibility and apologize for the dangerous situation he'd placed Scott in. "That was really nice of you. I'm sure Scott appreciated it."

"Yeah. I think he did. He's really sweet. After all the trouble I've caused the both of you, I wouldn't've thought he'd spend time giving me advice." Tim smiled, although his slumped form belied sadness. "You guys are so lucky to have each other."

"What'd he say?" Derek hadn't pried, yet Scott's comment about understanding and fearing at the same time weighed on him. Maybe whatever Scott said to Tim would shed some light on what was going on in his head.

"He said a bunch of stuff about believing in myself and having faith. He told me to work with the counselors to figure out how to let my parents know about me."

Tim prattled on, but Derek didn't hear past the first few words.

Scott had told Tim to believe in himself and to have faith? Just a month earlier, he never would've guessed Scott would give such advice. Maybe he finally believed Derek would be there no matter what. For the first time since the school year began, a weight lifted from his shoulders. He'd put his own needs aside to give Scott space to figure things out. From what Tim said, it sounded like Scott had figured things out far more quickly than Derek dared hope for.

Derek shook his head, realizing he'd been ignoring Tim. "Do you think he will?" Tim folded his hands on the table.

Heat rushed along Derek's neck and to his cheeks. Shit. So lost in thought, he had no idea what Tim was talking about. "Oh, yeah. Of course." He hoped his response appropriately answered Tim's question.

Apparently it had. Tim's entire body relaxed, his shoulders lowering and his head tilting to the side. Derek could even detect a hint of a smile from the curve of Tim's lips. "Good. Maybe someday we can all be friends."

Derek wasn't sure how soon he'd be willing to consider Tim a friend. He had a whole lot of things to forgive before he could let his guard down around the kid. Even then, he'd never forget the fear of worrying about Scott, despite the short duration of his panic. Tim had created the circumstances and would forever be the guy who'd dragged Scott through shit. "Yeah. Maybe."

The professor entered the class as well as a few other students. After another minute, class started.

~~~~~

Derek made a quick excuse why he couldn't go to the Student Center with Tim once class was over. After Tim's apology and knowing Scott had said something that seemed to get through to the kid, he couldn't wait to get back to the room and talk. If he didn't rush, he'd have to wait until Scott finished practice. As it stood, he'd only have an hour at the most before Scott had to leave for class.

When he arrived at their room, he found Scott at his desk, the tap of his fingers flying over the keypad of his laptop filling the room with a rapid *click, click, click*.

To interrupt such concentration seemed almost cruel, but curiosity barreled through Derek. "Hey."

Scott glanced up. "Hey." A brief smile crossed his lips, then he returned his focus to whatever he was working on.

Derek crossed the room, taking post next to him. "Whatcha working on?"

In a flash, Scott flipped his laptop cover closed. "It's secret." He stood and hugged Derek, kissing the side of his neck. "I love you so much, babe."

A hug and kiss, with a side order of adoration was certainly a pleasant greeting, although Scott's behavior added fire to the flames of the curiosity Derek had suppressed for the better part of the last two hours. "I love you, too."

"Tim stopped by earlier. Did he tell you?" Scott sat on the couch, patting the open spot next to him.

Derek knew a distraction technique when he heard one. If Scott wanted to keep his mix secret, Derek would allow it...for now. "Yeah. He said you were really cool with him. That you gave him some message about believing in himself and having faith."

"Isn't it great that he's finally getting counseling?" Scott grabbed a cup of coffee from the small table in front of the couch and took a sip, then winced. "Yuck, it's cold." He spit the liquid back into the cup. "Too bad about the academic probation, though."

"What academic probation?" Derek kicked himself for tuning out after the first few sentences of Tim's apology-confession.

"He didn't tell you?"

Derek shrugged. "He might have. To be honest, I stopped listening to him after he mentioned talking to you and hearing the message you gave him."

Scott shook his head. "You should lighten up on him. He's going through a lot."

If he hadn't been sitting he might've fallen to the floor. "All right. Who are you and what have you done with my boyfriend?"

Laughter did nothing to ease the rising tide of Derek's desire to get inside Scott's head. "Nothing. I'm right here."

"Seriously. Something's changed in you. I thought we promised no more secrets between us." Derek took Scott's hand in his own. "Tell me what's going on. Not that I'm complaining about this whole the-future-is-bright person who you've become, but it seems an awfully fast change of heart." Derek recalled their agreement from a few weeks earlier about not communicating. "Or do I need to punish you?"

Scott stared at him for a few seconds, then stood, dragging him to his feet as well. "All right. As tempting as a punishment sounds, I don't think my ass can take another pummeling after the way you've abused it this week." He strode over to his laptop and flipped it open. "I was saving this for a surprise, but you seem like you might explode if I don't share this with you now." Scott released his hand and slipped back into the seat at his desk. He clicked a few buttons, then stood. "Here. Listen to the mix. I finished it today."

Derek stared at him for a lingering moment, then turned his attention to the computer. He'd spied the *surprise* weeks earlier and had kept the information to himself.

Scott's first mix lay at his fingertips. All he had to do was hit play.

He hesitated, although he wasn't sure why. All his life he had used music to express his deepest emotions and feelings. The way Scott had taken to mixing, it made sense he would also be able to portray his feelings effectively though music. Fear and anticipation dueled inside him.

"What's wrong?" Scott placed a hand on Derek's shoulder, the warmth of the touch penetrating his shirt.

Derek shifted his gaze from the computer screen to Scott. Scott's eyes glowed, like a calm sea during a cloudless day. His olive toned skin lit up with vibrancy, no traces of worry or concern to be found in his expression. "Nothing. I'm just…you never stop surprising me."

A grin swept across Scott's face. "Listen to the mix." His gentle voice nudged Derek into action. Derek returned his attention to the laptop and hit play.

Sound swept through the room, doleful yet beautiful. Derek closed his eyes. He took in slow, easy breaths, his head growing a bit heavier. A slight constriction started in his chest. Although not uncomfortable, he had to work a bit harder to draw in breath. Words helped him to place his feelings. "Work. Hard. Lone." Derek imagined he was alone in the middle of a wooded area. It had to be somewhere in nature, beautiful and inspiring, yet isolated.

Slowly, a steady beat replaced the somber thud of the base percussion. The tempo of Derek's heart increased. He hadn't even realized the French horn in the mix until the monks' voices began to fade. Scott had managed to find the same pitch and entwine the two sounds together perfectly.

As the French horn's blare took center focus, the bands constricting Derek's chest released. A quiet metallic roll of a snare drum added an uplifting energy. Derek no longer felt alone. He could sense others, not exactly with him, but on the horizon.

Once again, words put names to the feelings. "Receive what is. Enjoy now. Be present." They weren't the only emotions the music evoked. With his eyes closed, Derek pictured himself standing taller, expectant. Hope for what might be on his horizon seeming bright.

The shift was subtle, yet powerful. Isolation had been a part of Scott's life. Derek knew that. But this, the empowering promise of a greater possibility, just out of reach, drawing closer, lifted Derek's spirit. The images of flowing water, like the stream on the mountain, dominated his thoughts. Had Scott become hopeful in this same way?

Derek wondered what role he'd played in bringing about the change. He'd always suspected his unwavering devotion was a likely ingredient to Scott's shift, but to hear evidence in the music turned a question into knowledge.

The tempo increased. The snare and steady thump of the bass shifted, becoming more technological, faster and faster, forcing Derek's heart into a staccato beat. And then music merged into the mix, the same pitch and tone as the French horn. After a few seconds he recognized the song.

Journey's "Don't Stop Believin,'" purely instrumental, started as a soft echo, winding in and around the triumphant blares of the horns. And slowly, the volume increased. Additional beats entered into the mix, rhythmic, similar to the kinds of beats Derek used for dances.

The lyrics weren't needed, yet they completed the shift, pushing Derek past the promise of a hopeful future straight into the joy of brightness and happiness. The words resonated in his soul, binding with his own belief in what the future held for him, for Scott, for anyone who could see the world through an optimistic lens. Even Tim could weather the storms ahead if he *believed*.

Derek could clearly picture Scott and Tim sitting in the room, Tim pouring his heart out and Scott building him up. If this was the song inspiring Scott, no wonder Tim seemed so upbeat in class.

Did the music represent where Scott was now? Did he truly believe in a limitless future? Was he accepting the stability and unconditional love Derek held for him? With the belief that his future promised happiness and connectedness, the opening sounds of sadness and isolation became a badge of honor, a storm Scott had weathered to arrive at this place where the sun shone bright, leading him on his journey toward his future.

Journey. That's what this song was about. Scott was sharing his journey. Derek had never considered the meaning of the band's name before, but what an amazing and simple concept. Scott's life had been a passage from darkness to light.

Derek opened his eyes and jumped to his feet. Sitting was an impossibility as his muscles quivered with energy needing release. He faced Scott, who simply stared at him, love bathing Derek like a warm shower. "That was so incredible."

Scott beamed, his hands clasped together. "Really? You like it?"

"No. *Like* is too weak a word." He hugged Scott. "I felt everything. The music told a story. Painted a picture with sound. You didn't even need the words, although I love how you infused them."

"I've been tormented trying to find the last song, but when Tim was here it just came to me. Everything I said to him was like I was speaking to myself." Scott held him at arm's length. "You know I made that mix for you."

"I could tell." For a week, hell, for the past few months, he had squirmed with need, struggling to contain his frustration at not knowing what Scott was thinking. "I'm so proud of you. Not just for the skillful mixing job, but…" He gazed at Scott, love and wonder mixing together and amping his already racing heart. "I'm so lucky to have you in my life."

"Babe, I think you've got that slightly wrong." Scott brushed his lips against Derek's cheek, then stepped back. "*We're* so lucky to have each other. I think *we* make a pretty amazing team."

"You're right." Nothing more needed to be said for the truth to fill the room. Derek sighed. Gravity seemed to lose some of its power over him. For the way Scott lifted him, time and again, he should've been floating miles above the ground. "You really meant what you said. In the mix, I mean? You really believe in our future?"

A momentary crease furrowed Scott's brow but immediately smoothed out. "Of course I do. I'm sorry I ever made you question it. Come on. Let's sit." He took Derek's hand and led him back to the couch. "I told you I needed some time. I didn't realize I'd come to such understandings so quickly, but then again, I never expected someone like Tim to inspire the kind of understanding he did.

"I'm not saying I'm all the way there, believing everything will be sunny skies and flower-lined walkways." Scott smiled, a dreamy expression on his face. "I know, more than I've known anything, that together we'll end up on top. You push me to grow and learn every day."

"You do the same for me." Derek rested his head on Scott's shoulder. "What's standing in the way of you letting go of old scars? What can I do to help?"

"Just keep on loving me." Scott kissed the top of Derek's head. "I may never figure everything out. I'm still pissed at my dad. He did a lot more damage than I realized."

Derek wasn't sure he knew what Scott meant, but there'd be plenty of time to figure it out. For now, there was one reassurance he could provide. "Loving you is as easy as breathing. That's one thing you can count on...forever."

Scott grinned. "Right back atcha."

Derek slid his hand behind Scott's head and tugged, sealing their mouths together. Only a gentle brush of lip on lip, feather-light touches, and then he withdrew, heat and blood flowing south. "We should celebrate you finishing your mix."

Scott chuckled. "Yeah? Any ideas on what we should do?"

Derek dragged Scott with him toward the bed. "Oh yeah. You bet your sweet ass I do."

Epilogue
A month later...

Derek bustled about the room in a frenetic whirlwind of activity. He'd spent the better part of a month putting together the mix for The Alliance's first dance. Coursework had, of course, taken priority, and finals were still a week away, but any spare moment he could find he used for mixing. Well, except for those moments when Scott distracted him. The dull ache in his ass reminded him of the most recent diversion the previous night.

The weeks since Scott shared his mix seemed a blur in a wonderful, peaceful, happy torrent of activity, but still hectic. Derek glanced at the sleeping form of his lover. After an hour of receiving hard pounding and an orgasm of seismic proportions, he doubted if Scott would get up before noon.

With the music done and too saturated with nervous energy to study, Derek slipped into sweats and donned his running sneakers. As quietly as possible, he left the room, taking extra care to close the door without a sound, and bounded outside.

December carried some of the bitterest cold weather Massachusetts had to offer, amplified by the fact the city sat next to a port. Unobstructed winds intensified the chill. Without taking the time to stretch or warm up, Derek started to jog toward the athletic complex.

So much had changed since the last time he'd made this same trek. Before, he'd run in order to deal with his frustration and sadness. He'd questioned Scott and the influence his boyfriend had on him. He'd actually viewed himself as broken and blamed Scott. Yeah right! What a stupid ass he'd been. As if he weren't the one making his own choices.

Now he ran to burn off excess energy. Not only because of the dance, although he was anxious to set up and wanted the event to be as big a success as the last one. Bigger even. No, he ran because running always cleared his head until he could narrow his focus to whatever really distracted him.

At eight o'clock on a Saturday morning, he didn't have to worry much about sidewalk or street traffic, so he made it to the athletic complex in about five minutes without having to stop too often along the way.

He maintained his pace for the first few laps around the track. With each circuit, he focused on a different thought. Finals. The dance. Scott's mix. Each of those was a good thing. He'd worked hard and was prepared for exams and the party. Scott's mix had shed light on questions Derek had pondered for the better part of the last two years. Even Tim wasn't a big concern anymore.

Tim failed all but the Rocks for Jocks class, and he was on academic probation, but he was now seeing a counselor twice a week. After six sessions, Derek already noticed changes. There were no lingering wafts of pot scenting the hallways. Tim had started attending The Alliance meetings and had even become the lead planner, second to Charlie, for the dance. Given some time, Derek could imagine being friends with the guy.

So why the uneasiness lingering in his chest?

He didn't have to dig too deep to answer his own question. Although Scott had made some breakthroughs, there were old wounds that would take time to heal. Twenty years of instability and rejection couldn't be wiped clean in a year or two.

Derek wished he could transport the two of them back in time. Change history. If he'd lived near Scott, if they'd been friends since childhood, maybe Scott would've had the consistency of someone who loved him all along. A ridiculous thought. Even if they'd been friends as kids and grown into their current relationship, the damage caused by Scott's unloving father would still be there.

Derek picked up his pace. No sense in wondering about what could have been. Better to focus on what he could actually do something about. Scott needed time, and Derek would stick by his side forever. So long as they continued to communicate, they'd end up just fine. Scott's mix proved that. Scott now believed in a hopeful future. That's all Derek had ever wanted for the two of them.

~~~~~

Scott kissed Derek. "You'll be great. I'll see you at the Student Center. Can't wait to hear this secret dance mix you wouldn't let me listen to…or help with."

Derek swatted Scott's ass. "You learn a little bit about mixing, and all of a sudden you're an expert, huh?"

"No. I didn't…I mean—"

"Relax. I'm fucking with you." Derek hugged him then took off. Once the door closed behind him, Scott sat down, wincing at the ache. Hell yeah, Derek had fucked with him…just an hour earlier.

When it was time for the dance, Scott threw on some jeans, his Taz shirt, and a coat. As much as he hated using the coat room in the Student Center, it was far too cold to weather the freezing temperatures of mid-December. The second he stepped inside the Student Center, he wished he'd reconsidered. A wave of heat, emanating from a sea of bodies, clogged the air.

He stared at the line to the coat room, which seemed to extend through the entire length of the main floor for at least fifty or sixty yards. "Oh, *hell* no." Scott bypassed the line and headed into the main auditorium area where the dance would take place. He scanned the room and found who he was looking for. Derek was set up on a dais at the far end of the room.

He wound through a web of students and climbed onto the platform. Derek smiled at his approach. "Hey!"

Scott shucked his coat and placed it over Derek's, which hung on the back of the chair by the mixing board. "At least there's one benefit of having you up here, even if I don't get to have you next to me on the dance floor."

Derek kissed Scott's cheek. "You'll survive one night without me by your side."

Scott pouted. "Maybe." He couldn't hold the expression for long. Pissy wasn't an emotion he could maintain unless he was actually upset. "Will I get at least one dance with you?"

Derek smiled. "Maybe."

Damn if Derek wasn't sexy when he teased. "I suppose you're not gonna tell me whatever you've got planned?"

Derek nuzzled into Scott's neck and bit with enough pressure to hurt for a split second. Just a love nip, but delicious nonetheless. "You've always been so smart."

Scott laughed. "All right, then, I'll let you get ready." He hopped off the stage and sauntered toward Marcus who he'd spotted entering the room.

"Scott." Derek's voice halted Scott's movement. He turned to face his lover. "Keep checking in with me. I want you nearby when the time is right."

Scott nodded, not knowing what to say to Derek's cryptic request. Luckily, Marcus clapped him on the back, giving him a reason to turn away without saying anything. Derek had something up his sleeve. Since the surprise camping trip Scott had planned for them before they started school, he'd been anticipating Derek returning the favor. Of course, Scott hated surprises. He'd lived with enough uncertainty.

The room quickly filled with students, the floor space congesting with bodies. Lights dimmed. The hum of hundreds of voices blended together, creating white noise. Derek stood on the stage, his sound system and mixing board before him. He wore headphones and worked the control panel.

Pride swelled within Scott as he watched the show of talent and concentration. Derek was never sexier than when he deejayed for a crowd. Well, almost never.

Marcus bounced like a drugged rabbit, his movements completely mismatched to the beat of Derek's mix. He slid an arm around his girlfriend's waist, the smile on his face spreading wide. He shifted his attention to Scott. "Your man sure knows how to play a party."

Scott shifted his attention to the person in question. Derek caught his eye and quirked the corner of his mouth up in a half-smile, then he refocused on the music.

Minutes stretched into hours. Sweat broke out over Scott's body as he danced, bumping against the other students crushed onto the dance floor. Finally, after a particularly energetic song, Scott weaved through the crowd to Derek.

He hopped up on the stage and slid behind Derek, resting his hands on slim hips and leaning his head on rounded shoulders. "You're smokin' hot. You know that?"

Derek pressed his ass against Scott's groin. Blood flowed south, filling out Scott's cock. He ground his hips, working his hardness into Derek's crack, keeping time with the electric beat. Despite the noise in the room, Scott could hear Derek's hum, just as easily as he could feel the trembling of Derek's muscles.

"I'm glad you joined me up here. I'm about to play a song I've been working on, and I want you close by when you hear it." Derek craned his head to the side and kissed Scott's cheek.

Scott lost himself in Derek's musky scent. He reveled in the heat passing between them. Sliding his hands up Derek's abdomen, he savored the taut muscles, undulating as Derek worked.

The current song, a fast paced dance number, slowly faded as a new and slower beat layered into the sound. Within seconds, Scott recognized the base song, "Happy," by Pharrell Williams. But the lyrics weren't included. Just the sound.

The students on the dance floor roared, flinging their arms in the air. Along with the music, the sound of clapping entered the mix. Two fast claps followed by a break and then one clap. The pattern continued, ramping up in speed along with the underlying percussive beat and the increased volume of the music.

Derek allowed the song to play out for a few stanzas before turning to Scott. "Pay attention to this."

When he returned his focus to the mix, he added a few more tracks. A tinny sound of sultry horns--saxophones, if Scott knew his instruments well enough--trilled in the background at steady intervals. Each booming burst of music served to punctuate each place where the word "happy" would have been in the mix.

The students cheered and ramped up their dancing pace. Scott watched them shift from individual people into a single mass of undulating bodies, arms waving, raised high in the air.

The introduction of a siren dragged Scott's attention back to the mix. Starting at a low timbre, the alarm rang, filling the room with a deafening blast. Scott's heart raced as the sounds mixed together. The theme of happiness reverberated through his bones as the sexy saxophone and powerful blare coalesced into a flood of energy.

Derek bounced on the balls of his feet, his smile stretching wide. Scott couldn't have dragged his eyes away from the vision of pure joy if he wanted to. Derek increased the volume with each new round of the chorus until the room thumped with the pounding beat.

Derek grabbed Scott's hands and stared into his eyes. No words passed between them. None were needed. His eyes sparkled, an amber fire burning into Scott, washing him in love and contentedness. So vibrant. So filled with power and optimism.

Derek rose onto his toes to place his mouth next to Scott's ear. "This is how being with you makes me feel."

Scott's breath caught in his chest. He'd always known Derek lived his life viewing the world as full and vibrant. The innocence and positivity leaked into Scott every day. But to feel Derek's happiness electrifying the air, pulsing against his skin, filling him with overflowing joy, lifted him higher than any words or promises of love Derek could possibly offer.

Gripping Derek, on either side of his face, Scott tugged at him, capturing Derek's mouth in a desperate kiss. Never before had the need for Derek's lips against his own filled him with such urgency. Derek wrapped his arms around him, squeezing tight as he kissed back, rolling his tongue in Scott's mouth.

Scott had no idea how much time passed, but somewhere in the distance he thought he could make out his and Derek's names sounding. Dragging himself from the kiss, he glanced in the direction of the call.

Marcus and a few other guys from the wrestling team stood by the edge of the stage, shit-eating grins plastered across their faces. They were accompanied by Derek and Scott's dorm mates. All of them were chanting, some of them whistling.

Scott hugged Derek close, laughing as their audience catcalled, "More, more, more!" When he returned his gaze to Derek, the grin adorning his lover's face matched the energy of the room. "Hey, we gotta give the audience what they want."

Scott didn't need any further invitation. He swept Derek into his arms, closing the gap between them and clamping his mouth over Derek's once again. The kiss wasn't fierce or fevered. Instead, Derek wove his fingers through Scott's hair, gently caressing Scott's scalp. The smell of sweat and cologne mixed together, creating a powerful aphrodisiac. Hugging Derek, tasting him, was all Scott needed to know his roots had finally taken hold.

Whatever challenges lay ahead, and surely there would be plenty as Scott worked through his own shit, he'd always have Derek, and, ultimately, he believed in the happiness pounding through the speakers.

He could hold off on dealing with his issues for another day. For now, the only thing that mattered was the man in his arms.

About the Author

D. H. Starr is a clean-cut guy with a wickedly naughty mind. He grew up in Boston and loves the city for its history and beauty. Also, having lived in NYC, he enjoys the fast pace and the availability of anything and everything. He first became interested in reading from his mother who always had a stack of books piled next to her bed. Family is important to D. H. and his stories center around the intricate and complex dynamics of relationships and how people work through problems while maintaining respect and love. His favorite books tend to fall in the genres of science fiction, fantasy, paranormal, and coming of age.

To learn more about D. H. Starr and his books, please visit his website at www.dhstarr.com.

Tell Us What You Think

We appreciate hearing reader opinions about our books. You can email us at Sedonia.guillone@gmail.com .

Ai Press Books by D. H. Starr

Meant For Each Other
Wrestling With Love
Variant Breed Book One: Chris and Zach
Feed. Prey. Love.